LET ME OUT

(An Ashley Hope Suspense Thriller—Book 2)

Kate Bold

Kate Bold

Debut author Kate Bold is author of the ALEXA CHASE SUSPENSE THRILLER series, comprising six books (and counting); and the ASHLEY HOPE SUSPENSE THRILLER, comprising three books (and counting).

An avid reader and lifelong fan of the mystery and thriller genres, Kate loves to hear from you, so please feel free to visit www.kateboldauthor.com to learn more and stay in touch.

ISBN: 978-1-0943-9380-3

BOOKS BY KATE BOLD

ALEXA CHASE SUSPENSE THRILLER

THE KILLING GAME (Book #1)
THE KILLING TIDE (Book #2)
THE KILLING HOUR (Book #3)
THE KILLING POINT (Book #4)
THE KILLING FOG (Book #5)
THE KILLING PLACE (Book #6)

ASHLEY HOPE SUSPENSE THRILLER

LET ME GO (Book #1)
LET ME OUT (Book #2)
LET ME LIVE (Book #3)

PROLOGUE

Thorns punctured the soles of Sarah Lester's bare feet, the sting from the cuts shooting up her legs as she careened through the thick forest underbrush, dodging trees and bramble bushes. Her limbs ached from being bound for hours in a cramped space and her core throbbed from abuse. Still, she forced herself to plow forward.

Fear numbed the pain.

Her pulse pounded in her ears as she pushed her muscles to their limit, increasing her speed.

Faster! Faster!

She dared not look back.

The hideous face flashed in her memory. The red synthetic hair, the white rubber skin, the red U-shaped mouth. The macabre Halloween mask bore a testament to the wickedness hiding beneath it.

"Run," the clown had commanded, *"if you want to live."*

She had to find her way out of the forest, had to stay alive. For Bobby's sake. If she died and her bones were buried in a shallow grave or scattered deep in the woods, the five-year-old would never understand why Mommy had left him.

He'd grow up feeling abandoned. Just as she had.

The crack of gunfire echoed through the trees behind her. She recognized the blast of a high-powered rifle.

Terror gripped her heart.

The clown had lied. Had promised that if she ran as fast as she could and didn't look back, if she kept her mouth shut about her ordeal, she wouldn't die. Now it was clear her abductor had planned to kill her from the beginning.

Why hadn't she listened to Dewayne?

Her boyfriend had warned her—time after time—that someone might break in. But she'd been careless. Had once again forgotten to lock the trailer door. A simple oversight that had sealed her fate.

But the clown knew things about her. Had taunted her with her past. The abduction wasn't random.

How long had this been planned?

Her lungs burned as she raced past an outcrop of limestone and over a fallen log. A break in the tree line loomed up ahead as the sound of flowing water rushed toward her. The river. Or a fast-moving stream. She wasn't sure which. Water could mean the presence of people. Maybe a fisherman. Someone who could help her. But she couldn't risk leaving the cover of the trees. Not with the clown at her heels.

As Sarah veered to the left, the crack of the rifle split the air again. The bullet ripped through the thicket beside her, missing her torso by mere inches.

Adrenaline whisked through her veins as she angled toward the edge of the tree line. The river popped into view down the embankment to her right. There were no people in sight. No one to save her.

Keep moving!

She zigzagged between the trees, resisting the urge to run in a straight line, as she attempted to stay out of the clown's crosshairs. She prayed she'd find a road ahead, that she'd be able to flag down a passing car. Or that she'd stumble upon a house or a cabin. A place where there were people. Or a place where she could hide.

Rifle fire ricocheted through the woods a third time, the source of the blast much closer now than before. The clown had gained far too much ground. She needed to push harder. Had to run faster. As she wound past a red maple, an exposed root snagged her left foot.

Sarah stifled a scream as she toppled forward, her ankle twisting in the maple's grip. Her right elbow slammed against the forest floor followed by the weight of her body. Stunned by the fall, she glanced behind her. She knew she had to get up. That she had to move—now.

Pain radiated from her ankle through her calf as she pulled her foot free from the root's grasp. Blood stained both her soles and briars had ripped the legs of her black polyester slacks. She struggled to stand.

Panic surged in her heart as she realized she could no longer run.

She hobbled forward, balancing her weight on her right foot. She scanned the woods ahead. There was no place to hide.

Crack! The rifle exploded behind her.

The bullet pierced Sarah's back like a hot needle. Her breath caught in her throat as a sting akin to a thousand hornets erupted in her chest. She fell to her knees, gasping for air.

It hit my lung! The thought reverberated through her brain.

Fighting for each shallow breath, she crawled toward the edge of the tree line. Her vision began to blur. But across the river, on the other bank, she thought she saw a figure. Could it be a man?

She needed to get his attention. Had to get help.

As she scooted forward, the earth dissolved beneath her. Sarah tumbled down the side of the embankment. Rocks bit into her flesh as she rolled, her body coming to rest at the shoreline. Cool water lapped at her side as she attempted to sit up. A metallic-tasting liquid flooded her mouth.

Blood.

Her lungs were filling with blood.

She coughed, spitting out the blood, trying to clear her airways. She struggled to take another shallow breath as the world around her began to spin. She fell back on her side and closed her eyes. Her son's innocent face floated through her mind. His big brown eyes. His sweet smile.

Please let them find my body. The silent cry echoed through her soul.

For Bobby's sake.

A shadow drifted across her face. Feeling a presence beside her, she opened her eyes. Her vision had dimmed, all the colors of the world faded into a hazy gray, but she could still make out the image of the one looking down on her. The terrifying mask was seared into her memory. The shocking hair, the evil smile.

She realized the man she'd thought she'd seen on the other bank didn't exist. There was no one here to help her.

Only the clown.

Sarah's eyelids fluttered shut as the darkness pulled her under.

She never even heard the shot that pierced her heart.

CHAPTER ONE

Police cadet Ashley Hope's sparring opponent faked a move to her right and then struck like a cyclone. Cadet James Mobley slammed his palm against the side of her head, hooked his right foot behind her left ankle, and jerked her leg out from under her. Ashley fell backward onto the exercise mat, her pride injured more than her body.

The gaze of a gymnasium full of students burned into the side of her protective helmet.

"Watch your stance, Hope," Sergeant Paul Newell, their defensive tactics instructor, barked from the sideline. "Those pretty blue eyes won't protect you. Keep your feet apart. Your center of gravity low."

Ashley's cheeks flushed. She'd realized her mistake the moment it was made, a split second too late to defend against the attack.

One of the most important lessons she'd learned from her nine weeks at the Highland Rim Law Enforcement Academy in Cedar View, Tennessee, was to anticipate the actions of the people around her. To prepare for any and all moves they might make. In this case, she'd broken that rule. She'd allowed her opponent to lead her in the wrong direction. Had brought her feet too close together, her center too high, instead of sprawling low to guard against the takedown. As a result, she'd been forced to the ground. A position that could prove fatal for a police officer.

Her sparring partner leaned over and offered her his hand.

"You make a tough opponent," he said, his voice just above a whisper.

The encouraging assessment surprised her, but the kind words didn't dull the sting of her defeat.

The compassionate expression on Cadet Mobley's face revealed that he took no particular satisfaction in his victory, unlike some of the other students who'd managed to wrestle her to the mat. She grasped his palm and pulled herself up. Not because she needed help standing, but because she didn't want the added attention that refusing his gesture would create.

One of only five women in the current class of forty-one students (shaved down from a starting count of fifty), she tried to keep a low profile. She trained hard, followed the rules, and never complained about the sexist remarks uttered by a few of her male instructors.

Sergeant Newell—tall, bald, and at least twenty years her senior—ranked at the top of the offenders' roster. His comment regarding her eyes was the latest in a long list of references he'd made to her physical features. Whether his behavior was a tactic to give her a taste of the real world and help make her a stronger officer, or if it was an attempt to force her into another profession, didn't matter.

She'd realized early on that ignoring the innuendoes would be the key to her staying focused. She wasn't about to let the sergeant's attitude—regardless of the reason behind it—prevent her from reaching her goal. She planned to become one of the best cops the state of Tennessee had ever employed. And she'd already gained a fair amount of experience.

Ashley had been instrumental in ending the bloody reign of serial killer Ethan Barrett—who also happened to be her ex-husband. Her involvement in the case coupled with her master's in criminal justice put her well on her way to achieving her dream.

"Listen up, cadets," Sergeant Newell shouted. A hush fell over the gymnasium. "Give me twenty push-ups, then line up and wait for dismissal. Except for you, Hope."

Ashley's face grew warm again as the instructor singled her out, directing the attention of all the other students her way.

"I've got something for you when you're done," he said, his dark eyes boring into her skull.

She slipped off her protective headgear, dropped to the floor, and began the exercise, wondering what the sergeant had planned. Probably an additional three-mile run. It seemed to be the punishment he favored for students who dared to disappoint him—which wasn't hard to do. It was as though his life's mission was to weed out the weak. He'd already been the catalyst responsible for nine cadets in her class quitting the academy. With three weeks left to go until graduation, she wondered how many more would fall.

As her push-up count hit seventeen, she caught sight of Sergeant Newell's black athletic boots out of the corner of her eye, just beyond her elbow. He was obviously waiting for her to finish. After her twentieth rep, she took a deep breath and pushed herself to her feet, bracing for the penalty she would have to pay.

Whatever the physical activity consisted of, she could handle it. She'd amazed herself by the level of strength she'd achieved. The first week of the academy she could barely complete five push-ups. Now, pumping out twenty was a breeze.

"Cadet Hope, meet your new sidekick," Newell said.

Ashley's eyes widened as the sergeant passed her a black kettlebell. The cast iron weight tipped the scale at eight kilograms, equivalent to eighteen pounds.

"What do mean by sidekick, sir?" she asked, gripping the handle with both hands. Was he adding an additional workout to her daily schedule?

"For the next week, everywhere you go on campus, the bell goes with you. Unless you're running or doing PT, it can't leave your side."

Seriously? He expected her to lug the weight around the campus along with her laptop and stack of books? Her classrooms lay scattered across the sprawling grounds the academy shared with Highland Rim State University, each several minutes apart. Her Ethics and Professional Conduct class was located at the top of three flights of stairs. The building—constructed in the late 1960s—lacked the convenience of elevators.

She glanced at the line of students forming at the side of the gym. Cadet Mobley met her gaze and rolled his eyes in a conspiratorial gesture, as if he thought Newell had gone too far.

The sergeant continued, "When the week is up, maybe you'll have a better understanding of how gravity works. Now join the lineup."

"Yes, sir."

Struggling to keep her irritation from showing on her face, Ashley took her place in the line and stood at attention, the kettlebell dangling from her right hand.

Sergeant Newell paced in front of the group assembled in rigid format.

"Next week we'll focus on baton maneuvers," he told them. "As always, I suggest you lay off the alcohol this weekend. And come to class prepared for battle. Cadets dismissed."

Ashley glanced at the clock hanging above Newell's head. It was already fifteen minutes past three. The class had run long, which seemed to be a pattern on Fridays. As if the sergeant found joy in delaying the students' highly valued time off.

With a sigh, she headed for the women's locker room. She didn't normally shower at the academy, preferring to wait until she got home. But today, with little time to spare, she didn't have a choice.

As she strode toward her locker, she yanked the white scrunchie from her ponytail and let her blonde tresses fall to her shoulders. Sergeant Newell had suggested she get her hair cut on more than one occasion. A short style would be more practical for the academy; the fact was obvious. But she refused to give her instructor the satisfaction of following his recommendation. She stripped off the gray athletic shorts and T-shirt with her last name emblazoned on the back, and stepped beneath the ancient shower stall's lukewarm spray.

Bruises covered her arms and legs. The result of her defensive tactics training. If a stranger were to see her, they would most likely jump to the conclusion that she was a victim of domestic abuse. Ashley realized that the assumption wouldn't be too far from the truth.

Just a few short months prior, her ex-husband had broken out of prison and embarked on a killing rampage, stalking Ashley and her then fiancé, Brett. The couple had barely escaped with their lives. Bringing Ethan down, making sure he would never kill again, had been the most challenging thing she had ever done.

Actually—the second most challenging. The hardest thing was getting over Brett—something she hadn't quite managed to do yet. Although finding out about his infidelity had cut deep—was something she couldn't force herself to forgive—a part of her still loved him.

After toweling off, Ashley dressed in a pair of chocolate slacks and a silk blouse. It was important she look her best for her appointment. For her own peace of mind. She blow dried her hair and applied her makeup under the harsh fluorescent lighting, careful not to go too heavy.

Once she was finished, she pulled her cadet uniform—a pair of navy BDU (battle dress uniform) pants and a white polo—from the hanger in her locker, folded it, and placed it in her duffel bag along with her gym clothes. The kettlebell sat on the bench in front of the row of lockers, taunting her.

"I hate you," she said out loud.

The stress of the academy had finally reduced her to berating a hunk of metal. But since she couldn't voice her opinion to the real object of her ire—Sergeant Newell—harassing the weight would have to do.

Her hands full, she shouldered her way through the locker room door, cut a sharp right, and almost plowed headlong into Cadet Mobley.

"Sorry," she said, stepping to the side.

"It's okay. I was waiting for you."

She noticed a sparkle in his hazel eyes and her stomach fluttered.

He continued, "I was wondering if you'd like to have dinner with me tomorrow night."

The offer flattered her. James Mobley stood around six feet tall with a runner's physique, strong jaw, and sandy hair a tad longer than military style. His personality seemed just as attractive. Under different circumstances, she'd be quick to say yes. But with the wound of her last failed relationship still fresh, dating wasn't on her current agenda. It would probably take months before she was ready to risk her heart again.

"Thank you for asking," she said, "but I've got plans with my family this weekend." A statement which happened to be true.

Mobley's smile faded. "Okay. Well, maybe a different night then."

He hesitated, waiting for her answer. She wondered whether she should say maybe, or if she should just confess that she had no interest in dating at the moment. The truth won out.

"I just recently broke up with my fiancé," she admitted. "And I'm not really ready …"

"Hey, I get it," he said. "Just … keep me in mind."

"I will." And she meant it.

He glanced at her duffel bag. "Do you need help getting your stuff to your car?"

"Thanks, but I've got it." She motioned with the kettlebell. "And I can't let go of my buddy."

Mobley smiled and nodded. "Well, I guess I'll see you Monday."

She watched his toned body retreat down the hallway before heading toward the exit in the opposite direction. She noted the time on the clock hanging above the door. Almost a quarter to four. With the afternoon traffic, the drive to Briarwood would span just over an hour and a half. She had to be at the attorney's office at six to sign the papers transferring ownership of the home she had shared with her ex-fiancé to the new buyers. Unless there was an accident on the highway to slow her down, she should make it in time.

A wave of dread washed over Ashley as her thoughts turned to Brett. Almost three months had passed since she'd last seen her ex-fiancé. And she didn't know how she was going to face him.

CHAPTER TWO

At the Laurel County sheriff's office, Special Agent Daniel Lansing shoved the case file into his briefcase and snapped it shut, a smile dancing across his face. The Amber Alert issued by the Tennessee Bureau of Investigations had paid off. A frightened seven-year-old runaway had been found near the small mountain town of Mettler Ridge, unharmed, and was now overjoyed to be reunited with his parents.

Sheriff Hiram Vance stuck out his hand. "We really appreciate everything you've done," he said, the sentiment reflected in his gray eyes.

Daniel had personally coordinated the search for the child, careful to keep the involvement of local law enforcement in the forefront so they didn't feel as though the Tennessee Bureau of Investigation was stepping on their toes.

"Glad the TBI could help," Daniel said, accepting the handshake.

He was thankful for the happy ending. Far too many missing children were never found. And a large percentage of those who were located didn't return home alive. With the county's rugged terrain, they were lucky the child had been spotted before he succumbed to hunger, the elements, or the forest wildlife.

Daniel remembered the last case he'd worked that stretched into Laurel County. The course of that particular investigation had not run smooth. He—along with the whole state—had been desperate to find escaped convict Ethan Barrett. The convict had murdered four people while on the loose. Fortunately, with the help of Barrett's ex-wife, the serial killer had been taken down.

Daniel glanced at his watch. The afternoon was fading fast and he had a two-hour drive back to his home in Briarwood, a suburb of Nashville.

"If you ever need anything else," he told the sheriff, "just give me a call."

As he turned to go, a loud knock reverberated against the door to Vance's office.

"Come in," Vance called out.

The door pushed open and a young freckle-faced deputy burst into the room, his eyes wide.

"Sheriff, a woman's body's been found along Chickadee River," he said, trepidation in his voice. "Deputy McConnell's there now."

Vance snatched his hat from the coat rack next to his desk, pressed it down over his salt and pepper hair, and looked at Daniel. "You feel like taking a ride?"

The special agent's plans of decompressing with pizza and a baseball game vanished.

He nodded. "Lead the way."

Daniel followed the sheriff to his county-issued Ford Interceptor Utility and climbed into the passenger seat. He listened as Vance radioed the deputy on the scene, getting directions to the body's exact location.

Deep in the heart of the Cumberland Plateau, Laurel County encompassed mountain forestland, jagged bluffs, and a fertile valley. The area once known for coal mining was both beautiful and remote, populated in large part by families who'd lived on the land for generations.

Vance piloted the Ford up a two-lane highway, heading northeast at top speed. The patrol car driven by Deputy Carter, the freckled cop who'd delivered the news to the sheriff, hugged their tail, sirens blaring and lights flashing. Daniel had heard stories of several people—mostly drug dealers, moonshiners, and car thieves—who had gone missing near the town of Mettler Ridge, never to be seen again. Abandoned mine shafts, secluded caves, and ancient wells dotted the landscape. Plenty of places to hide a corpse.

From the radio call, it sounded as if the body was fresh and had been found out in the open by two fishermen. This led Daniel to suspect the death may have been the result of an accident or illness. If foul play was involved, there was a chance it had been a crime of passion and not premeditated. The medical examiner had not yet made it to the scene, and it seemed the examination of the corpse had been limited thus far.

The Ford veered off the highway onto a narrow gravel road that snaked through a dense forest. Through the trees, Daniel caught a glimpse of water—which he assumed was a creek that fed from the river—outside the passenger window. The road jerked to the left and the water disappeared behind a wall of emerald leaves.

A couple of miles further up the road, Vance slowed the Ford to a crawl. The vehicle rocked as he steered the tires off the gravel and onto a dirt lane with a row of weeds striping the center. The canopy of trees overhead cast a heavy shadow over the cab's interior.

"Old logging road," the sheriff said.

Daniel nodded as the melody of "Dueling Banjos" popped into his mind. This was one of those days when he wished he'd never seen the movie *Deliverance*. He raked his fingers through his dark brown hair as he again realized the reasons the territory had been assigned to the TBI's newest agent. Contrary to his boss's explanation, Daniel was convinced the fact that he'd previously hunted an escaped convict in the area was only a minor factor in the decision.

As they topped a rise, two more police Interceptors came into view, parked on the lane. Vance rolled up behind the vehicles and killed the Ford's engine. Daniel hopped out and slammed the passenger door. From where he stood, he couldn't see or hear the river.

Vance motioned to the right. "We've got a bit of a hike. I hope you're wearing comfortable shoes."

Instead of his normal jacket and tie, Daniel had dressed in khakis, a button-down shirt, and black athletic boots at the motel that morning, thinking he would again be combing the area for the missing child.

"I'm good," he told the sheriff.

Joined by the freckled deputy, they tramped through the thick forest underbrush with no visible trail in sight. Although it was the end of the first full week of October, the temperature had reached eighty-three degrees, according to the thermometer in Vance's Ford. Sweat popped out on Daniel's neck and ran down his back as he maneuvered around trees and briar bushes, following the sheriff.

About a quarter mile into the hike, the sound of rushing water hit his ears. A minute later, a break in the tree line appeared up ahead. They'd reached the river.

Vance looked back over his shoulder. "Watch your step," he warned. "There's a pretty steep drop-off down to the riverbank."

Daniel heeded his words, approaching the border of the tree line with caution. In the distance below, he spotted a crumpled form at the river's edge. He inspected the ground, making sure there were no footprints or any evidence that would be destroyed before scooting down the embankment sideways.

Nodding at the two deputies already on the scene, he inched toward the body, scanning the ground for clues as he went. The sheriff stood back, choosing to speak with the fishermen who'd made the discovery.

The woman appeared to be in her late twenties to early thirties with light brown hair cut in a short bob. She lay on her side, right at the waterline. Her mouth gaped open, a stream of dried blood running from the corner of her lips down her cheek. Fresh scratches lined her arms. Daniel recognized her outfit: black slacks and a red cotton shirt. It was the uniform worn by the servers at the local diner.

A mix of indignation and sorrow flooded his chest. He was no stranger to the reality of murder, but to see someone cut down in the prime of their life was especially troubling.

He moved closer, minding his steps, and knelt next to the body. A bullet wound marred the center of her chest. He rolled up the legs of his khakis and moved behind her, wading into the cool water. Another bullet entry point dotted the left side of the woman's back, along with the exit wound for the bullet that had pierced her heart.

And she was barefoot. Dried blood caked her soles as though she'd been running along the rocky shoreline or perhaps through the forest. He peered up toward the trees and noticed an area where the earth seemed disturbed, as though it had caved slightly. The indentation was located in a direct line from the body. He realized the woman had most likely tumbled down the embankment.

Livor mortis—the way the blood had pooled in the body—indicated that the woman had died at the scene rather than being transported there. From the condition of the corpse, he figured her death had occurred sometime that morning.

He waded out of the river and stared at the woman's slacks. Snags ran from the knees to the hems. Likely caused by briars in the forest.

The sheriff appeared at his side. "Gunshot," Vance stated.

"Yeah. Two that I can see."

Daniel didn't want to touch the woman or roll her over to check her other side until the medical examiner arrived.

Vance rubbed his chin. "Do you think it could have been an accident?"

"No. The shot to her back was from a distance. But not the one to her heart. If you look close, you can see powder burns on her chest. Whoever fired that bullet knew exactly what they were doing."

Vance nodded. "She's a local. Twenty-seven years old. Her name's Sarah Lester and she's got a record—narcotics. Meth mostly. She's been busted a few times. Lost custody of her kid over it."

"So she's divorced?" Daniel wondered whether her ex could be responsible for her murder.

"She never married. Her grandparents have custody of her kid. Word around town is that the father was a man from Nashville. I don't think he's ever been in the picture."

"What about a boyfriend?" Nine times out of ten, the killer ended up being someone close to the victim.

"She's got a live-in. But he's been in county lock-up for the past three days. Drunk and disorderly."

"Does she have any enemies in town?" It seemed like the sheriff knew the woman's history.

"Nope. None that I'm aware of. I figure her death's probably drug related."

"Maybe." He guessed it was possible that the woman could have provoked her dealer's wrath in some way. But why was she barefoot out in the middle of nowhere? She was dressed for work.

"Have the deputies found her shoes?" Daniel asked.

Vance shook his head. "They haven't found anything yet. And likely won't ever."

The sheriff's defeatist attitude took the special agent by surprise. "Why do you say that?"

Vance stared at him, a strange look in his eyes. "Mountain folk protect their own. Even if one of their kin is a killer."

Due to the remote location of the body, it stood to reason that the person responsible for the crime was a local. Daniel knew the people living in the area tended to be clannish, but with proper detective work, most murders could be solved.

"Maybe one of the locals would crack if the right amount of pressure was applied," Daniel said, trying to keep the irritation from his tone.

"You're not from around here. You don't realize how life is. When it comes to something as serious as murder, nobody's gonna talk to the police. Not to me. Not to my deputies. And definitely not to you."

"But what about the woman's relatives? Don't you think they'd want to see her killer arrested?" It didn't make sense for her loved ones not to cooperate. Unless they were guilty.

"Folks in these parts have their own way of getting justice. If her kin finds out who's responsible for her murder ... well, that person will most likely disappear."

Daniel couldn't believe what he was hearing. He'd thought the days of vigilante justice were long gone. And for the sheriff to seemingly give up before even trying to solve the crime baffled him.

He looked back at the young woman, murdered in cold blood. She had a child. She was someone's daughter. Someone's girlfriend. Her life had value. Daniel wasn't about to let her killer go free.

"I'd like to investigate this case," he told Vance.

"You're more than welcome to take over. But I doubt you'll get anywhere."

Daniel was determined to prove the sheriff wrong. He'd find out who was responsible for Sarah Lester's murder and lock them behind bars.

But as Sheriff Vance had pointed out, getting through to the locals would be tricky. He needed someone they would trust. Someone who'd grown up in Laurel County. Luckily, he knew the perfect person to call on for help.

CHAPTER THREE

Ashley circled her sedan around the business complex in Briarwood for the third time. But not because she was having difficulty finding a place to park. With most of the offices concluding their business day an hour earlier, empty spaces abounded. Her reluctance to go inside stemmed from a case of nerves. The thought of seeing Brett again filled her with angst.

Her former fiancé's SUV sat directly in front of the real estate attorney's office. She wondered how long he'd been there and whether he was irritated that she hadn't shown up yet. She glanced at the clock on the dashboard: 5:59 p.m. One minute left until their scheduled appointment. She couldn't put off the meeting any longer.

Sighing, Ashley pulled her sedan into the space one car down from Brett's SUV. She'd been told by an administrative assistant that the buyers of the home she'd shared with her ex-fiancé would sign the closing documents first. She hoped they were finished by now. She wanted to get in and out of the office as fast as possible.

As she pushed her car door open, her cell phone chirped. A text message. She glanced at the screen.

Where are you?

The message was from Brett. She guessed she'd received her answer as to whether or not he was annoyed. She stuffed her phone back into her purse and headed up the winding sidewalk to the entrance of the real estate attorney's office. She stopped outside the raised-panel door and took a deep breath, wishing she had thought to ask whether it would have been legal for her to sign the forms by email.

Crossing the threshold, she scanned the room. Her stomach knotted when Brett's brown puppy dog eyes locked with hers. He sat alone in the traditionally furnished waiting area, handsome as ever in his charcoal gray suit and burgundy tie. She could tell his dark hair had recently been trimmed.

He stood. "It's good to see you, Ashley," he said, a wistful tone in his voice.

Maybe he wasn't too irritated with her after all.

"You too," she replied, out of politeness rather than a desire to be reunited.

Standing next to him, the warm scent of his cologne encircling her, she felt her heart break all over again. As though she was just now finding out that the love of her life had been unfaithful. She fought the tears threatening her eyes as she sank into the leather wingback chair next to the sofa where Brett had been sitting.

"How's the academy going?" he asked, returning to his seat.

"Good."

A one-word answer was the most she could muster. She knew it was impolite not to ask about his life as well, but she didn't trust herself to speak. She feared her voice would break. That her tears would flow.

The inner door to the waiting room pushed open and Ashley looked up to see an attractive older woman with graying hair, her hand on the knob.

"Mr. Holbrook, Ms. Hope, we're ready for you now," the woman said.

Ashley was relieved to be rescued from the torture of small talk with her ex-fiancé. She followed the woman down a long corridor, Brett close behind. At the end of the hallway, the woman motioned them toward an open door.

The closing attorney, a short man with wire-rimmed glasses, was already inside the small conference room. Three stacks of papers topped the table before him. Ashley assumed one stack contained the original documents they would sign and the other two were copies for Brett and herself.

She shook hands with the attorney and then took her place at the table. She could feel the heat from her former fiancé's body as he sat next to her, mere inches separating them. The attorney's words floated past her, their meaning lost, as she reflected on her life with Brett. The closeness they'd once shared. The visions she'd had for their future. For a while, it had felt like she was living in a fairytale, as though it was the two of them against the world. She remembered the day they'd moved into the exquisite two-story home on Marigold Court—the exclusive neighborhood where she'd planned to raise a family. Now, the house would foster someone else's dreams.

The attorney flipped to the last page of the closing documents. A pang of sadness struck her as she signed and dated the line above her printed name. With all the required signatures collected, the attorney thanked them and then handed them their copies of the forms.

And just like that, it was over. The last tie binding her to Brett severed.

She kept her head down as she hurried back through the corridor and waiting room. With her former fiancé at her heels, she jerked the entrance door open and bolted down the sidewalk heading for the parking lot.

"Ashley, wait!" Brett called from behind her.

She slowed her pace but refused to turn around. Didn't want him to see her cry.

A second later, he was at her side. "Can we talk for a minute?" he asked. "Please?"

There was nothing left to discuss. She'd heard everything he had to say—more than once. Still, choking back a sob, she felt herself nod an agreement. She stopped next to her sedan and leaned her back against the driver's door.

"I've missed you, Ash," he said.

The same words he'd texted several times before. Words that no longer felt genuine.

Steeling herself against the pain, she tilted her head up and met his gaze. "Is that all you wanted to say?"

"Don't be like that. You know I still love you."

"I'm not sure you really understand what love is." His version of the word had proven to have a different meaning than hers.

He sighed, clenched his bottom lip between his teeth. "I can't stop thinking about the baby."

Her hand snapped to her stomach, an unconscious reflex. She'd only been seven weeks along when she'd suffered the miscarriage. It was her second. The first time Ashley had been pregnant, she was only eighteen. With her track record, she was beginning to worry she'd never be able to carry a child to term.

"I think about the baby too," she said. The truth was she dreamed about the child she and Brett had lost almost every night.

"We can try again," he told her. "I know we could be happy. Just give me another chance."

Ashley pressed her eyes shut. But a tear still managed to sneak out and slide down her cheek.

"It would never work out between us long term, Brett," she said, wiping away the tear. "I wish I was wrong, but I'm not."

"How can you be so sure?"

"Cherie."

Although the woman he'd had the affair with was no longer living, her ghost still stood between them, as real as flesh and blood. Ashley's psychopathic ex-husband had murdered Cherie—while the woman was in bed with Brett.

The color drained from Brett's face. Maybe it was a mistake for Ashley to mention the woman's name since she had only been gone a short time, but it was important to be honest.

Ashley sighed, feeling the need to explain her point of view.

"It would be different if it had been a one-time thing," she said. "Maybe I could have gotten past a slip-up of meaningless sex. But that's not what it was. Do you not understand how bad it hurt when you told me you were in love with her?"

"I only said I *might* be in love. There's a difference."

Whether he'd really been in love—or just thought he might be—didn't matter. The admission had ripped Ashley's heart into shreds. And it had made her realize one cold, hard fact.

"The problem is that you were able to fall for someone else. Your love for me wasn't strong enough to stop it. That means there was something missing in our relationship—for you, anyway. Whatever that piece is, the empty hole it's created would always be there between us. And consciously or not, you'd always be trying to fill it."

He stared at her. "How can I convince you that you're wrong?"

"I don't think you can."

"Won't you at least let me try?"

Not when she already knew how it would end. Although she still loved him—and a part of her always would—she couldn't put herself through the pain of losing him again. Their relationship might last a year or two, but she knew he'd always be searching for that missing piece.

"Answer one question for me," she said, "with one hundred percent total honesty."

He nodded. "Okay."

She braced herself for his answer. "If Cherie had never been attacked—if she was still alive—who would you be with right now?"

His gaze dropped to the ground, telling her everything she needed to know.

"I'm not sure," he finally mumbled.

Although she was expecting them, the words still hit her like a brick. Was he being honest? She wasn't sure. She realized that it was possible he knew exactly which woman he would have chosen—Cherie.

"And that's one of the reasons you and I will never get back together," she said, trying to keep her voice steady.

"That's not fair. Cherie's gone. She's no threat to you."

He didn't understand, or at least he pretended not to. If she stayed with him, there would always be another Cherie. Eventually, he'd find the one with all the pieces. With his looks, charm, and money, it shouldn't take him that long.

"I have to go," she said, knowing that they could talk all night and it wouldn't change things.

It was getting late and she had a two-hour drive back to the small trailer on her father's property in Mettler Ridge.

He looked at her, his own eyes watering. "Tell your family I said hello."

She knew his words were an attempt at humor to lighten the mood. Her family—who had never trusted her former fiancé—now despised him for breaking her heart. And Brett's family loathed Ashley as well, but for a different reason. She'd been born and raised in the backwoods of the Cumberland Plateau rather than the affluent suburb of Nashville they called home. As hard as she'd tried, she'd never been able to measure up to the wealthy Holbrook family's standards. In the end, she'd realized they'd never been worth her effort.

Ashley wished she could smile, but the ache in her heart wouldn't allow it.

"Goodbye, Brett."

He stepped back as she opened her sedan door. She noticed he wasn't smiling either. He stood there watching as she started the engine and backed out of the parking space. The urge to stop the car, jump out, and run into his arms rushed through her. But she knew it would be a mistake. One she would regret. As she pulled out onto the street, she glanced in her rearview mirror. Brett still hadn't moved, his gaze following her.

Tears flooded her eyes and streamed down her cheeks. She'd give anything to be wrong. But deep in her soul, she knew she could never trust his love.

Her phone chirped from inside her purse on the passenger seat. She waited until the traffic halted at a red light and then pulled a small box of tissues from her console and dried her face. She checked her phone's screen. It was a text from her younger brother, Shane.

Hurry home. U got a visitor.

The message puzzled her. She had no real friends left in her hometown.

Who? she typed back.

She watched the bubble of dots, indicating that her brother was tapping in his reply.

Wait and c

She sighed and shook her head. Shane loved to tease her. She should have known he'd keep her in suspense.

Ashley veered onto the interstate and sped toward Laurel County.

CHAPTER FOUR

With her heart still aching from her meeting with her former fiancé, Ashley steered her sedan onto the hard-packed dirt driveway leading to her father's house in Laurel County. Hearing Brett's voice again, gazing into his eyes, breathing in his cologne, and seeing him standing beneath the glow of the streetlamp, watching her as she drove away, had stirred up a host of feelings she'd tried hard to bury. Now, a sense of sorrow had settled into her soul, as deep and dark as the mountain night.

The sedan wobbled as the tires hit the wooden bridge that stretched across the creek on the one-hundred-fifty-acre property, passed down in the Hope family for generations. After her breakup with Brett, Ashley had moved into a small trailer located on the back corner of her father's land.

More than eight years had passed since she'd last been a resident of Laurel County. She'd left to attend college in Chattanooga, with no intention of ever returning to the remote area which had no employment opportunities to offer. From Chattanooga, she'd relocated to Briarwood with her former fiancé.

Her newest accommodations were a world apart from the luxurious house she'd shared with Brett, but she didn't mind. Her father and two brothers were here. And that's what made it home.

The tree-lined drive snaked to the left and then broke through the clearing. As she pulled into the parking area, her headlights flashed across an unfamiliar car parked beside her father's pickup. Shane had texted that she had a visitor. Wrapped up in her thoughts of Brett, she'd forgotten.

The light on the long narrow front porch of the Appalachian farmhouse her great-grandfather had built long before she was born glowed a soft amber, urging her to come inside. With the day she'd had, she would have preferred to skip past her father's house and retire straight to her trailer. She wondered who the visitor could be. She hadn't seen any of her friends from high school in years. The only girl she'd really been close to had moved away right after graduation. And the friends she'd had in college—at the University of Tennessee in Chattanooga—wouldn't know how to find her. She'd always been vague about her backwoods upbringing. A fact she now regretted.

As she swung her car door open, a familiar baying split the air. Her father's bluetick hound, Ace, ran to greet her.

"Hey, boy." She scratched his head. The dog acted as Spencer Hope's own low-tech security alarm, alerting anytime someone ventured onto the property, friend or foe.

Mounting the porch steps, she heard voices leaking through the window screens—one of them saying her name—followed by laughter. She hoped she was wrong, but it sounded as though her family was sharing embarrassing stories of her childhood. Her suspicions were confirmed as she pushed open the front door and caught her father in mid-sentence.

"… ol' billy goat butted Ashley right in her tail," Spencer said, a broad grin covering his face. "She went a-flying. Landed smack dab in the middle of the hogs' wallering hole."

Her younger brother, Shane, chimed in. "You should of seen her." He motioned, touching his auburn hair. "Mud done covered her head to toe." He slapped the arms of his wheelchair with glee.

Although she hated being the topic of their conversation, she was glad to see her father in such a good mood. She'd been worried about his health since his recent heart attack. He'd come a long way in the last few months, but he still hadn't regained all of his strength.

"Very funny—" Ashley began, but then her gaze lit on the visitor sitting on the sofa. His blue eyes sparkled, and a smile painted his dimpled face. He was obviously amused by the tale.

"Detective Lansing," she said, surprised to see him in Mettler Ridge. She wondered what had brought the police detective all the way out to the mountains.

"It's Daniel, remember? And I'm not a detective anymore."

She was stunned. She'd never met anyone as dedicated to law enforcement as Daniel Lansing. He'd helped Ashley a few months back when her ex-husband, Ethan, had escaped from prison.

"You mean you quit your job with the Briarwood Police Department?" she asked. She hoped his leaving wasn't due to the budget cuts the department had been forced to issue.

"The TBI made me an offer I couldn't pass up," he told her, the smile still lighting his face. "So now it's special agent. But still Daniel to you."

She knew the bureau was lucky to have him on their team.

"I'm sure the Briarwood PD is not too happy that they've lost their best detective," she said.

A slight flush crossed Daniel's face, and she realized he was too humble to acknowledge the compliment.

She changed the subject. "So what brings you all the way out to Laurel County?"

He glanced at Spencer and Shane, and then turned his gaze back to Ashley. "Could we step out onto the porch for a minute?"

"Of course." It was obvious his answer required privacy.

Her father rose from his recliner. "I reckon I'll be hitting the hay," he said. "Mighty good meeting ya, Daniel."

"You too, sir." The special agent shook Spencer's hand.

Ashley looked at Shane, her eyes hinting for her younger brother to head to his own bedroom, but his wheelchair didn't budge. Instead, he picked up the remote and switched on the television. Shane could be exasperating at times, but she always stopped short of being angry with him. Every time she looked at his chair, a bolt of guilt hit her. She still blamed herself for his injury. It was her ex-husband who had attacked her younger brother, smashing his neck with a rock.

Knowing Shane had understood her unspoken request that he leave the room, Ashley stifled a sigh and led Daniel out the front door to the glider seat on the porch. The cool night air penetrated her silk blouse, heralding the arrival of autumn. Within the next few days, the leaves would begin changing from shades of green to gold, orange, and red.

The agent waited for her to sit first, then sank down beside her. She wondered whether there were loose ends left to tie up regarding her ex-husband.

"So, I'm assuming you're here on official business," she stated. "Is it about what happened with Ethan?"

"Oh, no. That file's been closed. Don't worry about it anymore."

She was relieved to hear that the police department was satisfied with the results of their investigation. But with Ethan's case no longer open, she was even more puzzled by the agent's visit. Maybe it had to do with her ex-husband's cousin being involved in the operation of a chop shop. She remembered mentioning the shop to Daniel once.

"Are you looking for one of Ethan's relatives?"

He tilted his head. "Well, I'm not really sure," he said, a serious tone in his voice.

Now he definitely had her curiosity piqued. It was obvious the situation was puzzling to him as well. "So, you drove two hours from Briarwood and you're not sure of the reason?"

He looked at her, his expression grim. "I'm investigating a murder. A young woman was killed here in Laurel County."

Her breath caught in her throat. "How?"

"She was shot. Probably sometime this morning. Her body was found on the bank of the Chickadee River."

The river, teeming with bass, was one of her family's favorite fishing spots. They'd charted practically every bend.

Ashley knew a considerable amount of crime took place in Laurel County, but it mostly involved drugs, moonshine, and stolen cars. There were occasional rumors that circulated regarding criminals in the area bumping each other off, but bodies were seldom found.

"Is it possible that a hunter thought she was a deer and shot her by mistake?"

He shook his head. "One of the bullets was fired at close range. Too close to be an accident."

"Was the murder ..." She wasn't quite sure how to phrase the question. "Sexually motivated?"

"The woman was found clothed. So we won't know for sure until the autopsy is finished. From what we gathered from her family and coworkers, she'd been missing a little more than twenty-four hours."

Ashley sighed. It pained her to hear of the murder, but she still wasn't sure of the reason Daniel had come to see her. One thing she knew for certain: Ashley's family had nothing to do with the crime.

"I don't really understand why you're here talking to me," she said. "I haven't been anywhere near the Chickadee River in years."

"Because I need your help."

"My help?" She had no idea why the agent would need her.

Daniel nodded. "The body was found in an isolated spot. Whoever killed her is probably a local. According to the sheriff, the people here won't be willing to cooperate with the investigation."

If a local had killed the woman, there was no way anyone living in the area would talk to the police about it, even if—or especially if—

they knew the identity of the person responsible. The threat of retaliation by the guilty party's relatives would be too high.

"He's right. Snitches in Laurel County would need a whole lot more than just stitches. I don't know how you'll ever get the people around here to tell you anything."

He stared at her as though she was missing something. "That's where you come in."

The picture was becoming clearer. "So you want me to try and squeeze information out of the locals," she stated.

"I'm asking you to help with the investigation. It's already been approved by my boss."

Ashley chewed her bottom lip. Her first impulse was to agree. She would like nothing better than to help solve the woman's murder, to ensure justice for the family. But conducting an investigation would take time. Something she had very little of currently.

Her weekdays were filled with classes at the police academy, and her evenings and weekends were spent studying. And, most important of all, helping Shane. If her brother ever hoped to walk again, he needed constant physical therapy. The insurance coverage for his in-home care had ended weeks ago. Ashley had taken up where the physical therapist had left off, watching and learning all the exercises Shane needed to perform. He was relying on her to help him heal from his injury.

"I wish I could help you, Daniel, I really do. But between my classes at the academy and Shane's physical therapy, I just don't have the time."

But needing to save her spare hours for Shane wasn't her only concern. Ashley feared she wasn't qualified to take on the job. That her inexperience would somehow jeopardize the investigation.

Disappointment flooded Daniel's blue eyes, stinging her like an arrow to the heart. She hated letting him down. But she didn't see any way around it.

His gaze lingered on her, but she didn't know what else to say. "I'm sorry," she finally muttered.

Then, as if by magic, his expression changed. A confident look spread across his face. It was obvious that an idea had hit him. She wondered whether he'd thought of a way to get the locals to cooperate.

"What is it?" she asked.

"I'm pretty sure you're going to change your mind."

There was nothing she could imagine that would get her to take time away from Shane's therapy. Ashley had brought Ethan into their lives. She was responsible for the damages.

"Why do you think that?"

He hesitated, empathy creeping into his eyes.

"Because of your relationship to the victim," he finally said, his voice soft.

CHAPTER FIVE

A chill, far colder than the autumn night could ever create, raced down Ashley's spine when she heard Daniel's words. Did she know the murdered woman? She shifted her position on the glider seat and stared at the agent.

"Exactly what kind of relationship do I have with the victim?" she asked him.

"You went to high school together. Graduated the same year."

Although her graduating class from Laurel County High had been relatively small compared to other schools in Tennessee, there were still plenty of students that she knew by name only. It was possible she'd never even spoken to the woman.

"Who is she?"

"Her name was Sarah Lester," he said as though searching her eyes for a recollection.

Ashley turned her head as a pang of sadness ripped through her heart. She had known Sarah, though they had never been close friends. Ashley's older brother, Kyle, had dated the girl for a brief time. He'd taken her to Homecoming during Ashley's sophomore year. A picture of Kyle and Sarah that had been snapped at the dance was in one of their family photo albums.

Daniel was right about one thing. Knowing it was Sarah who had been murdered made it harder for Ashley to turn down his request to help investigate the case. But she still had to put Shane's needs first. There was no one else who could coach him. They couldn't afford a private nurse. Her father wasn't physically strong enough, and her older brother, Kyle, was shorthanded at the auto repair shop her family owned. With the amount of overtime he was currently pulling, there was no way her older brother could help.

And since the age of twelve, Ashley had felt responsible for her younger brother's welfare, practically raising him after their mother had died of cancer. She couldn't bail on him now.

"I'm really sorry, but I have to be here to help Shane with his physical therapy. He's counting on me and I can't let him down. I hope you understand."

Daniel nodded. "I do," he said, though she could tell he wished the situation was different. "Your brother's lucky to have you."

The agent rose from the glider seat. Ashley followed him down the porch steps.

"Congratulations on your new job," she said, hoping for his success in solving the murder and wishing she had the time to assist him.

"Thanks," he said. "And let's keep in touch."

She waited until the taillights of his sedan disappeared into the forest before heading back inside the house. When she walked into the living room, the TV and overhead light had been turned off. She guessed Shane had gone to his room.

"Why'd you say no?" her younger brother's voice boomed from the darkness.

Startled, Ashley jumped. She realized Shane had been listening to her and Daniel through the open window.

"Why were you eavesdropping on a private conversation?" she asked him.

"You think I ain't able to do them exercises by myself?"

She flipped on the light. If they were going to talk this out, she wanted to be able to see him.

"It's not that I don't think you're capable of doing your exercises. I promised you I that would help and I didn't want to go back on my word."

Although what she'd said was true, there was more to it than that. Ashley was afraid that if she wasn't there to encourage Shane, to push him forward, he would give up. There had been too many times when he'd wanted to quit. To let his spinal injury defeat him and rob him of any chance of ever walking again. She couldn't permit that to happen.

And there was the matter of her inexperience. The investigation was too important to allow a rookie like herself to come in and make a mess of things.

"Well, you ought to be helping Daniel," he told her.

"Shane, I don't think you realize how much time and effort goes into a police investigation. If I agreed to work on the case, there might be days when you didn't see me at all."

He was silent for a moment. "I remember Sarah," he finally said, his voice soft. "She was mighty nice to me when I was a kid."

Ashley had the same memories. A latchkey child who seemed to suffer from neglect, Sarah had gone out of her way to make Shane feel included, instead of treating him like a pest as the other girls Kyle dated had done.

Shane continued, "It ain't right to just let her killer go. Daniel ain't never gonna find out who done it."

"He might," she said. Daniel was an excellent investigator. Maybe he could come up with a way to get through to the locals.

"Nah. And you know it."

Guilt began to worm its way into Ashley's heart. But it wasn't as much guilt as she would feel if Shane stopped his physical therapy.

"It's late," she said. "We should go to sleep. And don't forget, the Nolan Arnold Band concert is tomorrow."

She'd promised to drive Shane to Cedar View to catch the southern rock group's performance. He needed to get out of the house. He'd been cooped up for far too long.

He rolled his wheelchair toward the hallway. It still pained her to see his six-foot-three frame confined in the metal cage. But she was grateful that her ex-husband hadn't killed Shane. The attack on her brother had been brutal, but at least he was still alive.

"Ashley, I can do them exercises by myself just fine," Shane said. "I won't be a missing any. I'll keep working hard. But you need to be finding out who shot Sarah."

If only the decision of whether or not to join the investigation was that easy.

"Goodnight, Shane."

Ashley grabbed her purse, switched off the living room light, and headed out the front door. It looked as though her anxiety-filled day would be followed by a restless night. With her mind swirling, it would probably take hours for her to fall asleep. She couldn't wait to get back to her trailer where she could attempt to destress with a cup of chamomile tea.

She climbed back into her sedan and navigated the winding dirt drive that led to the rear of her father's property. She steered past Kyle's trailer on the way. His pickup was parked outside, but the mobile home's lights were off. She knew he had to be at the shop early in the morning, so he was likely already sleeping.

As she parked and cut the sedan's engine, she wondered what her older brother would think about the situation. Would Kyle encourage her to investigate Sarah's death? Or would he believe that she needed to concentrate her energies on Shane's recovery?

Ashley pushed open the door to her trailer and was hit by a wall of stagnant heat. The window air conditioner had obviously gone on the fritz again. Although the night air outside had now dipped to a cool seventy degrees, the day's sun had baked the interior of the mobile home like a clay pot in a kiln.

She flipped on the overhead ceiling fan, trudged down the hallway to the air conditioner, unplugged the power cord, counted to ten, and then pressed the plug back into the socket. Nothing happened. She'd have to open all the windows, otherwise, she'd never be able to rest. And hot tea was definitely out of the question.

Opting for a cool shower instead of the tea, Ashley stood under the gentle spray in the fiberglass tub shower combo. She cursed the weak water pressure for the millionth time. The trailer was old and lacked normal conveniences like central air and a washer and dryer, but she couldn't imagine living anywhere else right now. Not until Shane's condition improved. At least the water from the well, fed by an underground spring, was good for her skin.

As she slathered conditioner onto her hair, her thoughts jumped to Sarah Lester. She hadn't seen the woman since her high school graduation. By the time they'd become seniors, the two had managed to gravitate into polar opposite crowds. Concerned more with her grades than popularity, Ashley had a small circle of friends who spent most of their weekends hanging out at the local diner or at the movie theater in Cedar View. And she had met Ethan senior year, who had sucked up her time like a sponge.

Sarah, on the other hand, had earned a reputation as a party girl, choosing her friends from a group known for excessive drinking and drug use. Given what Ashley knew of Sarah's dysfunctional family—and the rumors of her father's physical abuse of her mother—Ashley hadn't been surprised by the high school teen's downward spiral.

Ashley toweled off from her shower and slipped into a lightweight cotton nightgown.

Did Mr. Lester have something to do with the murder? She shuddered at the possibility that the man could have killed his own child. But he had a history of violence. He'd been arrested once for assaulting Ashley's Uncle Russ with a beer bottle. She couldn't remember whether the altercation had resulted in jail time.

With the ceiling fan in her bedroom whirring above her, Ashley crawled beneath her bedsheets. As she closed her eyes, Shane's voice echoed in her mind.

You need to be finding out who shot Sarah.

Was her brother right? Should she trust Shane's commitment to his physical therapy, put aside her doubts regarding her investigative abilities, and search for Sarah's killer? Maybe she'd have a clearer perspective in the morning.

Both mentally and physically exhausted from the events of her day, she snuggled into her pillow and began to dream.

Ashley yanked the door of her olive green locker open and stared inside. She couldn't remember which books she needed. What class did she have next? Was it English or algebra? Maybe it was biology. Or geography. To be safe, she piled all four textbooks into her arms along with her notebook. She shouldered the locker closed and glanced down the long hallway inside her high school. The classroom doors lining the corridor gaped open. But she didn't know which one to enter. There were no other students or teachers around, no one to ask.

Behind her, another locker door slammed shut. She turned around and saw Sarah marching toward her.

"Do you know where I'm supposed to go?" Ashley asked the slender brunette.

Sarah nodded. "Follow me."

As Ashley strode behind her classmate, the building began to shake. A sound similar to thunder boomed in her ears as the walls crumbled away. Her books slipped from her arms. A crack raced along the center of the floor toward them, a jagged line splitting the charcoal gray tiles.

"Sarah!" she called out, reaching for the teen's hand.

But it was too late. A wide crevice parted the floor beneath Sarah's feet. Ashley jumped to the right side and rushed toward the edge as her classmate tumbled into the chasm. She had to get Sarah out. Now!

A flash of lightning streaked across the sky and the remnants of the school building faded into a thick black smoke. As the haze cleared, she realized she was no longer on the school grounds. Headstones dotted the scorched earth around her. She was at the cemetery in Mettler Ridge.

"Ashley, help me!" Sarah's voice cried out.

She rushed toward the sound. An open grave marred the charred ground before her. She dropped to her knees and peered into the hole. Sarah's face stared back, terror in her eyes. The teen clung to a rock on the side of the seemingly bottomless abyss.

Ashley fell onto her stomach, balancing her body on the rim of the grave. "Grab my hand!" she yelled as she stretched her arm as far as it would go.

The earth rumbled beneath her as a gust of wind, with the strength of a tornado, circled up from the abyss, lifting her up and knocking her back. A swirl of dust stung her eyes as she struggled to crawl back toward the edge of the hole. She had to save Sarah.

"Help me!" the teen cried out again.

The ground continued to quake. Fear raced through Ashley's heart as she watched the earth swell before her. A loud moan escaped her lips.

"No," she sobbed.

Tears ran down her cheeks as the grave sealed itself closed, trapping Sarah inside for all eternity.

Ashley jerked awake and sat up in bed, her heart pounding. A cold sweat coated her face and chest. There was no question left in her mind. She knew what she had to do.

She grabbed her cell from the table next to the bed and fired off a text to Daniel.

I want to help.

Let me know where to meet you in the morning.

CHAPTER SIX

A red-shouldered hawk squealed overhead as Ashley picked her way through the forest underbrush with Daniel directing her path from behind. He'd asked her to go first, wanting her to get a sense of the area without interference, hoping she would catch something he had missed. So far, she'd found nothing. No clues to shed light on the last few hours of Sarah Lester's short life.

There were other investigators scouring the woods as well—TBI agents and sheriff's deputies had arrived at first light. But they had moved on from the line Ashley and Daniel walked, expanding their search in an ever-widening circle.

Looking up, her eyes following the flight of the screeching hawk, she noticed a break in the canopy of trees ahead. The sound of rushing water echoed toward her. The Chickadee River.

She pressed onward, dodging a thicket of briars. A cottontail rabbit scurried out of the tangled branches, startling her. She glanced back at Daniel, hoping he hadn't seen her jump.

She'd spent her childhood tramping through the woods. The sudden appearance of the rabbit should have come as no surprise, but her guard had been down. Images of Sarah running through the underbrush had consumed her mind instead. She wondered why the woman had been out in the middle of nowhere. What had happened to her shoes? And who was she running from?

Continuing her trek toward the river, she caught sight of a large maple, its exposed roots snaking across the ground. A yellow evidence marker stood beneath the tree. A portion of earth had been disturbed, weeds cut. She wondered what clue the foliage had held.

As she squatted next to the marker, Daniel appeared beside her.

"We think this is where the first shot hit Sarah," he said, his voice low. "Drops of blood were found on the ground."

Ashley winced at the thought. She'd been told the first bullet had punctured the woman's lung, causing it to collapse. Her heart ached as she pictured Sarah lying in the weeds, struggling to breathe.

Daniel pointed toward the tree line where another marker lay. "She crawled a few feet," he stated. "Then she rolled down the embankment."

Nodding, Ashley stood and inched closer to the forest rim. She peered down at the river. Two sheriff's deputies walked the shoreline, one with a metal detector dangling from a strap hooked over his shoulder. He'd probably been combing the ground for shell casings.

To her right, she spotted a makeshift ramp—a piece of plywood on top of a couple of two-by-fours—the investigative team had constructed to make getting up and down the embankment easier. It was a good idea. The drop-off was steep and the area below rocky. Her stomach clenched as she realized Sarah had rolled across the sharp stones. Ashley hoped her former classmate had been unconscious at the time.

Taking a deep breath, she shuffled down the ramp with Daniel following close behind. The early morning sun reflected off the river, the rushing water glistening white and gold. At the edge of the waterline three bright orange flags rippled in the breeze. A solemn reminder of the exact location Sarah had died.

Ashley swallowed hard and held back the tears that threatened her eyes. She had to project a professional image, to detach from her emotions. To try and forget that the victim was someone she once knew.

Daniel stepped toward the row of flags. "Her head was positioned here," he said, pointing to the flag on the far left. "The second bullet entered her chest and exited her back. A tech managed to dig it out of the river bottom. A thirty-caliber rifle cartridge."

"Where did you find the shell casing?" She glanced up and down the riverbank. The agent had told her the second shot had been fired at close range, but she didn't see any more evidence markers.

"It wasn't found. Looks like the unsub picked it up."

The killer probably knew that by leaving the casings behind, they risked having their fingerprints identified. Which could mean they already had a criminal record.

"So I'm guessing that your team hasn't been able to find any casings in the forest either."

"No," he said, disappointment clear in his eyes.

She sighed. "Do you have any ideas yet about who might have wanted to kill her?"

Questioning a victim's family and close friends was always first on the docket. Although Ashley knew he hadn't been able to pry any real information loose—or he would have told her—she thought maybe he had sensed a suspicious vibe from someone.

"There's a boyfriend, but he's in jail on a different charge. He claims they had a good relationship. He said Sarah didn't have any enemies. And we're still trying to ID her kid's father."

"She left a child behind?" The revelation that her former classmate had been a mother made it even harder for Ashley to keep her emotions in check.

"A five-year-old son."

She wondered where the child was now. Most likely with Sarah's parents. She hoped the years had softened the Lesters' rough edges, had curbed their wild ways and made them more attentive.

The two deputies ambled up next to Daniel. He swiveled to make introductions.

"Ashley Hope, this is Deputy Kevin McConnell."

"I knew it was you, Ashley," Kevin said, extending his hand.

"Kevin and I went to high school together," she told Daniel as she accepted the deputy's grasp.

If she had bumped into her old schoolmate on the street, she never would have recognized him. The long sandy hair she remembered had been chopped short and his once acne-prone skin had cleared. Kevin had been one of the local diner's weekend regulars. Not exactly a part of her close circle, but right on the cusp. He always been a bright student, and she was glad he'd chosen a career in law enforcement.

Kevin grinned. "And guess who this is," he said, motioning toward the other deputy.

She searched the second man's face. His green eyes seemed familiar, but she couldn't quite place him.

"Troy Luckadoo," the man said, stepping toward her. "We had Mrs. Greer for geometry."

The classmate's name clicked and a memory floated into her mind. Troy's brown hair had been longer back then as well.

"That's right, you sat behind me," she said, shaking his hand. "Your crew cut threw me off for a second."

Her recollections were a little cloudy, but she was pretty sure that geometry wasn't the only class she and Troy had shared. She seemed to remember him in sophomore English.

"Kevin and me have both changed," Troy remarked. "But not you—you look just the same."

She appreciated the compliment although she knew it wasn't true. "Don't I wish."

"So you're with the TBI now?" Kevin asked.

"No, not officially." She wasn't really sure how to explain her role in the investigation.

Daniel chimed in. "She's working as a consultant."

"Oh, okay," Kevin said, his eyes revealing his bewilderment. He paused, most likely waiting for Daniel to elaborate.

When no further explanation was given, Kevin continued, "Well, we're heading back up in the woods." He patted the radar detector affixed to his shoulder as though the tool was needed elsewhere. "But we just wanted to stop and say hello first."

In an attempt to be polite, Ashley forced her lips into a half smile. "I'm glad you did. It's really nice seeing both of you again." The sentiment was genuine, but with the location of Sarah's murder at their feet, the normal pleasantries were difficult.

Troy nodded. "Just wish it could be different circumstances," he said, his voice somber. "It's rough, you know. Investigating the death of somebody we went to school with."

She met his eyes. He appeared to be just as unnerved standing next to the evidence flags as she was. This was definitely not the time or place for a high school reunion.

Ashley watched the two deputies mount the ramp leading into the forest and then turned her focus back to Daniel.

"I know you said that Sarah was clothed when she was found, but have you ruled out the possibility of a sexual assault?" she asked. "That could be the reason she was in the forest without her shoes."

The young woman could have been attacked in a car up on the old logging road. Maybe by someone she was dating. She could have been running from a rapist.

"Yeah, I thought the same thing," he told her. "And there was evidence of recent sexual activity. But the ME can't tell whether it was consensual or not. And there was no semen found."

The fact that there were no bodily fluids left behind for a DNA comparison disappointed her.

"So basically, there are no real leads or suspicions yet as to who could have killed her."

Ashley had hoped there was at least one suspect in the agent's crosshairs.

"The sheriff thinks it's drug related. Sarah had a history. He thinks she tried to rob her dealer."

Although Ashley was sad to hear that Sarah still had a habit of drug use, it didn't really surprise her.

"I guess that means that the medical examiner found drugs in her system."

"We don't know yet. Still waiting on toxicology."

Unlike on television, she realized the tests could take several days. But they had no time to spare. They needed answers. And soon.

"So do you agree with the sheriff's assumption?"

Daniel looked at her. "It's possible. But it feels like there's more to it. Let's say she did rob her dealer. In my experience, dealers usually carry handguns, not rifles. They get the job done with one shot to the forehead. They don't chase barefoot women through the woods."

Ashley shared his doubts regarding the sheriff's theory. She chewed her bottom lip, reflecting on what she knew of Sarah's childhood.

"I think you're right—it feels more like Sarah's murder was personal," she said. "And I think I know who might have killed her."

CHAPTER SEVEN

Ashley's stomach dropped as she remembered the rumors that had plagued Sarah's family throughout the teen's high school years. Some of the stories may have been just that—tall tales and nothing more. But there had been too many accounts of abuse for all of them to have been false. And she'd seen the bruises staining the arms of Sarah's mother with her own eyes.

An expression of surprise lit up Daniel's face. "You think you know who killed her?"

"I'm just saying that I have an idea of who *might* be responsible," she replied, glancing down at the three orange flags marking the position where Sarah's body had lain.

Of course Ashley couldn't be positive. But she knew that in most murder cases, the killer proved to be someone close to the victim. Sarah's boyfriend had been in jail during the time of the murder, therefore he was excluded from being the actual triggerman.

Because the killing felt personal, Ashley's suspicions had settled on a family member with a known history of violence.

"Who?"

"Sarah dated my older brother, Kyle, when she and I were in tenth grade. I remember that her parents would go to Mississippi to gamble and would leave her alone for days, without any food in the house. I can't count the number of times she ate dinner with us. And Daddy would always send her home with leftovers, claiming that we had more than we could eat in order to keep her from going hungry."

"You think her parents were involved."

Daniel had cut right to the heart of the matter, not waiting to hear the rest of Ashley's recollections. But she didn't suspect both of Sarah's parents—just one.

"Her father was physically abusive toward her mother and he's been arrested for assault on at least one occasion," she said. "I think it's possible that he may have shot Sarah."

Daniel shook his head. "He didn't have anything to do with it."

She was surprised that the agent had dismissed her idea without a second thought.

"How can you be so sure that her father's innocent?"

"Because he's dead. Sarah's parents died in a car accident five years ago."

The news stunned her.

Ashley felt her cheeks grow warm. Just as she'd feared, she'd made a rookie mistake. She'd relied on years-old gossip as a source for naming a suspect. She should have known better. At the academy, she'd been taught to gather facts—to follow the evidence. Instead, she'd jumped ahead to a conclusion. Had pegged a man who wasn't even alive to defend himself.

She sighed. It looked as though they were right back where they started—with zero leads.

"So where do you think we should go from here?" she asked the agent.

"Her father's parents have custody of her son. I've talked to them once, but didn't get anywhere. Maybe they've remembered something by now."

Ashley followed Daniel back through the forest, this time on guard for woodland creatures that might jump out of the many hiding spots the underbrush offered. When they reached the old logging road, she caught sight of an orange flag rising above a patch of thistles at the woods edge.

"I didn't notice that marker when we arrived," she said, pointing toward the flag. She wondered whether a clue had been found while she and Daniel were at the river.

"It was a soda can. Riddle's Root Beer. It's probably not connected, but we bagged and tagged it anyway."

Daniel unlocked the doors of his sedan and Ashley climbed into the passenger seat. She'd never actually met Sarah's grandparents, but she'd seen them around town. Of course, that had been many years ago. She most likely wouldn't recognize them now.

As they headed toward Mettler Ridge, she tried to recall whether or not Sarah had talked about her father's parents. She couldn't remember anything—good or bad. But Ashley had to wonder where the elder Lesters had been while the teen was home alone with nothing to eat.

Daniel steered the sedan into the driveway of a small house with aging Masonite siding. Dark speckles from peeled paint marred the dusty beige exterior, reminding Ashley of chocolate chip cookie dough.

She followed Daniel up the front porch steps and stood to the side while he rang the bell. After a few seconds, she heard footsteps coming from inside. An elderly woman, her gray hair piled on top of her head, opened the wooden door, but kept the screened door latched tight.

"Mrs. Lester, could we have a word with you?" Daniel asked. "It will only take a few minutes."

"Ain't got nothing more to say," the woman replied, her lips in a firm line.

As Ashley had expected, it was clear Mrs. Lester didn't trust the special agent and probably never would.

A male voice boomed from inside the house. "Who is it, Flora Lee?"

"That city policeman that come by yesterday," the woman answered the voice.

An elderly gentleman with a white mustache, wearing denim overalls, appeared next to Mrs. Lester. Ashley assumed it was Sarah's grandfather.

"You got something new to tell us?" the man asked Daniel.

"No, Mr. Lester. We just wanted to ask you a few more questions."

"We done told you all we know. Good day."

He started to push the door closed.

"Please wait," Ashley spoke up.

If she could get the Lesters to understand that she knew and cared about their granddaughter, maybe they would be willing to talk.

"I went to school with Sarah," she said, stepping closer to the door. "I remember what a nice person she was and I wouldn't be able to live with myself if I didn't try to find out who hurt her."

Mr. Lester stared at Ashley, most likely wondering whether or not she was telling the truth about knowing his granddaughter.

"What's your name?" he asked her.

"Ashley Hope."

He rubbed his chin as though he was trying to remember whether Sarah had mentioned her.

"You Spencer Hope's young'un?"

"Yes, sir." She hoped that the fact Mr. Lester knew her father was a good thing.

Flora Lee Lester pressed her nose against the screen. "Land sakes, child. You're the spitting image of your mama," she said.

"Yes, ma'am."

Again, Ashley hoped that went in her favor. If for some reason it didn't, if the Lesters refused to speak with her as well, then she would be of no use to the investigation. She didn't want to let Daniel down. And more important, she didn't want to let Sarah down.

Mrs. Lester shook her head. "You was born in these parts," she said to Ashley. "You done know we got to be protecting Sarah's boy. We go running our mouths and he's liable to get hurt."

It was just as Ashley had expected. The Lesters feared that if they cooperated with the investigation, they would receive retribution from the killer's family.

She nodded. "I understand how you feel and why you're afraid to get involved, but keeping quiet won't guarantee your great-grandson's safety. The only way to make sure the person who killed Sarah never hurts her son—or the two of you—is to put them behind bars."

Mrs. Lester stared at her as though she was trying to make a decision.

"Let her in, Flora Lee," Mr. Lester said. "But just her."

Ashley glanced at Daniel. He nodded his approval and then headed back to the car. She felt certain that Sarah's grandparents possessed more information than they had admitted. Now the burden of uncovering whatever it was they were hiding was on her shoulders.

She'd never conducted an official interview before. What if she said the wrong thing?

Ashley knew she would only get one shot to win over the Lesters.

CHAPTER EIGHT

The eyes of Mr. and Mrs. Lester drilled into Ashley as she crossed the threshold of their modest home. Although the couple had agreed to speak with her, she knew they were still suspicious. Ashley had grown up on the mountain and she understood the locals' ways, but she was also working with the TBI. And in Laurel County, the police were often thought of as the enemy.

Flora Lee motioned toward the cinnamon-brown upholstered sofa pushed against the far wall of the small living room.

"Have yourself a seat," she said, as she settled onto the adjacent wooden rocking chair.

"Thank you."

Mr. Lester claimed the armchair that matched the sofa.

As Ashley eased down onto the cushion, a clamor rang out from the next room. She looked up to see a young boy with dark hair bust through the doorway, riding a stick horse.

"Papa, Papa!" the young boy shouted. "The cows done got loose. We gotta round 'um up."

She felt her heart break at the sight of the boy, knowing he would never see his mother again.

"We got company, Bobby," Mr. Lester said. "Come say hello to Miss Ashley."

On the mountain, it was customary to refer to women as Miss, a southern title meant to show respect.

The boy stared at her, his brown eyes sparkling. "Hello," he said.

"Hi," she replied, smiling. "That's a really nice-looking horse you've got there."

"Uh-huh. His name's Flash cause he goes fast."

She had the sudden urge to scoop Bobby into her arms and hold him tight. She wondered whether his great-grandparents had told him about his mother's death yet. But how do you explain such a serious concept to one so young?

Mr. Lester touched Bobby's shoulder. "We got us some talking to do. You go play in the backyard and we'll round them cows up later, okay?"

"Okay, Papa."

Ashley watched as Bobby trotted out the front door, pulling it closed behind him. The Lesters obviously doted on the boy. He seemed happy and healthy. Again, she wondered where the couple had been during Sarah's childhood. If they had stepped in, their granddaughter's life might have turned out differently.

Photographs of Bobby dotted the living room walls and lined the bookshelf situated across from the sofa. His mother appeared in a few of the shots with her son. But there were none of Sarah as a child, nor were there any pictures of her parents. Maybe the Lesters had been estranged from their son. Ashley wanted to get an understanding of the family dynamic, but she couldn't just rush into questions of such a personal nature. She would have to gain their trust first.

"When was the last time that you saw, or spoke to, Sarah?" she asked.

Flora Lee glanced at her husband. "We seen her last Sunday," she said. "She come by to see Bobby."

"Did she seem upset or nervous? Or act like she was afraid of someone?"

Ashley wondered whether Sarah could have been a victim of stalking.

"Naw. She was just normal acting."

"Did she ever mention anyone giving her unwanted attention, maybe following her around, asking her for dates?"

Both the Lesters shook their heads. "She never said nothing like that," Flora Lee stated.

If Sarah had caught the attention of a sexual predator, it was possible she had no idea. Many women who were stalked were unaware of the fact until they were attacked.

There was also the possibility that Bobby's father may have had reason to kill her. If she indeed had a drug habit, maybe she had needed money. Maybe she had threatened to take her son's father to court to either seek larger support payments, or to begin support payments.

"Do you think that Bobby's father could have wanted to harm Sarah?"

Flora Lee exchanged another glance with Mr. Lester. "We ain't sure," she said after a pause. "We don't know nothing about him."

"He's never been here to visit Bobby?"

"We ain't never seen him. We don't even know his name. Sarah run off to Nashville one summer. She stayed gone a few months. When she come back, she was in the family way. She wouldn't tell us who the daddy was, just that he didn't want no kid."

"Do you know whether or not he's been paying child support?"

"Naw. He ain't sent her a dime—that's for sure."

Ashley wondered if Sarah could have been receiving payments that the Lesters didn't know about. Spending the money on drugs instead of her child. At this stage, nothing could be ruled out.

"Have you ever seen Bobby's birth certificate?"

"We got us a copy. Had to have it for his kindergarten. But there ain't no daddy's name on it, if that's what you're asking."

That's exactly what she had wanted to know. If Sarah had failed to list the father on Bobby's official birth certificate, Ashley feared it would be next to impossible to track the man down.

With that lead exhausted, it was time to switch gears.

"What kind of relationship did Sarah have with her boyfriend? Did they fight a lot?"

Flora Lee sat back in her rocking chair and crossed her arms. "Ain't saying nothing about Dewayne."

Ashley had hit a nerve. Maybe the boyfriend wasn't so innocent after all. Or maybe he just had a lot of unsavory relatives living in the county.

Mr. Lester spoke up. "He ain't the one who done it. And I ain't just saying that cause I fear his kin."

She searched the elder man's face. His jaw was set, as though he was confident in his words. And it was true that Sarah's boyfriend had not fired the shots himself, but he could have had someone else do it. The fact that he had been in jail at the time afforded him the perfect alibi.

"But is it possible that Dewayne asked one of his friends to harm Sarah?"

"Look, I've been knowing that boy since he was just a tadpole," Mr. Lester said. "Dewayne ain't perfect. He's got a lazy steak a mile wide, but he ain't no killer."

Although she still wasn't convinced that the boyfriend was not in some way complicit, she'd let the matter drop. Otherwise she risked alienating the Lesters. And there was a much touchier subject she needed to broach. One which called for finesse.

"I have really fond memories of Sarah from high school," Ashley told the Lesters, attempting to set them at ease. "She used to come to my house for dinner a lot when we were in tenth grade. She was always so nice to my little brother, which had to have been hard because he could be a brat. But she could always make him laugh."

Flora Lee began to relax in her chair, rocking at a gentle pace. "We didn't never get to see her back then. Her daddy kept her from us. I don't like speaking ill of the dead, 'specially since he's our own, but her daddy was no good. Gambled away ever dollar he made. Then he wanted what little we had. When we stopped giving him money, he took Sarah away. Threatened us with a shotgun once when we showed up at his place."

At least she finally had her answer as to the reason the Lesters had not been there to support Sarah. They probably never even knew the teen had gone hungry. And Ashley wasn't about to add to their pain by sharing the information with them now. The next few questions she had to ask would be difficult enough.

"Sarah and I lost touch our senior year," Ashley said, choosing her words carefully. "Some of the people she'd become friends with were a bad influence on her. They got her involved in things she wouldn't normally do."

She looked at Flora Lee. The woman's gaze dropped to the floor, as did Mr. Lester's. They were obviously aware of their granddaughter's drug problem.

"Can you give me the names of her current friends?"

"She ain't got none," Flora said. "Just Dewayne. Bobby and us. That's all. She didn't have no other real friends anymore."

Ashley sighed. Had their granddaughter really been without friends, or had she just kept their identities a secret?

"Do you think it's possible Sarah's death could have been drug related?" she asked the elderly couple.

Neither of the Lesters spoke for a moment.

Flora Lee stopped rocking, her eyes watering. "That girl had a good soul. But problems had a way of finding her. It ain't easy raising a young'un on your own. That's how come we took over."

Her heart went out to Flora Lee. She hated to remind the woman of Sarah's faults, but she had no choice.

"Yes ma'am, I understand. And I can see that you've done a wonderful job with Bobby."

"That boy's everything to us." A tear rolled down Flora Lee's face.

Ashley slid to the end of the sofa and grasped the woman's hand, holding it tight.

"I promise you that I will do everything in my power to make sure Bobby stays safe," she told Flora Lee—and meant it. "That's the reason we have to catch Sarah's killer."

The elderly woman nodded. "We thought she'd quit them drugs. But I guess we was wrong. She was supposed to have been here on Thursday for supper. But she didn't never show up. When we didn't hear from her, we figured she'd done backslid."

"Do you think she was getting the drugs from Dewayne?"

If that had been the case, it was possible the person supplying Sarah's boyfriend could have been responsible for the murder. Her death could have been payback for something Dewayne had done.

"Naw, not him." Flora Lee shook her head. "He done tried to get her to quit a bunch of times. Dewayne likes his whiskey ever now and then, but he don't do no drugs."

It was beginning to seem like Sarah's boyfriend might have been one of the best things she had in her life, even if he was in jail on a drunken and disorderly charge.

"Do you have any idea where she was getting the drugs?"

The elderly woman shook her head. "We don't know. She'd get all riled up anytime we said anything about it. We was afraid she'd steal Bobby and run off somewhere. So we minded our own business."

Ashley could understand the Lesters' reasoning. And if Dewayne had wanted Sarah to break her habit, she probably wasn't getting the drugs from one of their friends.

"Squeaky," Mr. Lester said, his voice booming.

She turned to look at the elderly gentlemen, not sure she'd heard him right. "Pardon me?"

"Sarah was talking to a man on the phone one day. All quiet like," Mr. Lester stated. "They was setting up a meeting. She called him Squeaky."

Hope surged in Ashley's chest. Finally, a lead. Her first official interview hadn't been a total disaster after all. A nickname wasn't as good as having a real first and last name, but she would take what she could get.

"I'm going to do my best to find this person," she told Mr. Lester. "And if he's responsible for Sarah's murder, I promise you, he'll be sent to prison for a very long time."

Ashley thanked the Lesters and headed back outside. Daniel locked eyes with her through the windshield of his sedan. She hoped the agent wasn't irritated with her. The fact that the Lesters had welcomed her into their home while refusing him entry must have stung. She climbed into the passenger seat.

"How'd it go?" Daniel asked, seemingly unscathed by the Lesters' rebuff.

"We need to find a man called Squeaky."

The agent smiled. "That's a name I haven't heard," he said. "Let's head over to the diner. See if any of Sarah's co-workers know him."

CHAPTER NINE

Ashley and Daniel arrived at the diner during one of the least busy times. The breakfast crowd had mostly cleared out and the lunch crowd had not yet started rolling in. The official name of the local hangout was Mettler Ridge's Finest Diner, evidenced by the red and yellow neon sign out front. The slogan was true, purely because of the fact it was the only establishment of its kind in town. But the name didn't really matter as the locals all simply referred to the joint as The Diner, and nothing more.

Sarah had worked as a server here for the last four years.

A search of the law enforcement database had failed to identify any suspect with the known alias of Squeaky. Although Daniel had questioned Sarah's coworkers the day before—without gaining any useful information—it was possible one of them knew the person Sarah had spoken with on the phone.

Ashley led Daniel to a corner booth flanked by windows on two sides. She'd chosen the location—farthest away from the door and serving counter—out of a concern for privacy. If she planned to get any information out of one of the employees, she knew they would need to feel as though the conversation wouldn't be overheard.

She slid onto the red vinyl bench that backed against the window and picked up one of the menus lodged between the napkin dispenser and the wire condiment basket. But instead of browsing the food selection, she scanned the area behind the counter. A lone server poured coffee into an elderly gentleman's cup. The woman was a heavyset brunette whom she had never met. Over eight years had passed since the last time Ashley had been inside the diner, but even so, she had counted on finding a familiar face.

Ashley's hopes sank. It would be difficult enough to get someone she knew to open up about Sarah, but it would be near impossible to convince a stranger to talk. She drummed her fingers on the tabletop, trying to think of a strategy.

Daniel looked at her, his blue eyes reflecting the slightest hint of irritation.

"Sorry," she said, realizing the constant tapping could be annoying. "But I was—"

A long red ponytail caught her attention. Another server stood at a booth on the other side of the diner, taking an order, her back toward Ashley.

Lou Ann.

Hope surged in Ashley's chest again. Right after Ashley graduated high school, she had moved into the trailer next door to the woman and her boyfriend. They hadn't been the closest of friends, but Lou Ann knew her.

Daniel turned his head, following her gaze. He turned back to Ashley. "You were what?"

"That's the woman we need to talk to—the redhead."

"Yeah, your expression pretty much gave it away."

She made a mental note to work on her poker face.

Scooting toward the end of her bench, she stared holes in Lou Ann's back, waiting for her to turn around. But when the server finished taking the order, she headed straight behind the serving counter, never looking in Ashley's direction.

Ashley sighed.

"Give her a minute," Daniel said, scouring the menu. "She's working the tables. She'll be here soon."

She knew Daniel was right, but patience wasn't her strong suit. She glanced down at the menu. It was only ten-thirty and they didn't start serving lunch until eleven. She was hungry, having been too anxious about visiting the location where Sarah had died to eat that morning. But she wasn't really in the mood for breakfast food.

"Here she comes," Daniel announced.

Ashley slipped her menu back into its resting place.

"Hi, Lou Ann," she said, smiling at the server.

"Well, hey, Ashley. I heard you was living over at your daddy's place now. How y'all been doing? How's Shane?"

Although Lou Ann was in her mid-thirties, she appeared much younger. Her creamy skin glowed without a blemish or line in sight. And she possessed the slender, well-toned build of a ballerina. Ashley assumed the server's diet did not include the diner's greasy fare.

"Shane's improving every day—thanks for asking," Ashley said. She motioned toward the agent. "This is my friend Daniel Lansing."

"Yeah, the cop," the server said, the smile disappearing from her face. "We met yesterday." She tapped her pen on her order pad. "Y'all want coffee?"

"Lou Ann, I was hoping you could answer a few questions about Sarah," Ashley said.

"I done told him everything I know," she replied, referring to Daniel. "Which ain't nothing."

"But there's a good chance that you have more information than you realize. Sarah may have said something that you didn't pick up on at the time. Something that could lead us to her killer."

The server shook her head. "I ain't got no idea who done it."

"Did you ever hear her mention someone named Squeaky?" Ashley prodded.

Lou Ann's eyes darted toward Daniel, a nervous expression crossing her face.

"Are y'all gonna order?" she asked, her voice strained. "Cause this booth's for paying customers."

Ashley could tell the name had sparked a recollection in the server's mind. But she also knew Lou Ann wasn't about to talk with the TBI agent present. She'd have to find a way to get the woman alone.

"I'll have the southwestern omelet, with coffee," she said.

Lou Ann nodded and scribbled on her pad, her nervousness still apparent.

"How 'bout you," she asked Daniel, without ever looking at him.

"Give me two scrambled eggs, an order of turkey sausage, hash browns, biscuits and gravy, three buttermilk pancakes, coffee, and orange juice. Oh, and can I get extra syrup please?"

Ashley stared at the agent. She wondered how he managed to stay so fit.

"What?" he said, his dimples showing. "My wakeup call came at four-thirty this morning. All I've had is coffee and a pack of peanuts from the motel vending machine."

"I didn't say a word about your order."

He smiled. "No, but you were thinking it."

Lou Ann stuffed her pen into the pocket of her apron and headed back behind the serving counter. Ashley watched her pin the order ticket to the carousel in the pass-through window and then lean against the wall, as though unsteady on her feet.

"Well, it's obvious that she's heard the name Squeaky before," Ashley stated.

Daniel nodded. "After we eat, I'll head out to the car. Maybe she'll tell you something."

The clatter of dishes hitting the floor echoed toward them. Ashley caught sight of a red-faced Lou Ann as she bobbed up from behind the counter. The server then bee-lined toward the restrooms.

The agent cocked his head. "Looks like you won't have to wait."

Ashley slid out from the booth and angled her way to the ladies' room. She pushed the door open and found Lou Ann washing her face at the sink. The two bathroom stalls behind her stood empty.

"Sarah has a five-year-old son who will never see his mother again," Ashley said, her voice soft.

"I can't help you, Ashley."

The woman was obviously afraid. And Ashley didn't want any harm to come to her.

"No one will ever have to know that I got the information from you," she assured the server.

Lou Ann jerked a paper towel from the dispenser and dried her face. She remained silent.

"Please—for the sake of that little boy—talk to me."

"I really don't know who done it. Honest," she said, her eyes meeting Ashley's.

It was clear the woman was telling the truth about not knowing the identity of the killer; however, it was also obvious that she possessed information that could help the investigation.

"But you have heard of Squeaky, haven't you? What did Sarah say about him?"

The server stared at her reflection in the mirror, her lips in a thin line.

Ashley pushed further. "Was Sarah buying her drugs from Squeaky?"

Lou Ann sighed. "I don't know. Maybe. He used to work here, but he don't no more."

"What's his real name?"

"You can't tell nobody that I told you," she said, fear crossing her face.

Ashley couldn't think of any reason she, or Daniel, would ever need to divulge the source of the information. "I won't, I promise."

Lou Ann turned away from the mirror. "Owen Sullivan. He lives out on Turkey Creek Road."

A small sense of accomplishment stirred in Ashley, lightening the burden of her self-doubt. She had a real name now. One she'd never heard before.

"Do you think he's the type of person who could murder someone?"

She shook her head. "I don't know." Her expression implied that she felt she'd already said too much. "I need to be getting back to work."

"Thank you, Lou Ann. And don't worry; I'll make sure that you won't regret talking to me."

The server nodded and then headed back through the restroom door.

Ashley pulled her cell phone from her purse and checked the time. She hoped Daniel was a fast eater. She wanted to get to Squeaky's house as soon as possible.

CHAPTER TEN

The tall grass skimmed Ashley's knees as she walked from the driveway to the front door of Squeaky's trailer. A single cinderblock served as the home's front porch. Balling her hand into a fist, she knocked on the door and waited.

She glanced back at Daniel sitting in his sedan. After their experiences with the Lesters and Lou Ann, she'd convinced him to let her speak with Squeaky alone. The nine-millimeter handgun holstered in the waistband of her jeans would serve as backup should the need arise. Tennessee was a constitutional carry state. She didn't need the TBI's blessing—or even a permit—to protect herself.

Ashley pounded on the door a second time. A rusty pickup sat in the drive, indicating that someone should be home.

"Squeaky?" she called out, banging on the door again, louder this time.

She heard movement inside the trailer.

The door opened just enough for a man with shoulder-length blond hair to stick his head out. Red sores dotted his thin face. His hair appeared rumpled and his eyes heavy as though he'd been sleeping.

"Who are you?" the man asked, his voice scratchy and high-pitched.

Now she understood how he'd acquired his nickname.

"I'm one of Sarah Lester's friends."

She'd decided to wait until after they'd talked a while before telling him she was working with the TBI.

"What do you want?"

His scowl revealed that he was missing at least two of his top teeth.

"I was hoping I could come in and talk to you about Sarah."

Squeaky looked past her toward the driveway. She was thankful that Daniel's boss had assigned him a confiscated Toyota. The Ford sedan he had driven when he worked for the Briarwood PD had screamed undercover officer.

"You a cop?"

Somehow she knew he would ask anyway.

"Me? No, I'm not a police officer." Which was technically true.

"I don't know nothing. Why do you wanna talk to me?"

"Because Sarah mentioned you." Actually she'd been overheard talking to him on the phone, but the difference could be considered minor.

He looked at her as if contemplating the idea of allowing her inside. Or maybe he was trying to figure out whether or not she was lying.

"Please," she said. "I'll only stay for a few minutes." She didn't want to be there any longer than absolutely necessary.

"What's your name?" he asked, searching her face.

"Ashley Hope."

Since her father owned an automotive repair shop in Mettler Ridge, her family was fairly well-known in the area.

"You kin to Kyle Hope?"

"Yes, he's my older brother."

Kyle had taken over the management of the shop since her father's heart attack. Hope Automotive had a reputation for fairness and honesty—unlike the other automotive repair business in the county that sourced its parts from a local chop shop. Whether or not this would be beneficial to her depended on which side of the law Squeaky favored. From where she now stood, the odds seemed stacked against her.

Squeaky stepped back, pulling the door open. She guessed that meant he deemed her trustworthy. At least for the moment.

"What's Sarah been saying about me?" he asked, his hand still clasping the doorknob.

Ashley glanced around the dim living room. The only light filtered in through a tattered set of blinds on the double window. An empty pizza box and fast food wrappers littered the floor. Cigarette butts overflowed the ashtray perched on a scarred coffee table, the air stale with leftover smoke. She inched toward the only seat in the room—a sectional sofa that had seen better days.

"You and Sarah used to work together at the diner, right?" she asked him.

"Yeah. So?" He pushed the front door shut, adding to the gloom.

"I'm guessing that the two of you were pretty good friends as well."

More like fellow addicts. She could tell by Squeaky's physical condition that he was most likely not the person supplying Sarah with drugs. Dealers didn't normally consume large quantities of their own inventory. They were in it for the money.

He shrugged. “If you say so.”

“When was the last time you saw her?”

“I ain’t the one that shot her,” he stated, his voice shrill.

Ashley smiled, hoping to put him at ease. “I’m not accusing you of anything more than being her friend.”

Squeaky nodded, seeming to calm down a bit. “She was a good person.”

He collapsed onto the sofa. “You can sit down,” he told Ashley.

She eyed the crumb-laden fabric and chose to remain standing. She ambled past the end of the L-shaped couch, pretending to be interested in the poster of a rock band plastered on the wall.

“Can you think of any reason that someone would want to hurt Sarah?” she asked.

He shook his head. “Naw. Everybody liked her.”

It was obvious that at least one person had a problem with the young woman. Maybe someone she had crossed.

“Is it possible that she stole something from someone—like maybe her dealer?”

Ashley looked down and saw a glass pipe sticking out from beneath the back of the sofa, a small bag of crystal meth beside it. Squeaky must have moved his stash out of sight when he heard her knock on his door. He’d picked a poor hiding spot.

“Sarah wouldn’t steal nothing,” he said. “Not unless she was tweaking real bad. Even then, she ain’t stupid enough to rob the ice man.”

Ashley assumed ice man was slang for a person who sold crystal meth—or ice. She supposed that Squeaky was right. Stealing from a dealer would be a very desperate act and seemed out of character for Sarah.

“Do you think it’s possible that she owed her dealer money? Could he have tried to collect from her and things got out of hand?”

He shrugged again. “Ain’t got no way of knowing that.”

But he knew the identity of her dealer and should know whether or not the person was prone to violence.

“You and Sarah both purchased your meth from the same person, right?”

“No, uh-uh,” he said, shifting into a more upright position on the sofa. “You got that wrong. I ain’t never bought no crystal.”

Ashley looked at him, wondering if he realized how ridiculous his denial sounded.

"But you do know who Sarah's dealer is—or was."

"Nope," he said, shaking his head. "Can't help you."

She moved to the end of the couch, between Squeaky and his stash.

"You told me that Sarah was a good person, and you know that she has a five-year-old son. Don't you want Bobby to know the truth about what happened to his mother?"

"It ain't worth my life," he stated, eyeing Ashley as though he thought she was crazy.

He pushed himself up off the sofa. "Time for you to get out," he said, his voice seeming an octave higher.

She should have known that self-preservation would be the first thing on Squeaky's mind. Fear was a powerful motivator. But the drug dealer wasn't the only one who could wield that kind of pressure.

"I know you saw the man waiting in the car outside," Ashley said, holding her ground. "He's a special agent with the TBI. Is the meth under the sofa the only thing he'll find when he turns this trailer upside down?"

Squeaky's eyes narrowed. He started toward her.

Ashley's hand snapped to the pistol in her waistband. "Don't be stupid," she warned.

The addict stopped short when he caught sight of the weapon.

"You said you weren't no cop."

"I'm not. I'm just helping out."

He held her gaze, frozen in place, as if he knew there was no way he could run.

"We can handle this one of two ways," Ashley told him. "You can tell me the name of Sarah's dealer and then I'll leave. No one—including her drug supplier—will ever know that I was here."

She tightened her fingers around the grip of her pistol to make a point. "Or, the agent waiting in the car can arrest you for drug possession, tear your trailer inside out, and make it known on the street that you've been cooperating with the police."

Ashley knew that labeling Squeaky as a snitch for the TBI was a threat he wouldn't take lightly.

He shook his head, a grimace further deforming his sore-ridden face. "How can I be sure you won't rat me out?"

"The only guarantee you have is my word. And I can promise you that your nickname will change from Squeaky to Squealer if we have to take you into custody."

He turned around and dropped back onto the sofa. He tapped out a cigarette from the pack on the coffee table, lit the end, and took a long drag.

"Clay Grimes," Squeaky spat out. "He's the ice man."

Ashley smiled. She remembered the cockroach from high school. It shouldn't be too hard to track the man down.

And she'd squash him this time.

CHAPTER ELEVEN

Violet Perry forced her heavy eyelids open and tried to focus on the yellowed ceiling above her. A misty haze clouded her vision.

Am I dreaming?

Where am I?

She swallowed. Her tongue pressed against dry cotton, her throat parched. She jiggled her head, trying to shake the fog from her mind. Her vision began to clear. The unfamiliar surroundings—the stained ceiling, a cardboard-covered window to her right—morphed from their fuzzy dreamlike state into cold reality.

Panic rushed through her.

She screamed—the sound muffled into a whimper. There was something stuffed in her mouth. A gag. Either drool or sweat—she wasn't sure which—had plastered strands of her golden brown hair to her cheek. Her arms stretched behind her head. Her wrists had been bound, fastened by a chain to a cabinet above. She struggled against her restraints, but her tugging proved useless. How did she get here?

Think.

The laundry.

That's right. She'd gone out into the backyard with a basket of wet towels and sheets. Had started hanging them up to dry. A soft breeze rippled a worn dishtowel as Florida Georgia Line's "Always Gonna Love You" blared through her earbuds. She'd pinned one corner of a pale blue cotton sheet to the clothesline, had stretched the fabric and secured the middle. And then …

Something stung the back of her right thigh. But not a bee or wasp. It had felt more like a needle prick. She'd watched a bright pink clothespin slip from her hand and fall to the grass. That's where her memory ended. And now she was here.

Why?

Violet wriggled on the bed. Her ankles were bound as well, and her thigh ached from the injection. Lifting her head as far as possible, she scanned the area around her. Walls touched the mattress on three sides. At her feet, a miniature sink and stove nested inside a row of cabinets.

To her left, the door to a small room—likely a bathroom—stood ajar. More cabinets lined the left wall of the cramped space, the oak finish scarred. Her prison was an old-model RV.

Who brought me here?

An idea hit her—ransom. Maybe that was it. She'd stolen some of his stash. But it had only been a small amount. Just enough to get her through. And in the past, he'd always let her pay him back. Her favors had been as good as cash. Why would he call in enforcers now?

Maybe he wanted a different kind of payment. Her sister didn't have any money to spare, but she was younger. Prettier. And would likely do anything he asked to ensure Violet's safety.

Anger flooded her heart. But her rage wasn't just directed at him. She was angry at herself. Eva had begged her to get clean. And Violet had tried—many times. But she was weak. And now her little sister would pay the price.

The side door to the RV creaked open and heavy footsteps jarred the floor, reverberating up through the bed where Violet lay. She strained her neck, trying to get a look at her abductor.

Frizzy red hair, a bulbous red nose, and an exaggerated painted-on smile hovered above her. A clown mask. Her captor wore a rubber clown mask.

That was a good thing, right?

If her abductor had gone to the trouble to hide their identity, that might signal that she would be set free. Once the debt was paid.

The clown stared at her and then held an index finger to its fake U-shaped mouth, as if instructing her to be quiet. A flash of metal caught her eye. A hunting knife in the clown's right hand.

Fear rose in her chest.

The clown rested its denim-covered knee on the bed.

The blade inched toward her.

CHAPTER TWELVE

A green pickup lumbered in front of the Toyota sedan, kicking up gravel dust that whirled outside the passenger window, reminding Ashley of miniature tornados. The single-wide lane that wound through Weaver's Cove Campground flowed in only one direction. Looping in a circle, the exit hit the highway just a few yards from the entrance.

Daniel wheeled the sedan into the parking lot of the recreation center, located in the middle of the loop. Few tourists passed through Laurel County, but the campground never seemed to lack occupants. The establishment served as a base for a small community of locals one step away from homelessness. The cheap campsite rental rates attracted those who teetered on the edge, offering restrooms and showers to anyone who owned a tent.

The fact that many of the campground's residents claimed a spot on Clay's list of clients had come as no surprise to Ashley. Although the man lived on the other side of the county, according to one of the sheriff's deputies, the drug dealer often held court at the rec center. Probably to spare his customers the trouble of searching for him.

Ashley spotted a red coupe parked in the far corner of the lot. The license plate number matched the DMV record for Clay Grimes.

"That's the sick little cockroach's car over there," she said, gesturing out the window. The deputy had obviously steered them in the right direction.

Daniel nodded. "Was that his high school nickname?"

"Yes, and he did everything in his power to earn it."

"Such as?"

Clay had been implicated in far too many schemes to list them all, so Ashley decided to recount the one she felt was most egregious.

"We had a bake sale my sophomore year to raise funds for a family who'd lost their home—and everything else they owned—in a fire. Clay stole all the money that we collected. Everyone knew he did it—some of his friends even said he bragged about it. But there was no proof. This was back before schools had cameras in every corner. So nothing happened to him."

"Ever sent to juvie?"

"No. Regardless of the number of crimes he committed—and there were a ton—he always dodged the charges. He'd scurry back under his rock and hide, planning his next hustle. He seemed indestructible, just like a cockroach."

Daniel smiled at her. "Looks like that may be about to change."

She hoped he was right. Even if Clay had nothing to do with Sarah's death, maybe the agent could find enough evidence to arrest the dealer on drug charges.

Ashley hopped out of the car and headed toward the entrance to the rec center. She edged past a wide trench that angled from the front of the building to the gravel lane, noticing a large pipe deep inside. A bulldozer sat next to the ditch.

"Looks like they're having plumbing problems," Daniel remarked.

Unlike a lot of the homes in the area that relied on private wells for their water, the county's utility district fed the campground.

She pushed through the door into the main room of the center. Everything looked the same as it had the last time she'd visited, over eight years earlier. A pool table stood at each end, an air hockey table wedged in between. A variety of vending machines and arcade machines—relics from the eighties—lined the walls. Ashley scanned the faces of the pool players, but none looked familiar.

Although she realized Clay's appearance would have changed over the years, she would never forget his dark squinty eyes. She guessed he was either in the bathroom or out back hanging around the basketball court.

She shook her head, indicating to Daniel that she didn't see their subject, and then motioned toward the double doors on the far side of the room.

Peering through the glass, Ashley watched a group of men engaged in a dunking contest on the aging asphalt court. Although she thought she recognized two of the players, neither of them was Clay. She shifted position and gazed along the back wall of the rec center. A short dark-haired man leaned against a picnic table, talking to two teenage boys.

Cockroach.

He'd better not be pushing his wares on the young men.

"He's outside at the picnic table and it looks like he might be conducting business—with two teenagers," Ashley told Daniel, her voice just above a whisper.

The agent's eyes narrowed. "I'll bust the scum now. We can talk to him at the station."

She glanced back through the door, her hand on the knob. The boys had disappeared. Clay was alone.

"Wait, the teenagers aren't there anymore," she said, scanning the area bordered by a chain-link fence. The boys must have gone out through the gate to her left.

"Did you see anything change hands?"

Ashley shook her head. "No, I didn't see them give him any money or take anything from him. They were just having a conversation."

She supposed the interaction could have been innocent, but knowing Clay, she was more inclined to believe the dealer was trying to entice the young men into a purchase.

"There's nothing I can do then," Daniel said, disappointment in his voice. "He's probably not stupid enough to be carrying."

She assumed the agent was right. Clay most likely had the drugs hidden somewhere on the property and would drop a buyer's purchase off at a predetermined location after he received payment. Since he'd made no effort to move from his perch on the picnic table, maybe the teens had declined his offer.

"I'll go talk to him and see what I can find out about Sarah," Ashley said.

"Signal if you need me."

Nodding, she pulled the door open and stepped out into the afternoon sun. Although Ashley's doubts regarding her interviewing skills were beginning to shatter, the thought of grilling a drug dealer stirred a sense of apprehension inside her. This man was a known criminal. Might be a murderer. If she said the wrong thing, not only could she jeopardize the investigation, she could end up on the dealer's list of targets.

But then she realized: all law enforcement agents were the targets of organized crime rings.

Cops put their lives on the line every day. Fear had no place in this—or any other—investigation. She'd gone up against a cold-blooded killer once before, and had won. No matter what she faced in the future, Ashley was determined to keep on winning.

As she neared the picnic table, Clay turned to look at her, his dark eyes narrow slashes on his tanned face.

"Well, if it ain't Ashley Hope," he said, hoisting himself up from the table.

The growth spurt he had no doubt prayed for in high school had failed to hit him. If she had to guess, Clay measured up to around five-foot-four in his designer high-top sneakers.

"How have you been, Clay?" she asked, forcing her lips into a smile.

Ashley knew that the drug dealer would run if she hit him with a barrage of questions about their dead classmate. She'd have to ease into it, put him off guard.

"Can't complain," he said, his squinty eyes raking over her. "You're looking good."

She wanted to pound her fists into the little cockroach's head, knock him down and squash him under her feet.

She motioned toward the basketball players.

"Are you waiting to get in on a game?" she asked, knowing the cockroach had never excelled in sports. He'd always seemed to gravitate toward things that took very little physical effort.

"Nah, just watching. Enjoying the weather." He leaned back against the table again.

He was most likely scouting for new customers. Or waiting to meet an old one.

"I always imagined that you would leave Mettler Ridge after high school and move on to bigger and better things," she said, implying that the town was too small to hold him. In actuality, she'd always thought he'd end up in a large prison somewhere.

"Yeah, well. Home is home."

She nodded. "And nothing seems to have changed here in all the years since graduation."

The observation was true. Laurel County seemed stuck in a time warp.

"You got that right."

Ashley regarded his stance. Noticed the way he lounged against the picnic table, the breezy tone of his voice. He seemed relaxed with her. It was time to go in for the kill.

"Did you hear about what happened to Sarah Lester?" she asked him, knowing that he had—the news had spread all across the county.

A nervous look flashed across Clay's face. He stood up straight. "Yeah, I heard."

"There's a rumor floating around town that she owed someone money."

Although the locals weren't actually talking, she wanted to gauge his reaction to the possible motive for Sarah's murder.

"Is that so?" he asked, his mouth now a thin line.

Was that guilt she saw written across his face? He was definitely hiding something. Whatever it was, she needed to chip away at it, and then pry it loose.

One of the men from the basketball group sauntered up to next to them. She recognized the player from high school, but couldn't remember his name.

"Hey bro," the man said to Clay, "she's working with the TBI."

Word that Ashley was helping the police had spread fast.

The drug dealer's face turned pale. His eyes darted behind her to the gate in the chain-link fence. She was standing in his path of escape.

Clay grabbed Ashley by the arms and shoved her to the ground. Her backside hit the hard-packed dirt, jarring her teeth. As she pushed herself to her feet, she saw the drug dealer struggling to open the gate's rusty latch. He must have information about Sarah. Why else would he run?

The gate finally swung open and Clay raced through, Ashley at his heels.

The dealer sped around the side of the rec center, obviously heading for his car. She was determined to stop him. He was shorter than her, his stride not as long. She'd catch up and drag him to the ground.

He weaved between a pair of swing sets and almost collided with a seesaw. Ashley cut to the left of the swings, skirting the side of the building, gaining on him.

As she rounded the front corner, she spotted the utility trench. Clay would have to jump over the ditch to get to the parking lot. Closing the gap on the dealer, she stretched out her hand.

Just as Clay leapt for the trench, she grasped the tail of his red T-shirt and jerked hard.

The dealer toppled into the channel, landing spread-eagle across the pipe.

Breathing heavy, Ashley slid to a stop at the edge of the hole. Daniel appeared on the other side.

"Clay Grimes, you're under arrest," the agent said. "For assault."

Ashley laughed as she stared down at the dealer, his narrow eyes now wide with shock.

The cockroach had finally been trapped. And she couldn't wait to see him behind bars.

CHAPTER THIRTEEN

Ashley peered through the one-way glass into the Laurel County Sheriff's Department's sole interrogation room. Clay Grimes slouched in a metal chair next to a dingy white table, unaware that her eyes were focused on him. He'd been booked and charged with assaulting Ashley at the campground. The charge was only a misdemeanor, but it was enough to hold him, at least for a short time.

The sheriff seemed convinced that the drug dealer was responsible for Sarah's murder. And the hint from Ashley that their classmate may have owed Clay money had definitely rattled him. Still, there was no hard evidence to implicate the man in the crime. But if Clay was innocent, why did he run?

Daniel pushed through the door of the observation room.

"You ready?" he asked.

The nervous energy balled in Ashley's stomach urged her to answer in the negative. It would be her first time in an interrogation room. Cameras were rolling. She would be on stage, her every mistake recorded. And now—unlike her previous conversations with the Lesters, Lou Ann, Squeaky, and Clay—Daniel would be watching and listening. She couldn't afford to screw up.

The agent had put his reputation on the line and obtained special permission from his superiors to allow Ashley to question Clay. Daniel felt that the dealer might be willing to divulge more information to someone he'd known since childhood. The fact that Ashley despised the man didn't seem to bother the agent, and obviously hadn't been relayed to the higher-ups at the TBI.

"Yeah, to see him behind bars for all the crimes he's gotten away with," she answered.

Daniel nodded. "His days are numbered," he said, conviction in his voice.

The agent held the hallway door open for her.

Ashley made her way into the adjacent room and took the seat opposite Clay. He kept his gaze focused on the middle of the table, his arms folded across his chest. If his posture was any indication, it appeared he had no interest in speaking with her.

From what she understood, it was her job to fill the "good cop" role. Although she knew the ploy was necessary, it was a task she wished she could avoid. She held no sympathy for the man, whether or not he was guilty of murder.

"Would you like something to drink—a soda or coffee?" Ashley asked him, masking her hatred.

She was met with silence.

"Look, Clay," she said, her tone earnest, "I can help you get out of this mess if you'll let me."

She was referring to the assault charge. If he confessed to murder, she was sure the misdemeanor could be bargained away.

He finally met her gaze, his squinty eyes cold.

"You don't wanna help me," he said.

In actuality, he was right. What she wanted was justice. To find out who had killed Sarah and why.

"Do you know the reason that I'm in here talking to you?"

"Cause your sorry ass landed on the ground," he replied, a slight smile tugging the corners of his lips.

If he had an idea of the serious charge he could face, it was apparent that he wasn't about to admit it.

"I really don't care that you knocked me down. In fact, I'm more than willing to ask that the assault charge be dropped."

And she would—if he agreed to tell her everything he knew about Sarah.

"Why?" he asked, confusion apparent on his face.

Could it be possible that he really didn't know the true reason he was being held?

"The sheriff thinks you're guilty of a much more serious crime."

He shook his head. "Y'all searched me. I didn't have no drugs on me, and there weren't none in my car."

It was true that Daniel had failed to find drugs on Clay's body, and a thorough search of his automobile had turned up empty. Ashley had hoped the man would be found with enough drugs in his possession to be charged with intent to sell, but the slippery little cockroach had been wise enough to hide his goods. And unfortunately, Clay's small-time dealing wasn't prominent on the TBI's radar.

He continued, "Y'all ain't got no other reason to keep me here."

Ashley looked at him, planting an empathetic expression on her face. "I said that I would try to get the assault charge dropped—and I meant it. But I need you to talk to me if you want my help getting out of jail."

"I done told you that you ain't gonna find no drugs." His eyebrows arched and it appeared as though an idea had struck him. "Truth is, I done got out of that business. I'm living straight now."

The obvious lie failed to impress Ashley. But she had to play her role as his "friend"—his only hope of staying out of prison.

"I'm really glad to hear that you've changed your ways," she said, pretending to believe him.

He smiled, his expression revealing that he thought he'd put one over on her.

She leaned toward him. "You and I have known each other since we were in first grade."

Clay eyed her as though he wondered where this was going.

"So?" he spat out.

"You know what kind of person I am—that I've always tried to help people. And now the family of one our friends from school needs help—your help."

She searched his face, waiting to see if a light would come on. It didn't. He either didn't understand that she was talking about Sarah, or he was deliberately hiding his thoughts. Most likely, the latter.

Ashley decided to try a more direct approach.

"I've heard that you were good friends with Sarah Lester," she said.

"You heard wrong."

"You're going to have to tell me the truth if you want me to help you," she told him, although she doubted he was capable of complete honesty.

"I don't know nothing about Sarah," he said, shaking his head.

"It's a known fact that she was a customer of yours and had been for a long time."

"That don't mean nothing. I got a lot of customers, but they ain't friends."

Inside, she smiled at the slip-up, wondering whether he realized he'd just admitted to still being in the drug-pushing business, but she kept her expression neutral. The camera affixed to the wall behind her was recording every word of the interview. She just wished that information could be used against him.

"There's a rumor going around that Sarah owed you money," she told him.

The statement didn't have the same effect on the dealer as it had at the campground. She guessed he'd had time to consider the matter and had realized that there was no proof.

Clay remained silent, his gaze directed back on the table.

"Look, I know you want to get out of here as fast as possible," she said. "And the best way to do that is to talk to me about your relationship with Sarah."

"Ain't got nothing to tell," he said, still avoiding her eyes.

Her intuition screamed that the man was holding back a key bit of information. But using a soft tactic to pry the evidence loose wasn't working. She'd have to push harder. But how could she put pressure on the dealer and still manage to convince him that she was on his side?

Ashley sighed. "I'm going to level with you, Clay. The TBI's not interested in your small-town drug racket. They're making plans to charge you with Sarah's murder."

Clay's hands flew to the armrests of his chair as he pushed himself into an erect position.

"I didn't kill that woman," he declared, anger in his tone.

"Then tell me everything you know about her so you can clear your name."

The dealer stared at her, his tanned face now ashen.

"I ain't saying nothing else," he stated, his lips set in a thin line.

"You're only hurting yourself by refusing to talk to me."

He shook his head and crossed his arms again. Ashley could tell that the interview was over. She wouldn't be able to get any information out of the dealer. And if she pushed further, he might ask for an attorney. If he invoked that privilege, Daniel wouldn't be able to question him.

"Let me know if you happen to change your mind," she said, scooting her chair away from the table.

Ashley headed back into the observation room, feeling as though she'd let Sarah's family down. She worried Bobby would have to grow up never knowing what really happened to his mother.

"I'm sorry I wasn't able to get him to tell me anything," she said to Daniel.

"You did a good job," the agent told her, his sincerity evident in his blue eyes. "He's just not quite ready to crack."

She hoped Daniel could use his weight as a TBI agent to scare Clay into talking. Ashley wasn't sure how much the dealer knew, but she felt certain he was holding back something important.

She glanced at the clock hanging above the agent's head. 5:57 p.m. Where had the time gone? She'd have to hurry or she'd be late.

"I really wanted to watch you shake him up and make him squirm," Ashley told Daniel. "But I can't stay any longer. I promised Shane that I would go to a concert with him in Cedar View."

She hated to skip out on the interrogation. For a second she considered calling Kyle and asking if he could go in her place, but she realized that would be a mistake. So far she'd been focused on Shane's physical health. But right now, it was his mental health that really needed a boost.

She knew Kyle wouldn't agree to go to the club without his girlfriend, Janet. Shane would no doubt feel like a third wheel tagging along. And being around the happy couple would remind him of his own recent breakup.

"Yeah, go ahead," Daniel said. "You did great today. You deserve a night out."

Ashley wasn't quite satisfied with her job performance—Clay had shut down on her—but it was nice hearing the agent's kind words. Making a silent vow to improve her interrogation skills, she smiled and headed out the door.

CHAPTER FOURTEEN

The narrow two-lane highway hummed with traffic as Ashley piloted her sedan toward Cedar View. With no real form of entertainment available in Mettler Ridge on Saturday night, the majority of Laurel County locals flocked to the neighboring town in Marcum County. Due to the exodus, the journey that took roughly thirty minutes during the week lengthened to forty-plus on the weekends. From their current location, they were still about ten minutes from Bobcat Saloon, a club that featured live music.

Tonight's headliner: The Nolan Arnold Band, a southern rock group based out of Atlanta.

She glanced at Shane, his six-foot-three frame stretched out in the passenger seat. He'd been quiet for most of the drive, his gaze focused on the scenery zipping past the side window.

"I heard on the radio that the crowd brought them back to play two encores in Nashville last night," she said, attempting to instill a bit of excitement into her brother.

Before his injury, Shane would have been eager to attend the band's performance. It had been almost a year since the group—which was starting to make a name for itself—had toured the area. Although the band ranked at the top of her brother's favorites, she'd had to practically drag him into the car.

"Yeah," he grumbled, as if he already knew, and continued to stare out the passenger window.

"Shane, you're going to have a good time tonight, I promise."

She would do everything in her power to make sure of it. Her brother had hidden himself away like a hermit since he'd returned home from the hospital, only leaving the house for doctor's appointments. Ashley feared the self-imposed isolation was hindering his recovery. Tonight she planned to break down the walls of self-pity she felt surrounded him and help him to see that his life was still worth living.

"You know *she's* gonna be there," he stated, his voice gruff.

He was referring to his ex-girlfriend. The ticket Ashley held, purchased several months prior, had been intended for Robin.

"Okay, I admit there's a good possibility that Robin will show up. But so what? Do you really want to be with a woman who runs whenever rough times hit?"

The woman her younger brother had dated for two years—and had planned to marry—had bailed when she learned Shane might never walk again.

Her brother remained silent, avoiding her eyes.

Ashley's heart ached for him. She knew what it felt like to have your soul crushed by the person who had promised to love you forever.

She wheeled her sedan into the packed parking lot of the Bobcat Saloon, concerned she wouldn't be able to find an empty space. Shane had refused to apply for a disabled person's hangtag—a choice she had supported, hoping that his condition would be temporary—so they would have to fight for a spot. She circled behind the building and finally found a space next to the fenced-off dumpsters belonging to the business next door.

At least there was one plus to the location: they were parked directly beneath a streetlamp. She popped the trunk and hoisted out Shane's wheelchair. By the time she made it around to the passenger side of the car, he'd already swung his door open and had his feet planted on the ground.

Steering the chair next to the sedan, she locked the brakes. She slid his transfer board—a wooden plank with cut-out handles at each end—onto the car seat, underneath his thigh. Without giving her time to position the other end of the board onto the wheelchair, her brother thrust his hips to the side.

The board slipped, tipping the chair, and Shane tumbled to the pavement.

"Dammit!" he yelled.

Ashley's stomach clenched.

"Are you okay?" she asked him, worried he might have injured himself further. She'd warned him many times before to wait until she had the board secure, but in his sour mood, he'd barreled ahead.

"Do I look okay?" he snapped. "Ain't even able to get my ass out of a car."

She wedged herself between her brother and the sedan door. "Let me help you get back into the car seat."

"Don't touch me."

He pressed one palm against the still plate and the other against the floorboard and tried to push himself up. Unable to get his hips high enough to reach the seat, he collapsed back onto the ground.

"Why'd you make me come here?" he barked.

Ashley understood her brother's frustration, but she'd been coddling him for too long. Maybe that was the problem. It killed her to see him suffering emotionally, but there was only one way she could help him now. It was time for tough love.

"You're not the only person on this earth who's had bad things happen to them," she told him. "And dwelling on your current condition won't make things any better."

Shane stared at the pavement, his jaw set.

"You've cut yourself off from all of your friends and spend most of your time playing pointless video games," she continued. "You can't keep feeling sorry for yourself—just existing from day to day. It's time to dust yourself off and start living again."

Ashley edged closer to her brother.

"Now, grab my arm and let me help you pull yourself back up onto the car seat," she instructed.

Without saying a word, her brother did as he was told. This time he waited until the transfer board rested securely on the seat of the wheelchair before scooting across.

Shane rolled through the parking lot toward the club. Ashley followed close behind, hoping her blunt words would sink in and that he'd be able to find joy in his life again.

All the tickets for the performance were sold as general admission with seating on a first-come, first-served basis. Ashley scanned the crowded room and finally spotted an empty table in the back corner. Not the best seats in the house, but they would have to do.

The warm-up band launched into a rendition of "Sweet Home Alabama" as the pair weaved through the club to the table. Ashley rearranged the chairs so Shane would have the best view of the stage.

"I really need me a beer," he told her, stress evident on his face.

She noticed the servers were attending tables on the other side of the room.

"Okay, stay here and I'll go get drinks from the bar."

As she made her way back across the club, a blonde head caught her attention.

Robin.

The woman sat next to a dark-haired man that Ashley didn't recognize, his arm draped around the pretty blonde's shoulders. Ashley hoped Shane wouldn't see the couple. It was the last thing he needed right now.

She had the sudden urge to purchase a pint of beer just so she could dump it on Robin's head. She was convinced her brother would be much further along in his healing process if his former girlfriend had stuck by his side. If he didn't have a broken heart to mend along with his spine. The woman had never deserved a man as loyal and good-hearted as Shane. Ashley was just glad her brother had found out about Robin's true nature before marrying her.

Not wanting to end up like Clay and be arrested for assault, Ashley pushed her desire to attack Shane's former girlfriend aside and approached the bar. She was met by a familiar face.

"Ashley?" the bartender said, his lips stretching into a grin. "How long has it been? Six, seven years?"

"I'm pretty sure it's been at least eight," she replied, returning the smile.

Randy Boatman had hardly changed at all since high school. He wore his brown wavy hair in the same short style and his clean-shaven skin appeared as though it had barely aged.

"Last I heard, you'd moved to Chattanooga," he told her.

"Yeah, I'm living back on my father's property now. I'm actually here with Shane tonight."

Randy had gained membership into Ashley's circle of friends during freshman year, so he knew her family well. Although there had never been any romantic feelings between the two, she had always enjoyed his company.

"What can I get you?"

"Shane wants a beer—whatever you have on tap, and I'll have a club soda with lime."

She wondered whether the bartender had kept in touch with Sarah over the years. After Kyle had broken off his relationship with their classmate, Sarah had dated Randy a few times.

"Here ya go," he said, sliding the drinks toward her.

"I guess you've heard the news about what happened to Sarah Lester," Ashley stated as she paid for the beverages.

A distressed look crossed his face. "Yeah. But it wasn't really a shock."

Not a shock? It sounded as though he might have still been friends with their classmate. How well had he known her?

"Did Sarah do or say something that would lead you to believe her life was in danger?"

"You know that crowd she ran with," he said. "All drug addicts. Something was bound to happen sooner or later."

Which group was he talking about? Ashley was well aware of the reputation of Sarah's high school friends, but was he referring to her current crowd? Did he have insight into her life just before she'd died?

"So did you and Sarah continue to be friends after graduation?" she asked him.

Randy shook his head. "No, but she came in here a few times. She always seemed high."

"Did you know the people she was here with?"

"Uh-uh. I just remember seeing her."

Ashley felt her purse vibrate against her side. It was her cell phone; she'd switched it to silent mode. She reached for the zipper intending to check her phone's screen, but behind her, another patron shot her an irritated look. She realized she was holding up the order line. She'd continue her conversation with Randy at a later time. Maybe he would remember something that could help.

"Thanks, Randy," she said, picking up the drinks.

Winding through the maze of tables, Ashley found her way back to Shane. Although her brother still didn't appear happy, the music from the warm-up band seemed to have relaxed him a bit.

She placed the beer in front of him and sank onto her chair.

"Did you miss me?" she teased, trying to lighten his mood.

Shane didn't seem amused.

She dug her cell phone out of her purse and checked the screen. It was a text from Daniel. Hope fluttered in her chest as she read the message.

Clay Grimes cracked.

She couldn't wait to find out what the little cockroach had spilled.

"I'll be right back," she told Shane. "I need to go make a phone call."

CHAPTER FIFTEEN

The crisp night breeze cut through Ashley's denim jacket as she settled onto the wooden bench outside Bobcat Saloon, sending a chill down her spine and making her want to run back inside. But at the moment, privacy ranked higher on her priority list than comfort, which was the reason she'd ventured outdoors rather than ducking into the ladies' room.

The text from Daniel had arrived only a few minutes earlier, and she hoped to catch him before he retired to his motel room. Although she didn't believe Clay Grimes had admitted to Sarah's murder—the TBI agent would have typed *confessed* instead of *cracked*—she was anxious to hear the information the drug dealer had divulged.

Unlocking her phone, she tapped Daniel's name on her contact list. He answered on the second ring.

"Hey, Ashley."

"So how much information did you squash out of the little cockroach?" she asked, hoping it was enough to solve Sarah's murder.

"Not as much as I wanted," he replied, disappointment in his voice. "Sarah did owe him money, but only a couple hundred bucks. Not enough to kill her over."

"So you don't think Clay was involved in her death?"

Daniel's instincts usually proved to be correct. If he suspected the drug dealer was innocent, then they'd have to focus their investigation elsewhere.

"Not directly."

"But you believe he could somehow be connected to the killer?"

She wondered whether Clay had underlings working for him. Maybe one of them had become overeager, decided to play muscleman, and things got out of hand.

"It's possible. But he didn't fire the gun himself. He's got an alibi for the time of death. Highway patrol in Georgia pulled him over for speeding just north of Valdosta."

Ashley was familiar with the Georgia town, having driven through the area on her way to Florida's gulf coast. Valdosta was located at least six hours away from Laurel County.

The agent continued, "He claims it's been over a week since he saw Sarah. And that he doesn't know who killed her."

"If Clay had nothing to do with her murder then why did he attack me and try to run off?"

The dealer hadn't been carrying drugs and there were none in his car. But he'd obviously felt threatened.

"He said he freaked when he heard the letters TBI. He thought there was some kind of undercover sting going on."

She guessed that made sense. The dealer may have thought they'd found his hidden stash at the campground. Her hopes sank, knowing they would have to start the investigation over at square one—with no solid list of possible suspects for her classmate's murder.

"Keep me posted and let me know if you find out anything else," she told Daniel, hoping he would get a new lead.

"Will do."

Ashley tapped off the call. She shivered as a cold gust of wind hit her. Rising from the bench, she stuffed her phone back into her purse. Although it was clear Sarah had drug issues, it felt as though the reason for her murder ran much deeper. Daniel had remarked earlier that people involved in the drug trade preferred handguns to rifles. She also believed that if organized crime—even a small organization in Laurel County—was involved, they would have disposed of the body. Nooks and crannies abounded in these mountains. Hiding a corpse would be child's play for the local criminals.

They should be searching for someone with a personal motive.

But with Sarah's live-in boyfriend still locked in jail and her grandparents claiming she had no other friends, who was left to suspect?

Ashley hurried back inside the club and flashed her blue handstamp at the doorman. Deciding to make a pit stop at the ladies' room, she wound her way between the tables toward the rear of the building. The hallway leading to the restrooms lay just beyond the bar. She rounded the corner and then stopped short.

Shane's wheelchair blocked the path ahead, his face red with anger. Robin stood next to him with her back toward Ashley. Her brother's ex-girlfriend shook her head and lifted her hands as if in a shrug.

Although Ashley could tell the two were shouting, the music from the warm-up band drowned out their words. She took a few steps backwards out of the hallway, not wanting to intrude on Shane's private conversation. From the way his chair was angled, it was clear her brother hadn't seen her. Maybe it would be best for her to head back to the table and wait for him there.

As she swung around, she almost ran head-long into a dark-haired man—the same man she'd seen sitting at the table next to Robin, his arm encircling the pretty blonde.

"Excuse me," the man said, pushing past Ashley.

"Wait!"

She rushed after the man, intent on stopping him before he caught sight of Shane and Robin, but the man ignored her plea and kept walking.

Robin's date obviously didn't care about the young woman's privacy. He plunged straight between his date and Shane.

"What's going on here?" the man demanded.

"It's none of your business," Shane barked.

Her brother was not one to back down from a fight, even though he could no longer stand up without help. She felt compelled to intervene. As hard-headed as Shane could be, left on his own, she feared the confrontation wouldn't end well.

Ashley moved next to her brother's wheelchair. "There's no reason for anyone to get upset," she told the man. "They were just having a conversation. Maybe it would be best if we let them finish it in private."

The man stared at her as though she was from another planet.

"I don't think so," he said, his eyes narrowed.

He grabbed Robin's arm. "Let's go," he ordered.

"Get your hands off her," Shane shouted, his face crimson.

"Or what? You gonna run over me with your chair?"

Ashley held up her hand, stepping between the man and Shane. She had to end this. Now.

"Stop it—both of you," she said, worried things were escalating out of control.

She shot her brother's ex-girlfriend an exasperated look. "Robin, I think you and your date should go back to your table before we're all kicked out of here."

Robin glanced at Shane and then nodded. “Come on,” she told the dark-haired man.

Ashley watched the couple disappear around the corner of the hallway before turning back toward her brother. With the club packed, she’d hoped Shane wouldn’t see Robin. But she knew her brother had probably scanned the tables searching for his ex. He had a habit of subjecting himself to torture.

“Why don’t you let me buy you another beer?” she asked Shane.

He shook his head. “Let’s go home.”

“But the Nolan Arnold Band will be taking the stage in just a few minutes. We can stay in the bar area if you want.”

She realized that seeing Robin with another man had stung Shane’s heart, but she hoped he would refuse to give in to the pain. That he could salvage his night and be stronger for it.

“No,” he said, his voice firm. “I’m ready to go.”

He rolled past her down the hallway. Ashley sighed and trailed behind. She wished she knew the right words to say, that she could convince her brother that he still had wonderful things to look forward to in his life. But now that Robin had moved on, she worried Shane would retreat further into himself, eventually even shutting out his family. Although tonight was a loss, she vowed to keep pushing him. She was determined to pull her brother out of his despair no matter how hard he fought her.

Ashley glanced at the bar as she walked past and her eyes locked with Randy’s. Her old friend smiled and waved. It had been nice seeing him again.

She thought back to her sophomore year in high school when her older brother, Kyle, had been dating Sarah. Kyle would pack Ashley and her friends in his car and drive them to the movie theater here in Cedar View. It seemed like a lifetime ago.

Pulling her denim jacket tighter around her, Ashley followed Shane out into the windy night. The movie theater sat just a block away. She could see the lighted marquee in the distance. Memories floated back as she crossed the club parking lot.

And then it hit her.

Ashley knew someone who might be able to provide a lead on Sarah’s murder.

She’d pay them a visit first thing in the morning.

CHAPTER SIXTEEN

The first light of dawn broke through the crack above the cardboard panel that covered the RV's window, stinging Violet's tear-swollen eyes. She'd fought hard during the night. Her wrists burned where the plastic zip ties had cut into her flesh and her jaw throbbed from the backhanded blow she'd received.

She licked her parched lips. At least her gag had been removed—cut from her face with the hunting knife. But screaming had failed to help her. Her captor had explained that they were parked miles from civilization. There was no one around to hear her cries for help.

The sheet beneath her reeked of blood and sweat. Her abdomen ached from the sexual torture she'd endured. But it was morning now. Was her ordeal almost over?

Although she'd struggled at first—vowing to die before she'd submit—a promise from her abductor had made her finally give in.

He'd stay away from her little sister.

And he'd let Violet go when the night ended.

There was no way for her to know whether he'd keep the promise or if he was lying. But what choice did she have? She would do whatever it took to keep Eva safe. Even if it meant surrendering to the twisted fantasies of a psychopath.

"Thirsty?" her abductor asked. The clown mask twitched as he spoke.

Violet had yet to see his face. But his voice sparked a memory in the far recesses of her mind. She'd met him before, but she couldn't recall where or when.

The clown pressed a can of Riddle's Root Beer to her lips. She hated the flavor, but she gulped the cool liquid, letting it linger in the back of her mouth. The carbonation burned away the stale taste of the cotton gag that had clung to her throat.

"You did good, Violet. So I'm gonna let you go."

He took the drink away and placed it on the counter behind him.

He picked up the hunting knife. The blade—struck by the stream of morning light—glinted in the gloom of the RV.

"Do you want to live?" he asked her.

Her voice seemed stuck in her throat.

"Yes," she finally said, the word sounding more like a sob.

"Then do what I say." He moved toward her. "I'll cut you loose, but don't move. If you do, I'll kill you. And then I'll kill your sister."

She could feel her heart pounding in her chest as he brushed the flat side of the blade against her cheek.

"Understand?"

This time she didn't hesitate to answer.

"I'll do what you tell me, just please, don't hurt Eva."

The thought of the man subjecting her little sister to a similar night of torture was more than she could handle.

He lifted the knife above her head and sliced through the plastic tie that bound her right wrist to the chain that dangled from the overhead cabinet.

"Remember, don't move," he instructed. "Not until I tell you to."

Although her muscles screamed at her to lower her arm and let it relax, she remained motionless, terrified the clown would follow through on his threats.

He slid the blade underneath the tie that held her left wrist and cut it apart as well. Her hands were now free, but she was still his prisoner. Still frozen in place.

She heard him laugh, the sound muffled by the rubber mask. He stepped away from the bed and gathered her clothes from the shelf next to the bathroom. He tossed the bundle onto her stomach.

"Get dressed," he ordered.

Violet scooted to the edge of the bed, keeping her eyes on him—on the knife. The clown leaned his back against the row of cabinets opposite the bed, watching her with just as much intensity. She slipped on her undergarments and her black cotton Jack Daniel's T-shirt. She slid her legs into her jeans, pulled the waistband up just past her knees, and then hesitated. She would have to stand to fasten the button. In the cramped space, that would place her body mere inches from his.

The clown seemed to realize her dilemma. She heard him chuckle again as he tilted his head. He refused to move to the side.

She gritted her teeth and pushed herself up from the bed. Avoiding his eyes, she jerked her jeans above her hips and pulled up the zipper. The heat from his body pressed against her. The sour stench of his sweat filled her nostrils, causing her stomach to churn.

He angled his hideous slash of a mouth next to her ear.

"That shirt doesn't suit you," he whispered. "You should have worn the pink G.R.I.T.S. one."

What?

She hadn't owned a *Girls Raised in the South* shirt in years. She remembered a pink one from long ago—high school maybe. How had he known? Who was he?

The man sidestepped to the right, his gaze still focused on Violet, and nudged the door of the tall cabinet behind him ajar. His arm disappeared inside.

Her eyes widened as he withdrew his hand. His fingers curled around the stock of a rifle, a scope mounted to the top. He'd promised to free her—had allowed her to get dressed. Why did he need a gun?

"Let's go," he barked.

The clown yanked her upper arm and pushed her down the aisle of the RV in front of him.

"I need my socks and shoes," she told him, trying to keep her tone from sounding like a whine. She didn't want to anger him by complaining, but she had no idea how far she'd have to walk to find help.

"Those are mine now."

His? He was going to make her go barefoot? It didn't matter; she was still alive. And she just wanted to go home.

Violet almost tripped as he shoved her down two steps and then out through the RV's door. As her bare feet hit the cold earth, her soul brimmed with hope at the promise of freedom. A heavy fog blanketed the forest. She breathed in the crisp morning air, clearing her lungs of the putrid odor of the motorhome's interior.

The clown pushed her toward the rear of the vehicle. She turned her head, surveying the area. They were parked on an old logging road. A memory tugged at the corner of her mind, like déjà vu. She felt certain she'd been here before.

"You know what'll happen if you talk?" he asked, his hand clamped tight around her arm.

She nodded. "You'll kill me."

"And who else?"

"My sister."

"So what are you gonna do?"

Violet wasn't completely sure. She knew she wouldn't go to the police—they wouldn't be able to keep her safe—but she had a few cousins who might be able to track the clown down. To make him pay for what he'd done.

One thing she did know: the right way to answer the question.

"Keep my mouth shut," she told him.

"Good girl."

Her eyes swept down the logging road as he walked her to the other side of the RV. The memory that had nudged her was starting to solidify; she was gaining her bearings. She realized exactly where she was.

Unlike her little sister, Violet had grown up a tomboy. Her father had taken her hunting many times during her childhood and early teen years. They'd parked on this particular logging road on several different occasions.

The clown was leading her toward the west. There was nothing in that direction other than dense forest, and the logging road stretched several miles long. But behind her, to the east—on the other side of the woods—ran a highway. She could cut through. That was the shortest route to civilization. With no shoes, it might take her a while to get through the underbrush, but she could do it. She could get help.

He shoved her forward, toward the gloom of the forest.

"Run," he commanded. "If you want to live."

Violet stumbled from his push. Regaining her balance, she swung around and sprinted behind the clown toward the rising sun.

"Dammit!" she heard him shout.

She zipped through the bank of fog and into the woods. Briars pierced the soles of her feet like tiny needles, bringing tears to her eyes. Willing herself to block out the pain, she focused on the horizon ahead. Winding between the trees, she ran as fast as she could, afraid that the man would follow her. That he would change his mind about letting her go.

The crack of rifle fire erupted behind her.

The clown.

He was chasing her. Fear ripped through her chest.

In an instant, everything became clear. The reason he'd pushed her toward the west. The reason for the rifle. The reason he'd taken her shoes.

The clown was hunting her. Like an animal.

Crack!

Tree bark exploded in front of her. She swerved to the right. She knew she couldn't run in a straight line—she'd make too easy of a target. But she also knew that running serpentine would slow her down. Still it was the better choice. Her pursuer would have to stop to take aim through the scope.

She jumped over a fallen log and almost slipped on the other side. Her feet had gone numb, both from the cold and from the dozens of cuts that had shocked the nerves in her soles.

Violet remembered that the woods between the logging road and the clearing next to the highway hadn't taken her and her father very long to explore. When you're a child, everything seems larger and time moves slower. She hoped that meant she was getting close.

She raced ahead, her heart thundering in her ears. As she snaked between two oaks, a break in the tree line popped into view. The highway was just up ahead. She could make it.

Crack!

Pain split through her right shoulder. She'd been hit.

Hugging her arm to her chest, she forced herself to push onward. If she stopped—if she even allowed herself to slow down—the clown would kill her.

Violet broke from the tree line. She could see the highway not more than a dozen yards away. Her leg muscles burned as she propelled herself forward, praying for a passing car.

Crack!

A scream caught in her throat as her right hip exploded and she tumbled to the ground.

Tears welled in her eyes and then spilled over her cheeks. A burning hot pain radiated from her hip down her thigh and up through her lower back. She clamped the fingers of her left hand around a clump of weeds and pulled, trying to drag herself closer to the road.

The tall grass behind her rustled. She looked back over her shoulder, already knowing what she would see.

The clown.

"You almost made it," he said, his voice taunting.

Her fear morphed into anger.

"You lied to me," she spat out, knowing it was over—that she had nothing left to lose. "You was gonna kill me from the start."

"That's right. I led you on. Made you think you had a chance."

He stepped closer to her and then squatted next to her head. "You thought I was a just a clown—a joke. Somebody to amuse you. But now, who's the real fool?"

What was he talking about? He wasn't making sense.

The man ripped the rubber mask from his face and stared down at her. Hatred beamed from his eyes.

Now she understood. It was *him*.

He stood upright. Smiled as he shoved the muzzle of the rifle onto the center of her chest.

Violet closed her eyes and waited for him to pull the trigger.

CHAPTER SEVENTEEN

Ashley woke her phone and scanned the text message again, checking to see whether Charlene lived in side A of the duplex or B. Daniel had plucked the address of Sarah's best friend during her senior year of high school from the DMV records. While the TBI agent had chosen to spend his Sunday morning at the Laurel County jail interrogating Clay Grimes, trying to squeeze out the name of his drug supplier, he'd given Ashley the go ahead to question Charlene.

Although Sarah's grandparents had insisted the friendship had dissolved, Shane remembered seeing the two women together in town in the not so distant past. He couldn't recall exactly when, but was sure it had been within the last couple of years. Even if the women hadn't been close in a while, it was still possible that Charlene might have information relevant to the case.

Side B.

Stuffing her phone into her purse, Ashley slid out of her sedan and mounted the concrete porch of the aging duplex. Built sometime in the eighties, the building—clad with gray vinyl siding—formed a rectangle with a shared porch and two front doors in the center. The residence on the left side reflected a mirror image of the one on the right.

She pressed the doorbell attached to side B.

Ashley heard a dog yapping inside. A moment later the door swung open.

"I was wondering when you'd show up here," Charlene said, obviously recognizing Ashley.

Always rail thin in high school, the woman had put on weight—but in a good way. Still far from being considered heavy, the added pounds made Charlene appear much healthier. The brunette cradled a white fluff ball. Maybe a cross between a toy poodle and a Maltese.

"You've been expecting me?"

She was surprised to learn the woman had been anticipating her arrival. Although they'd been acquainted in school, Charlene had been what Ashley's friends dubbed a "wild child," living her life in reckless abandon, oblivious to the consequences. They'd never been friends.

"It's all over town that you been helping the state police. Heard you got Clay Grimes locked up. 'Bout time somebody did."

News traveled at the speed of light in Laurel County.

"Then I guess you know that I came to talk to you about Sarah," Ashley said.

"Yeah." The fluff ball nosed Charlene's chin. "But there ain't really nothing I can tell ya. Sarah and me quit being friends a while back."

Ashley wondered what could have caused the split. Dewayne, maybe? Could the two women who had been so tight their last year of high school have fought over a man? Love triangles had spurred more murders than Ashley could count. And at this point in the investigation, all motives remained possible.

"I always thought that the two of you were as close as sisters," she remarked, hoping Charlene would elaborate on the women's relationship.

"Yeah, well … we was. But that changed."

She heard a hint of sadness in the woman's voice—not anger. If the former friends had fought over a man, Ashley would have expected to pick up a tone of resentment.

"Do you mind sharing the reason you ended your friendship?"

It was a personal question, but their classmate was dead. The seriousness of the crime should outweigh any offense at the intrusion.

Charlene chewed her bottom lip. "Just a minute," she said.

The woman disappeared inside the duplex. A moment later she returned, the ball of fluff traded in for a pack of cigarettes. She led Ashley to the concrete steps.

"Smoke?" Charlene asked as she plopped down on the top step.

"No thanks."

Cold from the chilled concrete seeped through Ashley's jeans as she sat down next to the woman.

Charlene tapped out a cigarette, pursed it between her lips, and lit the end.

"I ain't the same person you remember from back in school," she told Ashley. "I was messed up for a lot of years. Stayed high most of the time. Just cared about having fun. But two years ago, I seen the light."

From the weight she'd put on and the healthy glow of her skin, it appeared Charlene was telling the truth about kicking her habit. Ashley didn't want the woman to feel like she was the one being investigated.

"Charlene, I'm not here to bust you on a drug charge, I'm just trying to find out—"

"No—you don't get it. I seen *the* light. The one at the end of the tunnel. I died."

Ashley stared at her. She seemed serious. "You overdosed?"

"Yeah. It was just like in the movies. Only that big bright light went out and it got cold and dark. I heard screaming. I was so scared. Then I woke up in the hospital."

That was a twist Ashley hadn't heard before. But the mind was complex. And with the drugs in her system, and her neurons misfiring, Charlene could have experienced just about anything. If the ordeal had scared her straight, then she was fortunate.

"I don't want to die again," Charlene said. "Not like that. I knew I had to change my life. I told Sarah I couldn't get high no more. And she agreed to stop too. We was both good for a little while. But then Sarah started sneaking off. I knew what she was doing. It got to the point where I just couldn't be around her no more."

"So it's been two years since you last saw Sarah?"

If the woman had truly escaped from the type of life her former friend was still living, it made sense that she would go out of her way to keep her distance.

"I seen her a couple months ago. But it weren't social."

"Did you run into her in town?"

As small as Mettler Ridge was, it would be hard for the locals to avoid being in the same vicinity once they ventured into town.

Charlene flicked the ashes from the end of her cigarette. "Before Sarah hooked up with Dewayne, she lived with me for a while. I was cleaning out one of my closets and I come across a box of her stuff. Bobby's ultrasound picture was in there. I knew Sarah would want it. I didn't have her phone number no more, so I carried it over to her trailer."

"Did she do or say anything that would lead you to believe she was in trouble?"

"I didn't talk to her. I just seen her through the window. She weren't alone."

Charlene's tone made it obvious that it wasn't Dewayne that Sarah had been entertaining.

"Was she cheating on Dewayne?"

If there had been another man in the picture, that could put a whole new spin on the investigation.

Charlene shook her head. "She loved Dewayne." She sighed, apparently uncomfortable with what she was about to reveal. "I think she was trading favors."

"You mean she was exchanging sex for drugs?"

"Yeah."

"Was Clay Grimes the man she was with?"

The thought of the little cockroach using Sarah's weakness against her in that way made Ashley sick.

"I don't think so," Charlene said. "Sarah was sitting on the man's lap. I only saw his legs, but he looked bigger than Clay. Taller."

"How do you know it wasn't Dewayne that you saw with Sarah?"

"Cause Dewayne was roofing houses with my brother over in Cedar View. His truck was gone and there was a strange car in the driveway. A blue Dodge Charger. New looking."

Clay Grimes currently drove a red coupe. A newer model Dodge Charger sounded more like the kind of car someone higher up in the drug trade would drive. Maybe Clay's supplier.

"Do you remember anything about the license plate? Was it a Laurel County tag?"

She shook her head. "Naw, I didn't look. I seen Sarah had company, so I left her box on the porch and came home."

Ashley wondered whether Sarah's live-in boyfriend had found out that she was trading favors.

"Do you think Dewayne could have had something to do with Sarah's murder?"

"No way," Charlene said, a wistful smile forming on her face. "Dewayne loved Sarah like bears love honey. Ain't nothing he wouldn't do for her. He begged her to get clean."

So Sarah's grandparents weren't alone in believing that Dewayne was innocent of the crime.

"Who do you think could have killed her?" Ashley asked, locking eyes with Charlene.

"Ain't got no idea." She took a drag from her cigarette. "I done put out feelers. It weren't none of my kin."

Ashley could tell the woman was speaking the truth—at least as she knew it. The fact that her family was not involved was probably the reason she didn't mind being seen talking with a TBI consultant.

A Chevy truck pulled into the driveway, parking beside Ashley's sedan.

"Oh, shit," Charlene said, stubbing her cigarette out on the porch step.

A tall bearded man hopped out of the pickup, slamming the door behind him

Tate Barrett—the cousin of Ethan Barrett, Ashley's ex-husband.

"What the hell is she doing here?" he yelled at Charlene.

"I didn't invite her. She just stopped by."

"It's nice to see you again too, Tate," Ashley said, rising to her feet. She hadn't known that Charlene was involved with Ethan's relative. It seemed as though he lived here too.

The man stepped toward her, rage spreading across his face. "Woman, you're treading on thin ice."

For a second, Ashley thought Tate might strike her. On reflex, her hand snapped to the grip of the Smith & Wesson holstered in her waistband. She knew her ex-husband's family hated her—blamed her for Ethan's prison sentence and more—but she didn't know how far Tate would go to prove it.

His gaze followed her hand, stopping him in his tracks. "You best leave. Now."

Ashley nodded. "Charlene, I wish you would have agreed to talk to me," she said, covering for the woman and hoping Tate would believe the lie. Hoping that he wouldn't take his anger out on his girlfriend. "Let me know if you ever change your mind."

"She ain't got nothing to say to you," Tate barked, his hands balled into fists. "Don't you never come back here," he warned.

Ashley walked backwards toward her sedan, afraid to take her eyes off of the man until she was a safe distance away.

She slid into the driver's seat and locked the door. Tate glared at her through the windshield.

As she was buckling her seatbelt, her cell phone rang. She checked the screen. It was Daniel.

"Hello?" she answered, hoping the agent had learned something new from Clay Grimes.

"Ashley, we found another body."

The agent's words made her stomach drop. She hadn't expected another murder.

Ashley started the sedan's engine.

“Tell me where you are and I’ll be right there,” she said.

CHAPTER EIGHTEEN

Vehicles from the Laurel County Sheriff's Department lined the center of the highway, blocking traffic, their lights flashing, as Ashley maneuvered her sedan behind Daniel's unmarked Toyota. She'd been instructed to keep off of the shoulder to avoid destroying possible evidence from tire treads. Two more nondescript cars also hugged the road. She assumed they belonged to other TBI agents. She didn't see the medical examiner's van. But she knew the ME that served the county lived in Cedar View, so it might take him a while to arrive at the scene.

Mindful of where she stepped, Ashley crossed the ditch into the field roped off with yellow crime-scene tape. Daniel hadn't given her any details over the phone. Just that they had found another body—a female—and the location. She saw Daniel, Sheriff Vance, and Deputy Kevin McConnell huddled in the center of the cordoned area. She picked her way toward the trio, dodging thistles as she went.

As she topped a small rise, the land flattened and she spotted the woman's lifeless body lying a few yards to the left of the group. An evidence tech dressed in a white Tyvek suit squatted next to the corpse. Ashley paused and watched as the tech snapped photographs of the body from various angles.

The woman had died lying on her right side. Her back was toward Ashley. Her golden brown hair cascaded across her shoulder, the ends pointing to a gaping hole ringed with blood and bits of raw flesh. An exit wound. From the wound's location in the center of the woman's back, it appeared a bullet had pierced the victim's heart.

Just like Sarah Lester.

Ashley's attention zipped to the woman's feet. No shoes. Also just like Sarah. And this victim shared the same hair color. The same body type. Appeared to be roughly the same age.

A knot formed in the pit of Ashley's stomach. *Too many coincidences.* Were they dealing with a serial killer?

She looked up and saw the trio disbanding. Daniel walked toward her, scribbling on a note pad. Kevin met her gaze, nodded a greeting, and then followed the sheriff back toward the highway.

"Have you been able to identify the victim yet?" she asked Daniel as he approached.

The agent's eyes locked with hers. "Violet Perry," he said as though searching her face.

Ashley sighed, her gaze dropping to the ground. She knew the name. Like Sarah, Violet had attended high school with Ashley. The two had only been casual acquaintances, sharing few classes over the years. Still, the news stung.

She searched her memory, trying to recall whether Sarah had been friends with Violet. She couldn't remember seeing them together, and she didn't think Violet had shared the same party-girl reputation. But the women could have forged a friendship after graduation.

There had to be a connection somewhere. Maybe they were both just unfortunate enough to have crossed the same person. Or maybe Ashley was wrong about the murders being personal. If Laurel County was home to a serial killer, both murders could have been crimes of opportunity. The victims targeted based on their physical features.

"Who found her?"

Ashley glanced toward the highway. The way the land sloped, it would be difficult to see the woman from the road, so she doubted the body had been discovered by a passing motorist.

"A couple of teenagers on horseback. Their parents took them home. I sent a deputy with them."

She imagined the sight must have left the teens pretty shaken.

Daniel jotted something else down in his notebook and then flipped back a few pages.

"Violet had a history of drug use," he told her. "She was busted for possession."

Another thing the woman had in common with Sarah.

"Charlene thinks that Sarah was getting drugs from a man who drives a late-model blue Dodge Charger—in exchange for sex," Ashley said.

"Laurel County tags?"

"She didn't get a look at the car's license plate."

"I'll run a DMV search. See if we can get a hit."

Ashley didn't expect there to be many late-model Chargers registered in Laurel County. Although muscle cars were popular in the area, the majority of locals who drove them seemed to favor older, used vehicles. It was possible the man had come from Cedar View or even Nashville or Chattanooga.

She turned her attention back to Violet. The missing shoes puzzled her. With Sarah's murder, she'd thought maybe the killer had engaged the woman in a sex act and that her shoes had possibly been left in the killer's car. Now she wondered whether they had been taken as a trophy. But shoes seemed like an odd choice. Underwear she could understand. Maybe the murderer had some kind of sick foot fetish. She realized there were all kinds of crazies in the world.

A rustling noise interrupted her thoughts. She and Daniel both turned around at the same time. The agent had evidently been pondering theories of his own.

Kevin strode toward them. "One of your guys found tire tracks," the deputy told Daniel, pointing toward the highway. "On the shoulder at the bend in the road."

Ashley squinted, studying the position of Violet's body. The way the highway snaked around the field, it was difficult to tell whether the woman had been running from the direction of the forest or from the curve in the road.

"What's through those trees?" Daniel asked Kevin, motioning toward the woods that bordered the field. "Any homes or cabins?"

"No," the deputy answered. "No houses. Just forest. It's pretty thick."

Daniel nodded.

Ashley wondered whether the tire treads would match a Dodge Charger.

A scream shattered the stillness of the morning, raising goosebumps on Ashley's arms. She swung her gaze toward the opposite end of the highway. Sheriff Vance stood just on the other side of the crime-scene tape, his arms clamped around a young woman, barring her entry to the cordoned area.

"That's Violet's sister," Kevin said.

The woman cried out again. Ashley could hear her begging the sheriff to let her see Violet.

"Which one of your deputies notified the next of kin?" Daniel asked Kevin, his jaw set.

She could tell the agent was angry that Violet's sister had been permitted to visit the scene. The vision of her loved one shot dead in the field would likely haunt the woman for the rest of her life. Ashley knew Daniel would never allow Violet's sister to be subjected to the sight.

"The sheriff was gonna do it in person," Kevin said, "later this afternoon. I guess somebody leaked the news."

Ashley's heart broke for the woman. "I'll go talk to her and see if I can get her to calm down," she said.

Daniel nodded. "Don't let her come up here. Not for any reason."

Ashley made her way across the field with Kevin following close behind. The deputy lifted the yellow tape and held it while she ducked under.

"You don't understand!" the woman shouted, her face bathed in tears.

"Yes I do," Sheriff Vance replied, his voice soft. "It's gonna be okay."

The woman struggled in his arms. "No it's not. How can you say that?"

Approaching the sheriff, Ashley blocked the woman's line of sight toward the field. Then she locked eyes with Violet's sister. She guessed the pretty brunette's age hovered somewhere from twenty to twenty-two.

"What's your name, sweetheart?" she asked.

"Eva," the woman moaned. "I need to see Violet."

The young woman's pain radiated from every pore in her body. It cut through Ashley's soul like a knife. She grasped Eva's hand, shielding it between both of her own.

"You'll get to see Violet soon, but right now, the investigators are trying to find out what happened to her. So we need to stay down here out of their way. You want to know what happened, don't you?"

Eva nodded, sobs racking her bones.

Ashley looked at Kevin. "There's a cooler in the back seat of my car—the silver sedan. Could you bring her a bottle of water, please?"

She focused her attention back on Eva.

"Do you live nearby?" she asked, not because the answer was pertinent to the investigation, but as a distraction. Anything to divert the young woman's thoughts away from her sister's body.

Eva nodded again. "Over on Pine Hill Road."

"Is that the road that crosses over Laurel Creek?"

Ashley already knew the answer; she just wanted to keep Eva talking.

"Yeah."

The woman had relaxed just a bit. Ashley glanced at Sheriff Vance. He loosened his bear hug.

Kevin returned with the bottle of water. Ashley twisted off the cap and slid the bottle into Eva's hands.

"Do you think you can drink of few sips of this?"

Eva sighed. She closed her eyes and placed the bottle to her lips. Sheriff Vance released his grip on the woman. He looked at Ashley and mouthed *Thank you*.

She nodded. She waited for Eva to finish drinking and then took hold of her hand again.

"Come and sit with me for a few minutes, okay?"

She led Eva to her sedan and tucked the woman into the passenger seat. Ashley climbed in behind the wheel.

"I went to high school with your sister," she told Eva, hoping to establish some common ground—to let the young woman know she cared.

There were so many questions that needed to be asked. Questions that might lead to Violet's killer. But now was not the time. Eva was too fragile to be quizzed.

Ashley wondered whether the women's parents were still living. Or if Eva was married. She didn't want the young woman to have to suffer through the tragedy alone.

"Are you a cop?"

Ashley shook her head. "No. Right now, I'm just working as a consultant, but I hope to be a police officer one day."

Eva sighed. Her hand flew to the door handle.

"Then you can't arrest him," she said, pushing the door open.

"Wait."

Ashley clasped the woman's forearm. Eva knew something. Something important.

"Arrest who?"

Eva's blue eyes filled with tears.

"The man that killed Violet," she said.

CHAPTER NINETEEN

With her left arm wrapped around Eva, Ashley slid the woman's key into the lock of the double-wide trailer's door and then turned the knob. Eva leaned against her as they crossed the threshold into the home the young woman had shared with her sister, Violet. The air inside smelled of pumpkin spice. Ashley led Eva into the living room, navigating around a coffee table topped by a miniature scarecrow flanked on both sides by orange pillar candles—the source of the sweet scent.

"Do you want to sit here?" she asked.

She motioned toward a blue upholstered sofa that had been decorated for the season with throw pillows appliqued with autumn leaves.

Eva nodded, a vacant expression on her tear-stained face.

At the crime scene, the young woman had suffered a meltdown. Right after stating that a man should be arrested for killing her sister, Eva had hyperventilated, almost falling out of the passenger seat of Ashley's sedan. Alarmed, Ashley had jumped out of the driver's seat and rushed around to help. By the time she reached the open car door, Eva had fainted.

Ashley glanced at the cuckoo clock hanging next to the wide opening leading into the kitchen.

"Your Aunt Delilah will be here soon," she said. "Is there anything I can get you?"

Ashley had learned that both of Eva's parents were deceased, but her father's sister lived in Cedar View. Kevin had contacted the woman and informed her of Violet's death and Eva's condition. She was on her way to her niece's trailer.

Eva shook her head. She hadn't spoken a word since leaving the crime scene.

Ashley settled on the sofa next to Eva and clasped her hand, wishing she knew what to say to help alleviate the pain. The doctor that served as the medical examiner for Laurel County had given the woman something to calm her nerves. The drug had seemed to turn her into a zombie. Or was she in shock? Ashley couldn't tell.

Either way, she knew she couldn't question Eva about the man mentioned in the car—the one the woman believed killed Violet. If Ashley prodded, she feared the woman would suffer another episode.

Eva shivered, the motion so strong it jarred Ashley's body.

"Are you cold?"

There was no reply.

The woman wore a dark green sweater and jeans. The temperature in the room felt pleasant—neither too cool nor too warm. The chill most likely originated from deep within Eva's soul. Ashley stripped off her denim jacket and draped it around the woman's shoulders. She considered searching the bedrooms and bringing back a blanket, but she was afraid she'd make the mistake of choosing something that belonged to Violet, subjecting Eva to even more trauma.

From where she sat on the couch, Ashley held a direct line of sight into the kitchen. A coffee maker sat on the counter. She wondered whether she could leave Eva alone long enough to brew a pot.

"Would you like me to make you a cup of hot coffee? It might help to warm you up."

Eva sighed and then nodded, the blank look still in her eyes.

As she made her way into the kitchen, Ashley wondered what Eva knew about her sister's death. Had Violet been threatened? It was obvious that the person responsible for Violet's murder had also killed Sarah. Was it the man who drove the blue Dodge Charger?

She put the coffee on to brew.

At the same time Ashley had left the crime scene to drive Eva home, Daniel had headed back to the county jail to continue questioning Clay Grimes. Now that there had been two murders, the agent was determined to wriggle the name of the area's drug supplier out of the little cockroach. He felt it was possible the supplier might be the man Charlene had seen at Sarah's trailer.

Ashley found a plastic tray in the cabinet above the coffee maker. She placed a bowl of sugar, a container of non-dairy creamer, and two cups of coffee onto the tray and carried it into the living room.

She eased back onto the sofa and tucked one of the white ceramic cups into Eva's hand.

The warmth from the cup seemed to stir the woman's consciousness, bringing her focus into the here and now. She looked at Ashley, her blue eyes pleading.

"Will they arrest him?" she asked.

The question surprised Ashley. She knew she had to proceed with caution. One wrong word could trigger another meltdown. She felt it would be better to answer in the affirmative, to try and soothe Eva's worried mind.

"Yes, he'll be arrested."

And he would be—as soon as they could figure out who *he* was. She paused for a moment, gauging the woman's reaction. Eva seemed to have relaxed a bit as she stared into the dark liquid in her cup.

Ashley decided to press forward.

"But we need your help to catch him," she said, her voice tentative. "Can you tell me his name?"

Eva shook her head. "I tried to get her to stop."

"Do you mean that you asked Violet to quit using drugs?"

The young woman nodded. "She promised she would. She was going to take cosmetology classes. She wanted to work with me at the hair salon," Eva said, fresh tears sliding down her cheeks.

Ashley knew that Eva worked as a hairstylist in Cedar View. She glanced around the room, looking for a box of tissues, but saw none. She didn't want to leave the young woman's side. Not yet.

"We were saving our money for her tuition," Eva continued. "That's why she did it."

Ashley didn't follow. "What did Violet do?"

Eva pressed her eyes closed. Ashley didn't push; she waited for the woman to gather her thoughts.

"She stole from him," Eva finally said, opening her eyes.

Ashley assumed the person Violet had stolen from was either a drug dealer or supplier.

"What did Violet steal—drugs, cash?"

"Crystal meth. I found it in her bedroom. She never was good at hiding stuff. I knew she didn't have any money to buy it with. She admitted she stole it. I told her to take it back, but she said she couldn't. She'd already used some."

"So you believe that the man Violet stole from is the same person who killed her," Ashley stated.

She wondered exactly how much crystal meth Violet had taken. How much would be enough to commit murder?

"He kidnapped her," Eva said.

The woman shuddered, almost spilling her coffee. "Was my sister tortured?"

Ashley averted her eyes. She didn't know how to answer. Only the autopsy could determine what Violet had endured, but she'd seen the gashes on the woman's left wrist indicating she'd been bound and had fought. She'd seen Violet's bloody feet where she'd run through briars in the field trying to escape. Blood had soaked the woman's jeans on the right side, most likely from a bullet wound. And there was the fatal wound: a bullet had passed through Violet's heart.

"I'm not really sure what all happened to her," she told Eva.

She wanted to give the young woman solace, but at the same time, she refused to lie—to say that Violet had not been subjected to torture when it was possible that she had. And many forms of torture existed—not just physical. Mental and emotional torture couldn't be identified by the medical examiner.

"You said she was kidnapped?" Ashley nudged.

Eva nodded. "While I was at work yesterday. I came home and found a basket of wet laundry out by the clothesline. Violet's phone was on the ground. Her earbuds too. I knew right then that he'd taken her. I looked for her all night. Drove everywhere I could think of."

Ashley wondered whether Eva had slept at all.

"Did you call the sheriff's office?"

"I was scared to." A sob caught in the woman's throat. "I thought she'd come home. That she'd be okay."

She could understand the reason Eva had not wanted to involve the police. And this was Laurel County after all, where the majority of the people considered law enforcement to be the enemy.

"And you don't know this man's name or how to find him?"

"No. She didn't want me to know. Said it could get me in trouble."

"Did you ever see him, or the car that he drove?"

Ashley wondered again whether it was the man in the blue Charger that had visited Sarah.

Eva shook her head. "He never came here. At least, not while I was home."

It seemed they were at another dead end. Ashley needed to ask Daniel to send the TBI's forensic team to Eva's trailer to search the area where Violet was abducted. The kidnapper might have left a footprint or some other clue behind.

Eva shifted her position on the sofa, shoving her hand into the pocket of her jeans.

"I did find this," the woman said. "It was on the ground next to Violet's phone."

She uncurled her fingers, revealing a small silver-colored button resting on her palm. Black lettering spelled out Z.L. Holt. Ashley was familiar with the name. The company manufactured a men's clothing line sold mainly in sporting goods stores. The apparel wasn't expensive, but it tended to be more costly than clothing found at Walmart and other discount stores. However, the brand was so common, Ashley realized that unless they had a piece of apparel to compare it to, it would be hard to trace where it had come from.

Any fingerprints had likely been smudged or wiped away when Eva had picked up the button and slid it into her pocket.

"Can I take that and give it to the TBI?" she asked.

"Yeah."

Ashley didn't have an evidence bag. She dug in her purse and pulled out a small notepad. She ripped out one of the pages.

"Drop the button onto the middle of the paper," she instructed.

Eva did as she was told. Ashley folded the paper around the button, securing it as best as she could, and then placed it in the outer zippered compartment of her purse.

Ashley's cell phone chirped, signaling an incoming text message.

"Excuse me for just a second," she told Eva.

She checked her phone's screen. The message was from Daniel.

Got the supplier's name. Meet me at the jail.

It looked as though the agent had worked his magic on Clay Grimes. She tapped in a reply.

I'll leave here as soon as the aunt arrives.

Ashley shoved her phone back into her purse.

"Don't worry, Eva," she said. "We'll find the man who killed Violet and we'll lock him behind bars. I promise."

CHAPTER TWENTY

Ashley's body juddered as she squeezed the passenger handholds on the rear of the four-wheeler, her knuckles turning white. It wasn't hard to tell that this was Daniel's first time piloting an ATV. They wove through the trees, seeming to hit every bump and rut on the forest floor. She hoped they didn't have much further to go before they reached the cabin—if they reached the cabin. The way the agent drove, they might end up heading to the emergency room instead.

Daniel had acquired the location of the meeting place from Clay Grimes on a trade. After a TBI drug dog sniffed out Clay's goods hidden at the campground, his fingerprints all over the packages of crystal meth, the little cockroach had been eager to make a deal. Information in exchange for a lighter sentence.

Clay's supplier, a man named Wade Elkins, conducted a weekly meeting with his dealers at the hunting cabin every Monday at noon. Tomorrow, they were in for a surprise. Agents from the TBI's drug investigation division (DID for short) planned to have the cabin surrounded well before lunch. Daniel, who seemed to have an impatient streak that matched Ashley's, had decided to scope out the location now rather than waiting for the DID.

The four-wheeler topped a small rise, sailing airborne for a split second. The wheels slammed the ground on the other side, rattling Ashley's teeth. The jolt spurred a decision: she would insist on driving back—and wouldn't take no for an answer.

She wondered why she had ever agreed to climb aboard the passenger seat in the first place. She guessed she'd been fooled by the agent's expert ability at driving a sedan. The skill didn't carry over. But they couldn't just arrive at the cabin by car. Stealth was required. They didn't know who would be watching. The plan was to park the ATV in the forest, at far enough of a distance so the engine couldn't be heard, and then walk the rest of the way.

Ashley hoped they would find a clue in the cabin linking Clay's drug supplier to Sarah and Violet.

They were still no closer to finding the man who drove the blue Dodge Charger. A search of the DMV records revealed that Wade Elkins had never owned a Charger. He drove a white Mustang. But it was still a possibility that the supplier was somehow connected to the murders of Ashley's two classmates. And it was also possible that the driver of the Charger was completely innocent. At this point, everything remained speculative.

Daniel steered the four-wheeler next to a small outcropping of limestone and killed the engine. Ashley mouthed a silent *thank you* that they were both still in one piece. The agent dismounted and slipped off his helmet.

"That was fun," he said.

Ashley stared at him.

"Wait a minute," she said. "You're not telling me that you meant to drive like that, are you?"

He had to be kidding. Daniel didn't seem to be the reckless type. He had to be covering for his lack of experience with an ATV.

"Well ... maybe I didn't exactly mean to," he stammered, obviously embarrassed. "But we're here."

Ashley felt a smile cross her face. She was definitely driving back. She hopped off of the four-wheeler, leaving her helmet on the seat.

Daniel checked his handheld GPS unit.

"The cabin's on the other side of those trees," he said, motioning to a thick stand of cedars.

Ashley took the lead, plowing through the underbrush. Her legs were so shaky from the four-wheeler ride, she was grateful she could still walk. Dusk was beginning to fall, but they didn't need flashlights yet. A full moon hung just above the horizon to her left. The soft light leaked through the trees, painting the landscape with a silvery radiance.

With Daniel close behind, she circled around a felled tree that appeared to have been struck by lightning. Veering back on course, she found herself in the midst of the thickest part of the grove. A few moments later, she pushed aside a cedar branch, revealing a small clearing up ahead. The cabin sat in the middle. And it wasn't empty.

An amber glow lit the window on the side of the building. Ashley spotted a white Mustang parked on the dirt drive along with two pickup trucks. She glanced at Daniel as he trudged up beside her.

"Looks like they're meeting early," the agent remarked in a hushed voice.

"Should we get closer to the cabin and see if we can find out what's going on?"

Daniel nodded. "Elkins must be spooked. He's likely collecting cash. Handing out the goods for next week. DID's not in the area yet. I'll have to call my guys for backup."

The agent pulled out his phone and stepped back under the cover of the cedars. Ashley wondered how long it would take for the TBI agents to arrive. The cabin was located on the edge of the county—out in the middle of nowhere.

Headlights flashed through the trees to her right and she heard the hum of an engine. She knelt down, backing against a tree, hoping she wouldn't be seen. A car plodded up the rough dirt drive. In the darkness, she couldn't be sure of the color, but the shape matched the pictures of the Dodge Chargers she'd looked at online.

Daniel scooted up next to her.

"Well, look who's here," he whispered. "Mr. Charger."

The car door opened and the light flicked on inside. A dark-haired man that Ashley didn't recognize hopped out from behind the wheel. He sauntered up the porch steps and entered the cabin.

"Do you think anyone else will show up?" she asked.

The agent shrugged. "Clay said the number varied each week. All guys from surrounding counties. He claimed he didn't know anyone with a Charger."

The man who had been behind the wheel of the Dodge had a certain confidence in his gait, as though he were someone with authority.

"Do you think it's possible that the guy driving the Charger is Wade Elkins's boss?"

"Could be."

That might explain why Clay didn't know the man. The dealers may not have been allowed to meet him. But if that was the case, why was Elkins's boss here now?

Daniel looked at her as though he was debating something within himself.

"I'm going up to the window," he said. "You stay here."

Ashley grabbed his arm. "Please, Daniel, let me go up to the cabin with you. I'll be quiet and I'll stay hidden behind that bush."

She pointed toward the large native shrub growing next to the window. There was no way she was going to let Daniel take the risk alone. What if he needed her help?

The agent shook his head. “We don’t know what we’re up against. There are at least four guys in there. And you can bet your bottom dollar they’re armed.”

She hated the fact that Daniel felt he had to watch over her. That she wasn’t capable of taking care of herself. She knew how to use a firearm and she was getting pretty good at hand-to-hand combat. There was no reason for him to leave her behind. But the agent didn’t realize that yet—she’d have to find a way to prove it to him.

“I’ll be just as safe up there with you as I would be here in the woods by myself. What if they’ve got a scout patrolling the forest?”

Daniel sighed. She could tell by his frustrated expression that she’d put forth a worthy argument.

“Okay,” he said. “But stay close to me. And watch your back.”

With Daniel leading the way, they slipped out of the cover of the tree line and skulked toward the cabin. When they reached the building, Ashley crept between the wall of aged wood siding and the chokeberry bush as she’d promised. The window was raised and she could hear music playing through the grimy screen. An old country tune. Johnny Cash.

Daniel eased his head up and glanced through the window. With the darkness now pressing down on them, it was likely that they couldn’t be seen from inside the lighted cabin. The agent held up four fingers. She assumed that meant there were four men inside, as they had expected.

Ashley inched closer to the window and peeked into the room. She held her breath, fearing that even the slightest movement would attract the drug traffickers’ attention. That one of them would draw, fire, and blow her head off. She glimpsed a red-haired man sitting at a card table topped with stacks of cash and several brown paper bags which she guessed held crystal meth. From her angle, she could only see him in profile, but she recognized him from his mugshot. He’d done time for robbery. Wade Elkins. The supplier held a fist full of bills. He counted them off, piling them in front of him on the table.

Three other men sat in folding chairs scattered around the room. Mr. Dodge Charger, a bald man, and a man wearing a red ball cap. All three had their backs toward the window.

“So we ain’t gonna meet here no more?” baldy asked.

“No,” Elkins barked.

The supplier's tone exuded anger. It probably had something to do with the reason they'd decided to meet a day early.

"Clay done screwed us over, that's for sure," red cap said.

So that was the motive behind the change in plans. They were aware of the drug dealer's arrest and were afraid he'd talked. Which he had.

"You'll be notified and told where to meet and when," Mr. Charger told them. "But it won't be in Laurel County."

Elkins finished his counting, rolled up the cash, secured it with a rubber band, and then picked up another stack. She wondered how far away the TBI agents were. It wouldn't take the supplier that much longer to count the rest of the money. She worried the drug traffickers would be long gone before Daniel's backup arrived.

The agent slid down from the window, his back toward the wall. Ashley mirrored his movements. He looked at her, his bottom lip clenched between his teeth. He seemed to be sharing her thoughts—was likely concerned that the criminals would escape.

Daniel pulled her toward him and cupped his hand around her ear.

"I'm going in," he whispered. "Do not move from this spot. I don't care what happens. You stay put."

Fear that he might not make it out alive gripped Ashley's soul. She didn't want him to risk busting into the cabin alone. But she recognized the determination in his eyes and realized she wouldn't be able to talk him into waiting for backup. For a split second, she thought about demanding that he let her go with him. She could handle herself. And he needed her to cover his back. But even if she insisted, she knew he would never allow her to go inside. And they didn't have time to argue. Against her better judgment, she nodded.

A knot catching in her throat, she grabbed his arm and locked her gaze on his.

"Be careful," she mouthed.

Daniel smiled. "Always," he mouthed back.

He drew his weapon. Without making a sound, he disappeared around the corner of the cabin.

With her heart pounding in her chest, Ashley peered through the window and waited.

CHAPTER TWENTY ONE

As each second ticked past, Ashley's anxiety ratcheted up a notch. Her muscles tensed, she stared through the window into the cabin, waiting for Daniel to make his entrance. He had to act fast—before the group of drug traffickers disbanded. With the suppliers having decided to move the cash exchange to another county, the TBI might not get another chance to catch them. And any evidence tying the drug ring to the murders of Sarah and Violet could be lost.

Elkins continued to count the bills lying on the card table while Mr. Charger, the bald guy, and the guy in the red cap watched from their folding chairs.

Baldy started singing along with Johnny Cash.

"*I fell into a burnin'—*"

"Shut up," Mr. Charger ordered, his voice harsh.

The bald guy did as he was told. A sense of tension seemed to settle over the room which added to Ashley's nervous anticipation. The drug traffickers were obviously angry about Clay's arrest and the fact that they felt forced to abandon their weekly meeting location.

Ashley focused her attention on the front door of the cabin and held her breath, knowing that Daniel stood on the other side. She jumped as the door burst open.

"TBI!" Daniel shouted, his gun aimed at Mr. Charger. "Hands up where I can see them!"

An expression of shock spread across the faces of Mr. Charger, Elkins, and the bald man. It seemed clear they thought they'd outsmarted the police by meeting a day earlier. The guy in the red cap looked scared enough to pee his pants. One by one, the men raised their arms.

"The first person who moves gets a bullet in their head," the agent warned.

"Where's your tag-along blonde?" Mr. Charger asked.

The man's question surprised Ashley. She realized he was talking about her. The drug ring seemed to be well-versed in the details of

Clay's capture. They'd probably been filled in by the same basketball player who had informed Clay that Ashley was working with the TBI.

"Not here," Daniel said, "and none of your concern."

Although she had promised not to move from her hiding spot behind the chokeberry bush, Ashley wondered whether she should head into the cabin. Two guns aimed at the drug traffickers would be safer than one. She could also frisk each of the men and take away their weapons. She knew Daniel couldn't risk letting the men lower their arms to hand over their guns. One of them would no doubt draw on him.

She had to make a decision. Quick.

It was obvious the agent needed her help. The best choice was to go against his orders. She hoped Daniel wouldn't be angry.

Ashley caught movement out of the corner of her eye. Her gaze snapped to the open cabin door as a fifth man slipped through. She stifled a scream. She'd been right—they did have a lookout. A tall wall of muscle. And he was armed.

"Hold it right there, TBI man," the lookout ordered as he pressed a pistol to Daniel's back. "And drop your gun."

The agent placed his weapon on the card table and raised his hands.

Panic sliced through Ashley's heart. If she rushed in now, the lookout might shoot Daniel.

What was taking the other TBI agents so long to get here?

Mr. Charger stood up.

"Take off your belt," he instructed Daniel.

The agent unbuckled his belt, slipped it off of his waist, and tossed it onto the card table.

Ashley could tell by the expression on Daniel's face that he was chiding himself for not scoping out the property and checking to make sure there was no scout lurking around before going inside.

Mr. Charger moved toward the bald guy.

"Get up," he barked at baldy. "You take his seat," he told Daniel.

The agent dropped onto the folding chair. Mr. Charger wrenched Daniel's arms behind the back of the chair and secured the belt around the agent's wrists. The bald man drifted to the side and then made himself comfortable on the floor. He seemed to know better than to take Mr. Charger's seat.

The lookout holstered his weapon, crossed his arms, and sank down against the far wall. Ashley inched back from the window just a bit.

The lookout was facing her. She would have to make sure she stayed in the shadows while still maintaining a view into the cabin.

Mr. Charger kicked the leg of Daniel's chair.

"You got agents in the woods?" he asked.

Daniel remained silent. Ashley knew he would never offer up any information, especially the fact that she was hiding outside.

Mr. Charger drew back his fist and punched Daniel in the stomach.

An audible groan erupted from the agent's mouth. Ashley wanted to press her Smith & Wesson against the window screen and blow Mr. Charger's head off.

"Nobody's out there," Elkins said. "If he had help, they'd be yelling at us on a bullhorn by now."

Mr. Charger sneered at Daniel. "Is that right? Did you come alone?"

"Yeah. He's right," the agent said.

Ashley knew the last thing Daniel wanted was for the traffickers to know that help was on the way. They'd run. And likely kill the agent on their way out.

"But I bet you called your buddies for backup."

Daniel shook his head. "No cell signal."

No signal? Was Daniel bluffing or was he telling the truth? The cell service in Laurel County was spotty in areas, especially in the dales between the mountains. Like the valley they were in now. But if Daniel had failed to reach an agent for backup, he would have told her. Wouldn't he?

Fear spread throughout her as she realized she hadn't actually heard Daniel talking on the phone.

She fought the urge to pull out her cell and check for a signal. If she woke her phone, the light might attract the lookout guy's attention. And she didn't want to take her eyes away from the scene playing out in the cabin. If she did, she might miss her cue to rescue Daniel.

Ashley realized that the job of saving the agent had fallen on her shoulders. She couldn't count on the TBI to arrive in time—or at all. But she needed to wait for the right opportunity or she could end up getting both the agent and herself killed. She checked the stacks of money in front of Elkins. The supplier was almost finished counting.

The door to the cabin stood open. There was a window to the right of the door—the side closest to Ashley. The best way for her to surprise the traffickers—to keep from being seen—was to approach the porch from the other side.

Mr. Charger began to frisk Daniel, patting his jacket pockets.

"Where's your phone?" he asked.

"I lost it in the woods," the agent said.

Ashley knew that was a lie. She'd seen him slip his cell into his front pants pocket.

"Yeah, right."

Mr. Charger wasn't buying Daniel's explanation, but he seemed reluctant to touch the agent's front pockets. He pulled out his own cell. Ashley jumped backwards as the drug supplier headed toward the window, his eyes glued to his phone's screen.

"Well, what do ya know," Mr. Charger said. "No damn signal. Guess you're out of luck, TBI man."

Ashley's heart sank. If Mr. Charger had no service, there was a good chance that the TBI agents weren't coming. That she was on her own.

Elkins slipped a rubber band around another roll of cash. "Don't kill him here. We don't want him traced back to us."

"We'll take him out to that old mine shaft where we dropped the other guy. Do it there."

Mr. Charger put his phone away and eased back into his seat.

The fear that gripped Ashley's soul squeezed tighter. She couldn't wait any longer. She had to move now.

She backed away from the cabin and headed toward the dirt drive. She skirted behind the Mustang and then circled around the yard. With her hands sweating, Ashley crept toward the side of the porch. She knew she would only get one chance at saving Daniel. And she wasn't sure she could do it. But if she faltered—if she let her nerves get the better of her—both she and the agent would die. She had to be strong. Had to pretend she knew what she was doing.

As the full moon ducked behind a bank of clouds, Ashley hoisted herself up onto the porch. She pressed her back against the cabin wall and drew the Smith & Wesson from the holster in her waistband. Trying hard not to make a sound, she scooted toward the open doorway. She paused and listened.

Johnny Cash had been replaced by Loretta Lynn.

"Wouldn't wanna be Clay right now." The voice sounded like red cap guy.

"We'll handle him," Mr. Charger said. "And just remember, if you ever get arrested, keep your mouths shut. If you don't, you'll end up like Clay and the TBI man here. There's plenty of room in that mine shaft."

Ashley could feel her insides shaking. It was now or never. She took a deep breath and counted backwards. *Three ... two ... one.*

With adrenaline surging through her veins, Ashley swung around and plunged through the open door.

"Hands up—now!" she shouted, her Smith & Wesson aimed at Mr. Charger's chest.

The men raised their hands. A half smile tugged at Daniel's lips, as though he was glad to see her but wished she'd stayed outside.

"You," Ashley nodded toward the bald guy. "Untie the agent."

She'd noticed that the bald man's shirt was tucked in. Unless he had an ankle holster, he didn't appear armed.

The bald man hesitated, looked toward Mr. Charger.

"If you don't want me to shoot your boss then you'll untie the agent—right now," she warned. She didn't want to fire her weapon, but she would do anything necessary to save Daniel's life.

"She's not going to shoot me," Mr. Charger said. "Look at her, she's just—"

Ashley squeezed the trigger.

She had adjusted her aim. The bullet nicked the top of Mr. Charger's left arm before slamming into the wall behind him.

"Dammit!" the drug supplier yelled, clenching his shoulder.

A dark red stain spread across the upper sleeve of Mr. Charger's blue cotton shirt. The drug supplier had only suffered a minor flesh wound—definitely not fatal—but the action had made Ashley's determination clear.

The men appeared stunned—including Daniel.

"Get your hands back up," she ordered the drug supplier. "Next time I'll aim for your heart. And it might interest you to know that I'm a crack shot."

Ashley put forth a brave façade, but inside, her soul quaked. She knew she wouldn't kill the man—not unless she had no choice—but she wouldn't hesitate to graze his other shoulder.

The expression on Mr. Charger's face revealed he thought Ashley just might be crazy enough to follow through with her threat. He raised his hands again.

"Do it," Mr. Charger said. "Let the agent go."

The bald man pulled himself up off the floor and moved behind Daniel's chair. He unfastened the belt, freeing the agent.

Daniel bolted from the chair and grabbed his weapon from the top of the card table.

"Thanks," he told Ashley. He aimed his gun at Elkins.

Ashley's legs felt as though they were turning to jelly, but she tightened her muscles and held her stance. She heard movement behind her.

"TBI!" a male voice boomed. "Drop your weapon."

Relief flooded Ashley's body. She dropped her Smith & Wesson, sank to the floor, and crossed her hands behind her head. Daniel had contacted his agents for backup after all. He met her gaze and smiled.

"She's with me," he told the agents as they swarmed into the room, accompanied by deputies from the Laurel County Sheriff's Department.

Ashley pushed herself up. On shaky legs, she watched the agents cuff and frisk the drug traffickers. She'd had enough excitement for one day. She couldn't wait to head back to the county jail.

And this time—she would drive the ATV.

CHAPTER TWENTY TWO

The headlights cut through the darkness as Ashley steered the four-wheeler between ancient oaks and towering hickories. She handled the twists and turns with ease, like a professional skier in a slalom race. Thanks to her father, she'd learned to pilot an ATV when she was just a child. She hoped Daniel would be able to pick up a few pointers from the passenger seat behind her.

The agent had been acting strange since they'd left the cabin. On the walk back through the woods to the four-wheeler, he'd barely said a word. But his expression revealed that his mind was racing. Maybe he'd just been pondering the details of the case. However, it seemed as though he wanted to tell her something, but didn't quite know how.

She wondered if he'd spotted a clue at the cabin that she'd missed. A piece of evidence that would link the drug traffickers to Sarah and Violet. Could the women have been held at the cabin? The valley location was miles from where the two bodies had been found. But both women had been missing for twenty-four hours prior to their deaths. They had to have been kept somewhere. If they'd been at the cabin, the TBI's forensic team should be able to find DNA, hair, or clothing fibers—something they could use to identify the presence of Ashley's classmates. Wherever they'd been, whatever they'd touched, the women would have left a trace of themselves behind.

Ashley maneuvered the four-wheeler over a small rise. Beneath the glow of the full moon, the water of Mettler Lake glistened through the trees to her right. The parking area for the boat ramp—their destination—lay just up ahead.

The ATV belonged to the Laurel County Sheriff's Department. The low-pressure tires made it dangerous to operate the vehicle on asphalt. The tires could slip and regain traction in a split second, causing rollovers when turning. Because the sheriff's department was located at least twenty miles away, Daniel had hauled the four-wheeler to the boat ramp on a trailer attached to one of the department's SUVs.

Knowing that the agent was eager to interrogate Mr. Charger and Elkins, Ashley had offered to return the four-wheeler by herself in order to allow Daniel to accompany the drug traffickers to the county jail. But he'd refused. She knew it would take a little while to process the criminals—take fingerprints, mugshots, and fill out the arresting paperwork. She wondered whether that was the reason for his refusal to let her go alone. Or was there something else?

The four-wheeler plunged into the clearing, the tires biting into the gravel in the boat ramp's parking lot. Ashley veered to the left and pulled up behind the sheriff department's Ford Interceptor. She backed off the ATV's throttle and inched the vehicle onto the trailer.

As she killed the engine, the realization of the night's events finally hit her. They were safe now, but Daniel had almost been killed. A wave of nausea washed through her. What if Mr. Charger had sensed her fear? What if she had been taken hostage? Had she been stupid to rush into the cabin? If she had made one wrong move, both she and Daniel would have been murdered. She pressed her eyes together and took a deep breath, thankful that everything had worked in their favor.

Forcing her insides to stop trembling, she dismounted the four-wheeler and slipped off her helmet.

Daniel followed suit.

"I have to admit, that was a much smoother ride," he told her.

The journey had been a far cry from the white-knuckled, teeth-jarring experience she'd suffered on the way to the cabin with Daniel at the helm.

"All it takes is a little practice," she said, hoping he would train without her.

He nodded.

And there it was again—the concerned look had returned to his eyes. The same expression he'd worn on the hike from the cabin to the four-wheeler.

Ashley hopped down from the trailer.

"What is it that you're not telling me?" she asked.

Had the agent received news of another murder? Something had definitely unnerved him.

Daniel chewed his bottom lip. "Let's get in the car."

She circled around the trailer and climbed into the passenger seat of the Ford SUV. She waited while Daniel settled into the driver's seat and fastened his safety belt. It seemed to take him an unusual amount of time. Was he stalling?

"Have the sheriff's deputies found another body?" she asked, bracing herself for his answer.

"No. It's not that."

"Then why do you look like you've just lost your best friend?"

He raked his hand through his dark hair and sighed.

"Ashley, you saved my life tonight. You were brave. If you hadn't come into the cabin when you did …" His voice trailed off as though he were contemplating the worst-case scenario. "Well, Elkins probably would've finished his business before backup got there. And I'd be in that mine shaft right now. I'm grateful you were there."

He paused and stared at the Ford's instrument panel. Ashley knew it wasn't because he wanted to check the time or the outside temperature. Although the agent had praised her for saving his life, his tone and body language let her know something was wrong. A seed of self-doubt sprouted in her chest. She was in trouble. She'd screwed up at the cabin and Daniel was likely trying his best to find the right words to tell her. Was he disappointed that she hadn't followed his instructions to stay hidden behind the chokeberry bush? Based on what he'd said, that didn't seem to make sense. What had she done wrong?

"I know you told me to stay hidden no matter what happened," she said. "But I couldn't just let them take you out in the middle of nowhere and kill you."

"You were right to come inside," he said, still avoiding her gaze.

Then why was he upset with her? She didn't understand.

"I know that I messed up in some way tonight, Daniel, so please, don't try to sugar-coat it; just tell me what I did wrong."

He finally looked at her. "Did you mean to shoot that guy?"

He was obviously talking about Mr. Charger, the drug supplier.

"Yeah," she said, surprised that he would even ask. "I was telling the truth when I said I'm a crack shot. I wanted to graze his arm—inflict a little pain—to let him know that I meant business. And that's exactly what I did. It should only take a few stitches and he'll be as good as new."

"Why didn't you just hit the wall behind him?"

So that was it. She was in trouble for injuring a criminal. A man who wanted to kill both her and Daniel.

"Do you think he would have taken me as seriously if I had just fired past him?"

"That's not the point. The problem is: you deliberately shot a suspect. One who had his hands up."

One who had his hands up. The words burned through her brain like acid. Mr. Charger hadn't been pointing a gun. He'd been submitting to her. At that moment, the drug supplier had been the one who was vulnerable.

Ashley felt her face grow warm as a tide of humility engulfed her. She hadn't realized until now how egregious her action had been. She'd let her fear and adrenaline rob her of her common sense. She'd purposely shot someone who did not pose an immediate threat. She should have known better.

"You're right—I can see now that there's no excuse for what I did," she said, trying to keep her voice steady. "I should have thought things through—should have just shot the wall like you said."

"You're a civilian. And this is Tennessee. You've got a constitutional right to carry a firearm, and to use it to protect yourself. But the guy wasn't coming toward you. He wasn't threatening you right at that moment. I can't lie in my report. Can't say that it was self-defense. I have to lay out the facts. But since you're not an agent, and the man wasn't seriously hurt, I doubt there will be any charges. Not this time. But you need to realize that your actions have consequences."

She hated that she'd put Daniel in such an awkward position. That after all the faith and trust he'd put in her, she'd let him down. Why had she allowed herself to succumb to her emotions instead of acting logically?

"Nothing like this will ever happen again, Daniel—I promise you."

The agent nodded. "There's another thing. Anytime a cop discharges a firearm, it's a big deal. Even if no one is shot. So this won't sit well with my boss."

Ashley could feel the disappointment radiating from Daniel's body. He wasn't finished with his lecture, and she feared what his next words would be.

The agent sighed again. "There's a good chance you may be pulled off the case."

Her heart sank. She knew Daniel was counting on her to help him with the locals. And she knew she was under the agent's direct supervision. She hoped his boss wouldn't hold him responsible for her actions—that he wouldn't be reprimanded. Could Daniel be pulled off the case as well?

"Will you get in trouble because of me—for what I did?"

"Don't worry about that," he said, shaking his head.

She wasn't sure whether that meant he was in the clear or not. If he did receive some type of punishment, he would likely never tell her. He always seemed to want to protect her, which made her feel even worse for what she'd done.

"Ashley, you've got the instincts and ability to make a damn fine cop," he told her. "You just need to keep a level head. Always think about what your actions will look like to a jury."

She hadn't even considered the fact that she could be sued for shooting the drug supplier. Because she was a civilian, that most likely wouldn't happen. But members of law enforcement were sued all the time for injuring suspects. It was clear that even though she knew the right answers on paper—had aced every test at the academy—if she wanted to be a police officer, she needed to learn the proper way to conduct herself in real-life situations.

"I'm really sorry that I broke your trust and let you down, Daniel," she said, a lump forming in her throat.

The agent met her gaze, his blue eyes kind.

"Hey, you saved my life," he reminded her. "That's no small thing."

Afraid her voice would crack if she tried to speak, Ashley nodded. She appreciated the agent's attempt to lift her mood. But she couldn't get past the fact that her mistake might harm his career. He was the most dedicated cop she'd ever met. If her action led to Daniel's dismissal from the case, she would never forgive herself.

The agent slipped the SUV into gear.

"Let's go interrogate our suspects," he said.

As Daniel circled the Ford around the boat ramp parking lot, Ashley stared out the passenger window into the darkness. The ride back to Mettler Ridge wouldn't be pleasant. She'd be chiding herself every mile of the way.

CHAPTER TWENTY THREE

Ashley turned on the faucet in the ladies' room at the Laurel County Jail and soaked a paper towel with cold water. She stared at her reflection in the mirror hanging above the stained porcelain sink. Why had she felt the need to shoot Mr. Charger? In a split second, she had not only jeopardized her role in the murder investigation, but it was possible she had damaged Daniel's career as well. He had brought her onboard the team. Had vouched for her professionalism. But instead of behaving the way a decent cop should, she'd thrown logic out the window and had made a rookie mistake. A mistake that could have far-reaching consequences.

She wondered whether this was her last night on the case. If so, she'd not only let Daniel down, she'd let down the families of Sarah and Violet as well. Ashley remembered the look of trust she'd seen in Eva's eyes when she promised to find the man who had killed the woman's sister. Would her impulsive action tonight lead to a betrayal of that trust?

Wringing out the excess water, Ashley patted her face with the wet paper towel. She needed to make these last few hours count. She'd choose her words with care. Do her best to wrangle the truth out of Mr. Charger.

The drug supplier—who had been identified as Aaron Finney—was first up on the interrogation roster.

A knock on the swinging bathroom door startled Ashley.

"Yes?" she called out, finding it unusual that someone would knock on the door of a bathroom equipped with private stalls. It had to be Daniel. Or another male cop.

The door nudged open a crack.

"Ash?" Daniel's voice echoed into the room. "They've got Aaron Finney ready for us."

"Okay," she answered. "I'll be right out."

She wadded up the paper towel and tossed it into the trash bin. It was time to focus on the here and now. Dwelling on her failure would only hinder her ability to do her best work. And she couldn't afford to screw up again. Too much was at stake. Taking a deep breath, she pushed through the door and met Daniel in the corridor.

"Bad news," the agent said. "Finney lawyered up."

Ashley was disappointed to hear that the drug supplier had secured legal counsel. It made their job of ferreting out the truth much more difficult.

"Well, it sure didn't take him long to get his attorney here."

"He's got a rap sheet," the agent continued as he led her down the hallway. "White-collar crime. Did time in a cushy Fed pen. He lives in Marcum County, just outside Cedar View."

The fact that the drug supplier lived near Cedar View explained the reason they hadn't been able to get a DMV hit on the Dodge Charger in Laurel County. She was surprised to learn the nature of his former offense.

"Wait—are you telling me this is the first time he's been arrested on drug-related charges?"

"Surprisingly, yes. Believe it or not, Finney used to work as an investment broker. He conned a lot of people out of a lot of money."

She wondered what had caused the man to switch from white-collar crime to the seedy depths of the drug world. Opportunity, maybe. With his prison record, he likely couldn't find a job that would allow him to bilk other unsuspecting victims out of their hard-earned money.

Had Finney resorted to murder as well?

Ashley followed as Daniel turned left into a connecting corridor. It was her first time inside this part of the jail. The pale gray-green walls of the old building reminded her of moldy pea soup. The musty odor that permeated the hallway added another layer to the resemblance.

They stopped outside a door labeled *Room A*.

"Ready?" Daniel asked, locking eyes with her.

She could tell the agent still had faith in her even though she'd messed up in a big way. His encouraging expression bolstered her resolve to keep her promise to Eva. To find the person who murdered Violet and Sarah, and make sure the killer paid for his crimes.

"Yeah, I'm ready."

Daniel pushed the door open, letting Ashley enter first.

Aaron Finney sat at a metal table bolted to the floor, his hands cuffed in front of him. A white bandage peeked out from beneath the short sleeve of his orange prison shirt. Ashley had been right about the minor severity of his wound. It had only required four stitches.

Finney's attorney—a plump man with graying hair, wearing bifocal glasses—sat next to the drug trafficker.

Daniel made introductions as they took their seats.

"I'm Special Agent Daniel Lansing," he said. "And this is Ashley Hope."

The attorney nodded. "Let's get on with this. Mr. Finney has an early arraignment in the morning."

The agent snorted. "If your client will cooperate, it shouldn't take long."

Translation: If the lawyer would allow the drug trafficker to answer all of the questions she and Daniel asked, then it wouldn't take that long.

"Mr. Finney will be entering a plea of not guilty," the attorney stated.

Ashley didn't expect anything different. Finney would no doubt claim to have been at the wrong place at the wrong time, and that the drugs and money belonged to someone else.

Daniel met Ashley's gaze and nodded, as though telling her to proceed with the questioning. She felt a little uneasy with Finney's lawyer in the room. His presence made a world of difference. Going up against an attorney could prove to be a difficult task—one she wasn't quite sure she was ready to handle. She knew that trying to befriend or coax the drug supplier into a murder confession wouldn't work under the circumstances. Bluntness would probably be her best bet.

"Mr. Finney, tell us about your relationship with Sarah Lester," she said.

A puzzled expression crossed the drug trafficker's face. He glanced at his attorney and shrugged. The lawyer nodded his approval.

"What about it?" Finney asked.

"When was the last time you saw Sarah?"

His gaze shot up toward the ceiling as though he was trying to recall their last meeting.

"A month ago, maybe."

That fit within the time frame that Charlene had mentioned. She'd seen Finney at Sarah's trailer the prior month.

"Where were you this past Friday morning?"

The attorney interrupted. "What's all this about?"

Ashley glanced at Daniel. "We have reason to believe that your client was involved in a homicide," she stated.

"I didn't kill anybody," Finney said, his voice firm. "Not Friday or any other day."

Ashley guessed he'd forgotten about the guy the drug traffickers had dropped into the mine shaft. Finney may not have been the person who pulled the trigger, but he had implicated himself in the murder. However, since they didn't know the identity of the man, or the location of the body, it would be hard to press charges.

"Don't say anything else," his lawyer cautioned.

She had suspected that the attorney would shut down that line of questioning, but she was prepared to reason with the man.

"If you will let us establish Mr. Finney's whereabouts at the time of Sarah Lester's murder, then maybe we can eliminate your client as a suspect," Ashley told the attorney.

The lawyer nodded. "Can I have a minute alone with Mr. Finney?"

Daniel rose from his chair. "Of course," he said. "We'll be right outside. Just let us know when you're ready."

She hoped the lawyer would keep his conversation with his client short.

The agent held the door for Ashley and then followed her out into the hallway.

"Finney seemed to be surprised when I asked him about Sarah," Ashley said in a hushed voice. "It was almost like he didn't even know she was dead."

"Yeah, you're right. I don't think he was faking it."

The drug supplier's reaction had seemed genuine to her as well. She wondered if he had an alibi for the time of Sarah's death. Or Violet's.

"Maybe Wade Elkins is the person responsible for the two murders," she stated, referring to the trafficker who had been counting the cash at the cabin.

"Could be."

Daniel glanced at his watch.

"It's almost midnight," he said. "It'll be tomorrow before we get a crack at Elkins."

Ashley realized she would likely be in class at the police academy when Daniel interrogated the other drug supplier. She wished there was some way she could get an excused absence, but the academy didn't work that way.

The door to the interrogation room swung open.

"You can come back in now," the attorney told them.

Ashley and Daniel returned to their seats at the metal table, across from Finney and his lawyer.

"My client has informed me that he was in Nashville on Friday," the attorney said. "He checked into the Best Western on Division Street Thursday and didn't check out until Saturday. He has credit card receipts that will verify his stay. I'm sure there will also be surveillance video of his arrivals and departures."

If it could be substantiated, that alibi would cover Sarah's murder, but not Violet's.

"Will you allow your client to tell us where he was from midnight last night until eight o'clock this morning?" Ashley asked.

Finney looked at his lawyer and nodded, as though he had nothing to hide.

"I was at my girlfriend's house in Cedar View," the drug supplier said. "We didn't get up until around ten this morning."

Again, Finney seemed to be telling the truth.

"We'll need you to give us your girlfriend's name and contact information so we can verify your story."

"Sure. No problem."

The attorney patted the table, as though he was a judge banging a gavel. "Will that be all for tonight?"

Ashley looked at Daniel. He seemed tired—ready to call it a day.

"There is one more thing we need to address before we let you go," she said. "Mr. Finney, could you please tell us about your relationship with Violet Perry?"

"Who?" the drug supplier asked, confusion apparent in his eyes.

"You don't have to answer that question," Finney's attorney reminded him.

"It's okay," the trafficker replied. "I don't know who she's talking about."

Ashley and Daniel exchanged glances. It was clear from his body language that Finney was either telling the truth or he was one hell of an actor.

"Are you saying that you've never met a woman named Violet Perry?"

"That's right. I've never even heard of her."

The lawyer scooted his chair away from the table and stood. "I believe we're finished for now," he said.

Daniel nodded, standing up as well.

"An agent from the TBI's drug division will contact you tomorrow," he told the attorney.

Ashley rose and watched the lawyer waddle out of the room. The short, pudgy man reminded her of a penguin in his dark suit and white shirt.

Daniel leaned out of the open doorway.

"Guard?" he called to the officer stationed in the hallway. "You can take the prisoner back now."

Crossing her arms, Ashley rested her hip against the table and waited while Finney was escorted out of the interrogation room. The man was a criminal—guilty of drug trafficking for sure. But the murders of Sarah and Violet? It seemed unlikely.

Once they were alone, she met Daniel's gaze.

"I really don't believe that Finney had anything to do with either of the murders," she told the agent.

"My gut says the same."

"Maybe you'll get better answers from Wade Elkins tomorrow."

If neither Finney nor Elkins proved to be the man Violet had stolen the drugs from, then they would be back at square one.

Daniel checked his watch again.

"You've got class in the morning," he stated. "You should go home. Get some sleep. I'll let you know what happens with Elkins."

Ashley nodded, though she knew that after the day she'd had—after shooting Finney—her sleep would likely be interrupted by bad dreams.

"Good night," she said.

"See you tomorrow afternoon."

As she headed down the hallway toward the exit to the parking lot, her thoughts switched to Daniel's boss. How would the supervising agent react when he learned the details of the shooting?

Ashley just hoped that when tomorrow afternoon arrived, both she and Daniel would still be on the case.

CHAPTER TWENTY FOUR

Beth Holder scribbled down the answer to the last question of her assignment and then tucked her homework into the red notebook that rested on the edge of the kitchen table. She had an important test tonight. Surgical Procedures for Small Animals. The exam would constitute a major portion of her grade for the semester, but she was confident that she'd receive a high mark—maybe even a perfect score. Her job for the past three years—as a veterinary technician at the Gaines Animal Hospital in Cedar View—had prepared her well for all of her classroom studies.

On-the-job experience was the one perk she enjoyed while having to work her way through school. The downside being that a degree which normally took eight years to acquire had stretched into nine so far, and she still had two more years of credits left to go. But Beth knew that on the day she graduated, all her sacrifices and hard work would prove to be worth it.

Once she earned her D.V.M., she planned to open her own veterinary clinic right here in Mettler Ridge.

Beth groaned as Sebastian, her gray tabby, jumped onto the table top and snatched up a crust of toast that remained on her father's breakfast plate.

"You know you're not supposed to be up here, you silly cat."

Sebastian appeared to grin as he chomped the toast. It was as if he knew that as soon as Beth's parents left the house, he was free to do as he pleased without repercussions. Which was probably the reason he was a few pounds overweight. Although she realized it wasn't healthy—and she chided herself for her weakness—it was hard for Beth to deny the affectionate cat anything. Including carb-laden table scraps.

She glanced at the clock hanging on the wall beside the refrigerator. 7:19 a.m. Her shift at the animal hospital started at nine. She wanted to stop at Walmart in Cedar View first to pick up a binder for her report on soil-transmitted parasites that had to be turned in tonight. If she waited until after work to visit the store, she would likely be late for her first class.

"Come on, Sebby; it's time to get moving."

The cat ignored her as his tongue wiped the plate clean. She scooped Sebastian off of the table and nuzzled her cheek against his soft fur before placing him onto the floor. Her mother would have a fit if she found out that Beth had allowed the tabby to lick the grease from the stoneware plate.

But life was short—especially for a cat—and sometimes you just had to smile and let things go.

With the tabby winding between her feet, Beth crammed her notebook into her backpack and then gathered the breakfast dishes from the table. When she was a young teen, she'd worked out a deal with her mother. Yvonne Holder prepared the meals for their three-person family and Beth cleaned up afterward. Which was a wise move on her mother's part since everything Beth attempted to cook usually ended up too dry, or too salty, or burned beyond recognition.

After rinsing the dishes, she stacked them into the dishwasher. As she switched the appliance on, her eye caught movement outside the window above the kitchen sink. She leaned over and peered beneath the branches of a maple tree, across the side yard. Her car was still parked where it should be—on the gravel driveway. She didn't see any animals or people. Nothing out of the ordinary. The movement had most likely been a bird flying by.

Satisfied that the kitchen was clean enough to pass her mother's inspection, Beth grabbed her backpack and purse and headed through the living room toward the small entry hall with Sebastian trailing close behind.

"You be good and stay off the kitchen counters," she told the tabby as she rested her belongings on the floor next to the coat closet.

She slipped her arms into her new blue fleece jacket—a gift from her father. He'd said the color was a perfect match for her eyes. Over the years Frank Holder had become an expert at picking out things he knew the women in his life would enjoy, preferring to spend the meager amount of disposable income left over from his fireman's salary on gifts for Beth and her mother rather than on things for himself.

One day Beth hoped to meet and fall in love with a man who was as thoughtful as her father. But for now, she was too busy with work and school to even think about dating. And she realized that men like Frank Holder were few and far between. Maybe when she was closer to graduation, she'd allow herself to socialize. Maybe accept one of the many offers of dinner she'd received from clients at the animal hospital.

Smiling at the thought that she might even end up marrying another veterinarian, she slung her backpack over one shoulder and her purse over the other. She nudged Sebastian out of the way and then pulled the front door open and stepped out onto the porch.

The temperature had plunged during the night, painting the edges of the maple leaves a bright orange. She loved this time of year—crisp morning air, crystal blue skies, and abundant sunshine. She started down the porch steps and then froze.

The hairs on the back of Beth's neck tingled.

It felt as though someone was watching her. She scanned the yard and the long driveway lined with maple trees. A flock of blackbirds pecked at the ground down near the road. They were the only living souls she could see. Still, she couldn't shake the sensation of eyes surveilling her.

The events of the previous afternoon flashed into her mind. She'd been at the gas station in Mettler Ridge filling up her car, when out of nowhere, a man appeared beside her, causing her to jump. He hadn't made a sound as he'd approached.

"Can you tell me how to get to the diner?" the tall man with the scruffy beard and dark, greasy hair had asked.

"It's just two blocks over," she'd replied as she pointed toward the rear of the gas station.

The man had stared at her and smiled, never looking in the direction where she was pointing.

There was something in the man's eyes—a hint of wickedness—that sent a shiver down Beth's spine. Although her tank was not yet full, she'd pulled out the gas nozzle and returned it to the pump.

"Can you give me a ride, angel?" the man pressed, stepping closer to her.

"No," she'd said, hurrying around the side of her car. "I'm going in the opposite direction."

She'd leapt inside her Kia sedan and locked the doors. The man had stared after her as she'd driven out of the parking lot of the gas station and sped down the street.

Had the man somehow found out where she lived?

Was he here now, hiding behind one of the many trees on the property?

The urge to run back inside the house rushed through her. But she couldn't afford to miss work. And she had her test tonight. Her eyes searched the boundaries of the property again. The path to her car seemed clear. She'd be quick. She'd get inside fast and lock the doors.

Beth raced from the front yard toward the gravel driveway on the side of the house. She yanked her sedan door open, hopped into the driver's seat, and then slammed the door closed. Her finger hit the door-lock button less than a second later.

She took a deep breath and tried to calm herself down. With her heart pounding in her chest, she checked the yard again. There was no one in sight. Was she being silly? Paranoid?

Even if the strange man had followed her home, she was locked inside her car. He couldn't get to her now. She was safe. Still, an icy fear enveloped her like a thick blanket of frost.

"Get it together, Beth," she said aloud. "You're being ridiculous."

Once she got to the animal hospital, she'd tell her co-workers about the man from the gas station and ask them to keep an eye out for him. After class tonight, she'd ask one of the other students to walk her to her car. Everything would be okay.

As her nerves began to settle, she buckled her seatbelt, started the car, and shifted into reverse.

Beth glanced in the review mirror and screamed.

A hideous clown stared back.

Panic flooded her heart as she reached for the door handle. But she was still buckled in.

A strong arm clamped around her upper body. As she struggled to unfasten her seatbelt, a stinging pain shot through the right side of her neck. A wave of dizziness hit her. Her arms and legs went numb.

Beth heard the clown laughing behind her as she faded into unconsciousness.

CHAPTER TWENTY FIVE

Pain jolted through Ashley's right arm as she pulled open the glass door at the front entrance of the Laurel County Sheriff's Department. She gritted her teeth and choked back a curse word. The biceps and triceps in both her arms ached from hours of lugging the eighteen-pound kettlebell back and forth across the campus of the police academy, along with the backpack containing her books and laptop.

If her instructor, Sergeant Newell, was searching for a way to get Ashley to drop out, he may have found it. Only one day of her punishment period had passed and already, she could barely lift her hands above her head. She wasn't sure her muscles were strong enough to endure the week.

She strode past the reception desk and nodded at the deputy on duty. He smiled and returned the nod. She was becoming a regular fixture at the sheriff's department. She no longer needed to flash the TBI consultant ID that hung from the lanyard around her neck. Everyone knew her.

But she realized this might be the last day she enjoyed her privileged status.

Because of her rookie mistake, Daniel's boss may have already jerked Ashley off of the case.

The fact that she hadn't received any messages or calls from the agent today worried her. Was his silence due to the knowledge that she had been stuck at the academy? Was he just being polite—not wanting to interrupt her classes? Maybe he'd been too busy with the investigation and interrogation of Elkins to send her an update.

Or maybe—as she feared—he had been given bad news.

News that he felt should only be delivered in person.

Reaching an intersection in the hallway, Ashley turned right. She caught a glimpse of Deputy Kevin McConnell and Deputy Troy Luckadoo heading out a rear entrance that led to the parking lot behind the building. They were still searching the field and the surrounding area where Violet's body had been found. She wondered whether the

TBI had been able to match the tire treads they'd pulled from the shoulder in the bend of the highway to a particular manufacturer.

There was one thing she felt certain of: the treads wouldn't lead back to a Dodge Charger as she had once suspected. In her gut, Ashley knew Aaron Finney was not the killer.

That left Elkins as their primary suspect. At least he had been last night.

If the TBI obtained a warrant to search the drug supplier's home, would they find clothing branded with the Z.L. Holt label? Due to the widespread availability of the apparel, the button found near the clothesline in Violet's back yard would be hard to trace. Did the person who lost the button know it was missing? Was the item of clothing it had been ripped from now hanging in the killer's closet? Or had he disposed of the garment?

Ashley stopped outside the closed door of the small conference room the sheriff had loaned to Daniel for his use as an office. Bracing herself for the news that she'd been eliminated from the investigation team, she took a deep breath and knocked. The vibration shot another bolt of pain through her bicep.

"Come in," the agent's muffled voice called.

She stepped across the threshold and scanned Daniel's face, searching for an answer to her question. Was she still on the case? The agent didn't look up—his eyes glued to the screen of his laptop.

He motioned toward one of the metal chairs on her side of the scarred wooden table.

"Have a seat," he said.

Butterflies whirled in her stomach. Daniel's tone was too hard to read. Too neutral. The anticipation of finding out whether or not she'd been fired was almost too much to bear.

As she pushed the door closed, a wave of claustrophobia hit her, adding to her anxiety. The space felt more like a closet than a conference room. The worn table—pushed tight against the far wall—and four chairs were the only furniture the windowless room could hold.

She eased down onto the closest chair, wishing the agent would look at her. That he wouldn't keep her in suspense.

"How was the academy?" he asked, still focused on his laptop.

Really? He wanted to make small talk? She realized it was the polite thing to do, but under the current circumstances, the normal pleasantries felt like torture. The coil of tension inside her chest was ready to spring.

"It was fine—but what did your boss say about me shooting Aaron Finney?" she blurted out.

Daniel finally met her gaze.

"He wasn't happy. And he's worried about a lawsuit."

Ashley's heart sank. Her fears had been warranted. She'd screwed up in the worst way possible, letting Daniel down, and letting down the families of Sarah and Violet.

"So I guess that means that I'm no longer a consultant for the TBI," she stated, her hands clammy.

It was time to hang up her ID lanyard. She'd failed her first case.

"You're still on the team," Daniel said, a note of encouragement in his voice. "We need you. Maybe now more than ever."

How could that be possible? They'd busted the meth ring and likely had the man responsible for the murders of Sarah and Violet in custody. Why would Daniel's boss want her to stay on the case after the mistake she'd made?

"What do you mean—you need me?"

"A lot has changed since last night," the agent told her. "Elkins cracked under pressure. He admitted that Violet stole from him. But he said it wasn't the first time. It had become a habit with her. And she always paid her debts. Just not with cash."

"So Violet had the same type of setup with Elkins that Sarah had with Aaron Finney—exchanging sex for drugs," Ashley remarked.

If the situation with Violet had been ongoing, then what motive would Elkins have to kill her? It didn't make sense.

"Right. And Elkins has an alibi for the time frames of both murders. They're solid. He's not our guy."

It sounded as though they were back to square one. That's the reason the TBI needed Ashley. So she could continue to help with the locals.

Daniel opened a file folder and slid it across the table toward her.

"We got the toxicology screen back on Sarah," he said. "No drugs were in her system at the time of death."

Ashley wondered whether Violet's results would prove to be the same.

"What if we've been concentrating on the wrong motive this whole time?" she asked. "The fact that Sarah and Violet were both drug users may not be linked to their deaths at all. Maybe they were murdered because they fit a certain profile—not because they crossed someone."

Serial killers often had a certain type of victim that they stalked. For Ted Bundy, it was college-age women with dark hair parted in the middle. Sarah and Violet may have been targeted because they had a similar appearance.

"Yeah, that occurred to me too," Daniel stated. "Both women had light brown hair. Blue eyes. The same body type."

Ashley nodded. "And Sarah and Violet were also the same age. They were both missing for around twenty-four hours and neither one of their abductions was reported to the police. Do you know what that makes me wonder?"

"What?"

"Is another woman—another victim—missing right now at this very moment?"

It was entirely possible that the person who had killed Sarah and Violet was holding his third victim hostage and her family had not yet reported the abduction.

Daniel looked at her, a renewed concern apparent in his eyes.

"Let's hope not," he replied.

After pausing a second, as though he was pondering the possibility that another woman could be fighting for her life right now and he had no idea of how to help her, the agent nodded toward his laptop.

"I've been digging back through the county police records," he said. "I found something interesting in the database. Six months ago, a female camper, hiking in the forest, reported that she was attacked by a mountain man. She claimed he tried to kidnap her. Three months ago, another woman got lost on a camping trip. She reported the same thing. A mountain man chased her through the woods."

So that's what the agent had been studying on his computer when she'd walked into the room. No wonder his attention had been so focused on his screen.

"Did the police ever identify this so-called mountain man and arrest him?"

"He was brought in for questioning. But the sheriff let him go. The report states the man is a harmless recluse. That he was just trying to scare the women off of his property."

She'd heard about people living deep in the mountains who didn't trust any outsiders. People who resorted to extreme lengths to keep others off of their land. But from Daniel's expression, in this case, she could tell that he felt there was more to the story.

"Is there some reason you don't believe this recluse is really all that harmless?"

He nodded. "The DMV records for the women who filed the reports."

Daniel slid his laptop around so she could see the screen. The driver's license photos of the two women stared back at her. Both women had light brown hair and blue eyes.

Ashley was stunned.

"So what's the name of the mountain man and where exactly does he live?"

"Milner Stanton. He owns a cabin on Tucker Cave Road."

Milner Stanton?

Recognition flooded Ashley's mind. She knew the name—could almost remember the man's face.

"Did that report happen to list Mr. Stanton's place of employment?" she asked the agent.

"It says he's retired."

"Well, he was still working nine years ago—at Laurel County High School. He taught a machine shop class in the basement."

Now it was Daniel's turn to appear stunned.

Maybe this was the connection they'd been looking for all along. Although Ashley was pretty sure neither Sarah nor Violet had taken the machine shop class—in fact, none of the females she knew had signed up for it—Milner Stanton had been on campus at the same time as the women. He could have come into contact with them at some point. He may have become obsessed with Sarah and Violet, following them without their knowledge for the past nine years. Until finally, he worked up the courage to strike.

Daniel closed his laptop.

"Looks like it's time to pay Mr. Stanton a visit," he said.

Ashley pushed back her chair. "I'm right behind you."

CHAPTER TWENTY SIX

Ashley twisted in the passenger seat of Daniel's confiscated Toyota sedan and peered through the rear driver's side window. The dirt driveway behind them was easy to miss. No mailbox marked the way. Knee-high grass, weeds, and bramble bushes filled the shallow ditch next to the road. On the other side of the ditch, a host of oaks, hickories, maples, and pines crowded against each other, competing for sunlight. Daniel shifted the car into reverse and backed down the narrow road.

They were located in the heart of Tucker Holler. A place where ghost stories were born. During prohibition, lawmen working for the state had come here intent on shutting down the moonshine stills. They'd searched for mountain men making sour mash, but had met the grim reaper instead. Their bodies were never found. According to the local legend, on cold moonless nights, you could hear the screams of the lawmen's spirits echoing through the trees.

The Toyota rocked from side to side as it inched up the rut-laden dirt driveway. A search of the county tax records revealed that Milner Stanton owned a little more than three hundred acres that stretched from the bottom of the holler up the side of Tucker Mountain. It was family land. Passed down from the former machine shop teacher's great-great-grandfather. One edge of the irregular-shaped property bordered a small campground. Both of the women who'd filed reports against Mr. Stanton had wandered away from the safety of their tents and had become lost in the woods.

Ashley wondered whether Sarah and Violet had ever spent time at the campground.

She tried to conjure up an image of Milner Stanton in her mind, but her memory was fuzzy. However, she did recall the rumors that had circulated around the high school. The teacher had gained a reputation for being an odd fellow. Several students had reported that they'd snuck down the stairs into the oily basement classroom and caught Mr. Stanton talking to himself.

That particular quirk alone wasn't all that unusual. Ashley reminded herself that she'd recently scolded a kettlebell. If she'd been overheard, her mental faculties would likely have been called into question. But the habit seemed to be more intense with Mr. Stanton. If the rumors were true, the man possessed the eccentricity of carrying on two sides of a conversation. This led many of the students to believe that the teacher suffered from a split personality.

Mr. Stanton had also seemed to be a consummate loner, appearing to shun the company of the other members of the faculty and staff. He'd rarely emerged from his basement lair and was known to eat his brown-bagged lunch at his desk.

The canopy of tree branches parted and the Toyota rolled to a stop.

The sight ahead stunned Ashley. A wide creek intersected the dirt drive. On the other side of the waterway, Stanton had erected a wooden drawbridge. The design appeared to be inspired by the medieval time period. The bridge was raised, preventing them from crossing.

"Well, one thing's clear: Mr. Stanton takes his privacy very seriously," she said.

Daniel nodded. "The waterline's low," he stated. "I think we can wade across."

He was right. Laurel County had entered its dry season. Almost a week had passed since the last rainfall, and it had been light. From her seat inside the car, she could see the tops of several boulders peeking out above the quick-flowing water.

She slid out of the sedan and followed Daniel down the slope to the edge of the creek. She watched as he rolled up the legs of his chinos, taking particular note of his shiny penny loafers.

"You need to buy yourself a sturdy pair of boots if you plan to keep tromping around in the forest," she told him.

He smiled. "Yeah, I realize that. But I haven't had time to drive back to Briarwood. And I didn't see any shoe stores in town."

That's because there weren't any shoe stores in Mettler Ridge. They did have a cobbler though. A man in his eighties who worked out of his home. Ashley's family had been regular customers when she was young. Her father could better afford to repair church-donated, hand-me-down shoes than buy brand new ones at a retail store. But times had changed—at least in the world outside Laurel County. Cobblers had become rare relics.

"I think you might be better off crossing over in your bare feet," she said, kneeling down to fold cuffs into the right leg of her jeans. "I know the water's ice cold, but you'd have a lesser chance of falling on those slick rocks."

He looked at her; bit his bottom lip. Seeming to realize that she was right, he stepped out of his penny loafers and peeled off his socks. With a shoe in each hand, the agent maneuvered his way across the creek. He held his arms out for balance as he leapt from one boulder to the next.

By the time Ashley had finished rolling up the left leg of her jeans, Daniel was already on the opposite bank. Trusting the grip of her hiking boots, she hopped across the creek, following the agent's path. She was grateful she didn't have to brave the icy water barefoot. Although the agent hadn't complained, she'd noticed his feet had turned pink from the cold.

As she pushed off from the final boulder, the sole of Ashley's boot slipped. A cry escaped her lips as she felt herself falling forward. With the rocky creek bottom racing toward her, the agent rushed in, catching her before she hit the water.

His grip firm—and yet gentle—he lifted her up and pulled her onto the shore.

As he helped her regain her footing, Daniel's blue eyes locked with hers, reaching into her soul.

Ashley's heart fluttered in her chest.

She averted her gaze, trying to hold back the wave of emotion that had hit her.

"Are you okay?" Daniel asked, his strong arms still encircling her.

He smelled like bergamot and sandalwood.

"Yeah," she managed to say, as she pulled out of his embrace.

But she wasn't okay. What had just happened? Daniel was her colleague, her work partner. She respected him. Cared deeply for his welfare. But she couldn't allow herself to develop romantic feelings for him.

Office romances seldom ended well. And the friendship they'd built was too precious to lose.

Trying her best to shake off the strong sentiment that had surfaced, Ashley headed toward the drawbridge. Large metal support columns, featuring a counterweight, flanked the bridge on each side. Heavy chains connected the columns to the wooden bridge's metal frame. She realized Mr. Stanton had secured the chains with padlocks. Without the keys, there was no way they could lower the bridge and bring the car over.

"Looks like we'll have to walk," Daniel said.

His tone was casual—lacking any hint of awkwardness. She was thankful he hadn't picked up on her sudden attack of emotion. She'd obviously been the only one who'd felt the surge of electricity. To her surprise, a tinge of disappointment crept into her heart at the realization that Daniel hadn't shared in the moment.

But she knew it was for the best.

Ashley decided to push the unsettling incident aside and move forward.

She fell in behind the agent as he began the trek up the remainder of the dirt driveway. Three hundred acres covered a large swath of ground. She wondered how long they would have to walk before they reached Mr. Stanton's house. As they rounded the next bend, Ashley received her answer. She spotted an old log cabin in a clearing approximately a hundred yards up ahead.

As they neared the front porch, a second building popped into view through the trees to the right. It was another cabin. Almost identical to the first. She assumed that like most of the families with a long history in the area, more than one generation of Stantons had lived on the property together, each with their own humble abode.

Daniel stopped at the base of the porch steps of the first cabin, motioning for Ashley to take the lead.

She knocked on the rustic wooden door and waited. She couldn't hear any movement inside. Glancing at the agent, she knocked again.

After a few seconds with still no answer, she shrugged. Either Mr. Stanton wasn't at home, or in the manner of a true hermit, he'd decided to ignore their presence.

Daniel nodded toward the second building.

"I'll check out the other cabin," he told her.

Ashley wandered off of the porch and headed around the side of the first building. She noticed that all the windows were covered with what appeared to be aluminum foil. During the summertime, she guessed the foil could be used to reflect the harsh rays of the sun and help keep the interior of the cabin cool. But the mature trees that grew near the house provided an ample supply of shade, and instinct told her that the window coverings had nothing to do with the temperature. She wondered if Mr. Stanton had attempted to turn his cabin into a giant Faraday cage.

Or could there be a more sinister reason for covering up the windows?

Her pulse quickened as she realized the foil might have been applied to keep people from looking inside the rooms. To hide his secret—that he was holding women hostage. Torturing them. Was that the real reason Mr. Stanton had gone to great lengths to keep people off of his land?

Rounding the rear corner of the building, she found another porch tacked onto the back. As she approached the steps, she heard a faint noise behind her, like the snap of a twig.

"Hold it right there," a deep male voice ordered.

Fear raced through Ashley's bones as she felt the muzzle of a gun press against the middle of her back. A rifle, most likely.

Her sore muscles objected as she raised her hands.

"My name is Ashley Hope," she said to the person behind her, who she assumed was Milner Stanton. "I was a student at Laurel County High School back when you taught there. My younger brother, Shane, was in one of your machine shop classes."

The man kept his weapon fixed against her spine.

"What do you want?" he asked, his tone gruff.

She wanted him to put down his gun.

"I'd like to turn around and talk with you face-to-face."

After a short pause, she felt the man remove the barrel of the weapon from her back. With her hands still raised above her shoulders, she inched her body around in a circle, finally meeting his gaze.

He dropped the aim of his rifle toward the ground and Ashley lowered her arms.

Milner Stanton didn't look like she'd expected. Although the man's date of birth pegged him at fifty-seven years old, he appeared much younger. Only a few flecks of gray were visible in his dark hair. The uneven sides of his short cut suggested he'd done the job himself. His face was clean-shaven, and his broad muscular shoulders formed a perfect V above his chiseled waist.

"Start talking," he barked.

Ashley caught movement out of the corner of her eye. It was Daniel, easing up behind Mr. Stanton. She kept her focus trained on the former teacher, not wanting the man to detect the agent's presence.

"TBI—" Daniel shouted.

Before the agent could get out another word, Milner Stanton swung around, firing his rifle.

The bullet missed Daniel by a foot, splintering the bark of an oak tree.

Ashley drew her Smith & Wesson from the holster in the waistband of her jeans.

"Drop your rifle!" she yelled, her weapon aimed at the center of Mr. Stanton's back.

Daniel stood next to the oak, his Glock pointed at the former teacher's chest.

Realizing he was outnumbered, Mr. Stanton dropped his gun on the ground and raised his hands.

"Milner Stanton," Daniel said, "you're under arrest."

"On what charge?" the man asked.

"The attempted murder of a TBI agent."

Ashley let out the breath she'd been holding. She wondered whether they had finally caught the man who had killed Sarah and Violet.

She was anxious to get Mr. Stanton into the interrogation room at the county jail and drill him with questions.

Holding her weapon on the former teacher, she watched Daniel fasten handcuffs around the man's wrists. With their captive between them, they headed back down the dirt driveway toward the drawbridge.

This time Ashley would ask for the keys.

CHAPTER TWENTY SEVEN

Ashley unzipped the black padded case, pulled out Daniel's laptop, and placed it on the ancient wooden table in the observation room at the Laurel County Jail. While she waited for Milner Stanton to be processed, she wanted to read through the reports the two female campers had filed against him. She wondered whether the former machine shop teacher had been armed during the encounters. Although Daniel had given her the highlights of the alleged attacks, that was one detail he had failed to mention.

She booted up the computer and logged into the database that contained the police records for the state. Ashley had been given a temporary password that would be active for the duration of the murder investigation. While she was not permitted access to all of the TBI's files, she had enough information at her fingertips to make her head spin.

Ashley heard footsteps in the hallway.

Deputies Kevin McConnell and Troy Luckadoo appeared at the open door to the observation room.

"We just got word about Mr. Stanton," Kevin said, settling on the edge of the table.

She wondered how much time the deputy had spent around the former teacher; if he could give her any further insight into the man's personality.

"Were you—or Troy—in any of Mr. Stanton's machine shop classes?" she asked.

"Yeah, we both were."

Troy nodded in agreement and then pushed the door of the observation room closed.

"It's wild," Troy commented, his eyes expressing his surprise at the news. "I never figured Stanton for a killer."

At this point, they had no evidence proving the former teacher was involved in the murders. However, the TBI was working on getting a warrant to search his property and his rifle was being sent to the forensic lab in Briarwood. Testing would confirm whether or not the weapon had fired the bullets that had killed Sarah and Violet. But the tests could stretch on for days.

Kevin tapped the tabletop. His eyebrows rose. "The man always gave me the creeps. I bet he's guilty as sin."

"Do either of you ever remember seeing Mr. Stanton with Sarah or Violet? Not just at high school—but at any time?"

She doubted the former teacher spent much time in Mettler Ridge, but he would have to come into town for groceries at least once in a while. And Sarah had worked at the diner. Maybe he had been spotted with her there.

Both deputies shook their heads.

"I don't think any sane woman would want to be around him," Kevin said. "The guy's got a screw loose."

"I'm guessing you're one of the students who caught Mr. Stanton talking to himself down in the basement," Ashley told Kevin.

And if that was the case, he'd probably been responsible for many of the rumors.

"Yep. I'll never forget it. He'd be facing one way and he'd ask a question. Then he'd turn around and face the other direction and give the answer. Like he was two different people."

"Do you remember what type of questions he was asking himself?"

"Crazy shit. Like, '*When are they gonna come for us?*' And then he'd answer, '*Any time now. We have to be ready.*' Paranoid stuff like that."

She had to admit, the words sounded like the ramblings of someone on the verge of insanity. But mental illness alone didn't make Mr. Stanton a murderer.

Noise from the adjacent room echoed through the speakers beneath the observation window. Ashley looked up and peered through the glass. A guard led Milner Stanton into the interview room. The officer cuffed the former teacher's wrists to a restraint ring built into the frame of the metal interrogation table. Because he had been arrested for shooting at Daniel, the TBI most likely considered the man to be a threat to the agent.

"We better get out of here," Kevin said, pushing himself up from the table where Ashley sat.

"Thanks for the information," she replied, wishing that Kevin and Troy had more recent recollections about their former teacher.

She watched the deputies as they exited through the doorway.

Focusing her eyes back on the laptop's screen, she pulled up the complaints filed by the two campers against Mr. Stanton. She read each report along with the notes taken by the sheriff and his deputies. Both of the women had stated that Mr. Stanton had brandished his rifle, but it had only been a threat. He had never actually pulled the trigger.

Ashley remembered being on the wrong end of the former teacher's gun. Although she was armed herself, she'd been helpless to stop Stanton from doing whatever he'd wanted to do with her. There was no mention in the reports of either of the women being armed. They'd had no weapons to protect themselves. Which begged the question: if Mr. Stanton had wanted to kill or abduct the women, why didn't he fire his rifle?

And it seemed obvious that the women—each weighing less than one hundred twenty-five pounds, according to their DMV records—were no match physically for the fit, well-muscled former teacher. He could have overcome them easily.

So why did Mr. Stanton let the two campers get away?

Hearing movement in the hallway again, Ashley glanced toward the open door.

Daniel poked his head inside the observation room.

"Let's do this," he said.

Ashley closed the laptop. She followed Daniel into the interview room and took the seat directly opposite Milner Stanton. She was starting to get used to the interrogation process. While she still felt it was by no means easy, she was far less intimidated now than she had been at the start of the investigation.

"Would you like something to drink, Mr. Stanton?" she asked. "We can get you a cup of coffee, or a soda, or some water—just about anything you'd like."

If Milner Stanton was mentally ill, she wanted him calm for the questioning. If he felt trapped, he would most likely retreat into his own mind and they wouldn't be able to get any real answers. They had many things at their disposal to help make the man morc comfortable.

"Can you uncuff me?" he asked, his voice flat. "I'm no animal."

She glanced at Daniel.

The agent pulled a set of keys from his pocket and placed them on the table in front of Ashley. She guessed Daniel was letting her do the honors so that he wouldn't have to get too close to the man who had fired a bullet at him. But unlike Stanton, the agent was still armed. He could protect himself if things went south.

She moved to the other side of the table and removed the cuffs.

"Thank you," Mr. Stanton said, massaging his wrists.

Ashley returned to her chair.

"There are a few questions we'd like to ask you regarding a case we're working on," she said.

"Yeah? Like what?"

She opened the manila file folder that Daniel had placed on top of the metal table. She slid pictures of Sarah and Violet—taken while they were still alive—toward Mr. Stanton.

"What can you tell us about these two women?"

The former teacher picked up the photo of Violet first. There was no hint of recognition in his eyes. Then he picked up the picture of Sarah. He studied both of their faces for a few seconds before placing the photos back onto the table.

There was nothing in the man's body language to indicate that he knew either woman.

"I can't tell you anything," he said. "I don't recognize them."

Daniel lifted a piece of blank paper inside the file folder and pulled out two photos that had been underneath. Photos of Sarah and Violet that had been taken by the medical examiner after the women's deaths. He slapped the pictures down in front of the former machine shop teacher.

The act produced a reaction.

An expression of shock flashed across Mr. Stanton's face, followed by sadness.

"Where were you Friday morning?" Daniel asked.

"Where I always am. At home. And no, nobody was with me."

"What about Sunday morning?"

Mr. Stanton sighed. "I didn't kill these women. And I don't know why you would think I did."

Ashley focused on the man's eyes. He seemed to be relaying the truth as he believed it. Of course, if the former teacher suffered from a split personality, it was possible that the other identity inhabiting his body was guilty of the murders. And he might not be aware of it.

"Mr. Stanton," she began, "six months ago you were brought into the sheriff's office for the attempted assault of a female camper. And then three months ago, you were called in again for the very same thing. Both of the campers bear a strong resemblance to the women who were murdered."

He nodded. "I know it looks bad. But I never would have hurt those women. I was just trying to scare them off of my land. I just want to be left alone. To live in peace. Just me and nature."

She stared at him, searching his face.

Mr. Stanton met her gaze.

"You said you went to Laurel County High School," he said. "Well, you probably heard a few things about me. Strange things. Things that might make you think I'm crazy. And the truth is—there for a little while—I was. But that was long time ago. I was under a lot of stress back then. To get better, I had to separate myself from the world. Now that it's just me and nature, I'm healthy. I just want to keep it that way."

Ashley could see the sincerity in the man's eyes. She believed him. At least, she believed this particular version of him. They had yet to meet his other personality—if he still had one.

Daniel's cell phone rang. Ashley glanced at him and waited to see if he would take the call or send it to voice mail.

The agent checked his cell's screen. He must have felt the call was important because he rose and started toward the door of the interrogation room.

"Lansing," he said into the phone as he stepped out into the hallway, closing the door behind him.

Ashley turned her attention back to Mr. Stanton.

"Why did you fire your rife at Agent Lansing?"

"That was a mistake," he said. "A reflex. When the agent yelled out, it startled me. I had no idea what he'd said. I just heard a loud noise behind me, and then my finger hit the trigger. I didn't even aim. I wasn't trying to kill him."

The explanation made sense. She knew how easily things could go wrong in the heat of the moment, with adrenaline pumping.

Mr. Stanton leaned toward her. "And I'm sorry that I scared you. I never would have shot you either. I just wanted you to leave."

The interrogation room door pushed open. Ashley looked behind her and saw the guard who was responsible for transporting Mr. Stanton to and from his holding cell. The officer walked around the table.

"Stand up," he told the former teacher.

Ashley wondered what was going on. Why was the interview being shut down? Confused, she rose from her seat.

Mr. Stanton did as he was told. The guard fastened the handcuffs back around the man's wrists and then led him out of the room.

Daniel appeared a second later, before she could get to the doorway. She could tell by his pained expression that something was very wrong.

"That was the sheriff on the phone," he told her. "Another woman's been abducted."

CHAPTER TWENTY EIGHT

Ashley shoved her aching arms into her denim jacket and then climbed inside the passenger seat of Daniel's Toyota. While she was sickened by the fact that another woman had been abducted, the news hadn't shocked her. A part of her had been expecting it. Dreading it. She wondered how long the woman had been missing.

How much time did they have left to find her?

"What all did the sheriff tell you about the abduction?" she asked Daniel.

The agent shifted the sedan into reverse and backed out of the parking space at the county jail.

"Not much," he replied, concern covering his face. "Just a name and address."

Ashley pressed her eyes shut. She was afraid to hear the name. Afraid that it was someone from her past whom she knew and cared about.

"Who is it—who's missing?"

"Her name is Beth Holder. She lives with her parents on Iris Hill Road."

The memory of a shy, pretty brunette popped into Ashley's mind. She could only recall one class that they'd shared—chemistry—but like Sarah and Violet, Beth had attended Laurel County High School with Ashley.

The three kidnapped women had graduated the same year. Was that fact just a coincidence?

She couldn't help feeling that there might be something about the high school that tied all three abductions together. Was the other personality who inhabited Mr. Stanton's body the source of the common link? Was that unknown entity the killer?

She knew the TBI was working on obtaining a warrant to search Mr. Stanton's property. If the missing woman was being held captive there, they would find her. Ashley just hoped it wouldn't be too late.

"You probably won't be surprised by this—Beth was another one of my classmates."

Daniel nodded.

"I thought so. And I pulled up her DMV photo. Light brown hair, blue eyes."

Beth's physical characteristics definitely matched the previous victims. But unless the woman had made a drastic change over the years, the similarities seemed to stop there.

"Beth was known as a real straight arrow back in high school," Ashley said. "It's hard for me to imagine her getting involved with drugs."

Daniel chewed his bottom lip. She could tell that his mind was racing.

"What's your verdict on Stanton?" he asked.

Ashley sighed. The truth was that she hadn't made her mind up quite yet.

"I believe that the person we talked to in the interrogation room was telling the truth," she stated. "But I also think Mr. Stanton could still be guilty—that his alternate personality could have murdered Sarah and Violet."

"You buy that identity disorder stuff?"

She was surprised that he would question a well-documented form of mental illness.

"I read through several case studies on the subject when I was studying for my master's in criminal justice. Of course I think it's real—don't you?"

He glanced at her. "I'm not saying it doesn't exist. But I've come up against criminals trying to use it as a defense. More than a few times. They were all faking it."

Ashley could understand his skepticism. His opinion was based on his real-life experience, not something he'd read in a textbook.

Daniel steered the Toyota onto a long gravel driveway lined with maple trees sporting bright orange and yellow leaves. At the top of the hill rested a charming ranch-style house with well-trimmed boxwood shrubs planted around the foundation. The light from the front porch blended with the glow from the landscaping lights dotting the edge of the sidewalk. From what she remembered of Beth, it was the exact type of home Ashley would expect the woman to live in. Traditional and tidy.

In the parking area to the right of the house, large halogen lights had been set up to aid a group of TBI agents in Tyvek suits. The forensic team had started work collecting evidence from a white Kia sedan. She assumed it was Beth's vehicle.

As the Toyota rolled to a stop, Ashley unfastened her seatbelt. She headed up the sidewalk to the front porch with Daniel close behind. Before she could ring the bell, the front door opened and she was greeted by a man wearing navy pants and a light blue shirt bearing the logo for the Laurel County Fire Department.

"Mr. Holder? I'm Ashley Hope and this is Special Agent Daniel Lansing," she said, shaking the man's hand.

"Come in," the man said, his face creased with worry.

He ushered them across the threshold, through a small entry hall, and then into a living room.

"I'm Frank and this is my wife, Yvonne." He motioned toward an older version of Beth, standing just inside the room.

"Please, have a seat," Yvonne told them, her voice weak.

The woman's eyes appeared red and swollen, as if she'd been crying for hours.

Ashley chose a spot on the brown leather sofa. Daniel sat next to her. Although Frank Holder eased down onto the edge of one of the matching chairs that flanked the sofa, Yvonne remained standing. It seemed the woman was filled with nervous energy. She kept looking out through the front window as though she expected her daughter to return home at any second.

"When did you first realize that Beth was missing?" Ashley asked.

The question was directed at Frank, but Yvonne answered.

"I got home from work a few minutes after six," she said. "I saw Beth's car and I knew something was wrong. But I just thought she had gotten sick and stayed home from school. I didn't know …"

The woman's voice broke and she began to sob.

Ashley wanted to wrap her arms around Yvonne and tell her that everything would be okay, but the truth was, she couldn't make that kind of promise. Not yet.

Frank took over for his wife.

"Yvonne called me at the station. I work twelve-hour shifts. When she told me Beth was gone, I got home as fast as I could. Beth's keys and her purse—her cell phone—were all in her car. I called the vet's office in Cedar View where she works, and they said she didn't show up this morning. She was supposed to be there at nine."

That meant that Beth had likely been abducted as she was leaving the house for work.

"Mrs. Holder mentioned something about Beth going to school."

Frank nodded. "The veterinary college in Cedar View. She takes evening classes after work."

It seemed the missing woman had more ties to the neighboring county than she did to Laurel County. Randy Boatman, the bartender at Bobcat Saloon in Cedar View, had mentioned that he'd seen Sarah at the club several times. Ashley wondered whether Violet had any links to Marcum County. Maybe the women had met their abductor in Cedar View.

"Does Beth have a current—or any ex—boyfriend?"

"No. She doesn't have time to date. She's always studying."

"Do you know whether or not she has any enemies?"

Frank shook his head. "She gets along with everybody."

Daniel exchanged a glance with Ashley.

"Have you ever heard the name Milner Stanton?" the agent asked.

Frank paused for a moment, as though he was searching his memory. "No, I can't say that I have."

Yvonne cut in. "I bet it's the man from the gas station," she said, as if the thought had just struck her. "I bet he took Beth."

Frank appeared surprised by her words.

"What man?" he asked his wife.

"Beth didn't want you to know. She was afraid you'd get upset and go looking for him. She told me that a man had asked her for a ride at the gas station on Sunday. She said he was acting strange. That he scared her."

"Did she tell you what this man looked like?" Ashley asked.

"He had dark greasy hair and a beard. She also said he was wearing a green canvas jacket with a skull on the back."

Mr. Stanton's hair was peppered with gray, and his face was clean-shaven.

Ashley thought about the button that had been found at Violet's home. She tried to recall whether Z.L. Holt manufactured canvas jackets. The skull didn't seem to fit with the brand, but she supposed the decal could have been ironed on after the garment was purchased.

"Did she tell you how old she thought the man might be?"

"No. That's all she said about him."

They didn't have the man's age, weight, and height, but the detail of the clothing made for a fairly decent description.

"Do you know which gas station Beth was at when this happened?"

"The minimart on Spring Street."

Ashley glanced at Daniel. He had pulled out his notebook and was writing down the information.

"Around what time?" the agent asked.

"It would have been between two and three in the afternoon," Yvonne said. "You have to find this man. He has to be the one who took her."

Tears spilled from Yvonne's eyes and streamed down her cheeks. Again, Ashley felt the urge to comfort the woman, but at the same time, she didn't want to provide false hope.

Frank rose from his chair and wrapped his arms around his wife.

"They'll find her," the man said, his voice soft and soothing.

Ashley hoped Frank Holder was right. That they would find Beth before it was too late.

Daniel slipped his notebook into his jacket pocket and stood up from the sofa.

Ashley stood as well.

"We're going to do everything in our power to bring your daughter home safely," she told the couple.

It was the only promise that she was certain she could keep.

Frank nodded, tears welling in his own eyes.

Ashley followed Daniel back through the entry hall. The agent opened the door and then stepped back, letting her go first. Her heart ached for Mr. and Mrs. Holder. It seemed obvious that their family was close-knit. She just prayed it would stay that way. That the three would be reunited.

As she settled back into the passenger seat of the Toyota, Ashley glanced at the clock on the dashboard. 8:24 p.m. If the killer stuck to his previous schedule, they had less than twelve hours to find Beth.

Daniel must have noticed Ashley checking thc time.

"Do you need to go home?" he asked her.

A vision of her unfinished police academy homework flashed through Ashley's mind. If it came down to it, she'd just have to take a lesser grade. A woman's life was at stake.

She shook her head.

"The only place I need to be right now is the minimart on Spring Street," she said.

Daniel smiled. He maneuvered the Toyota back down the Holders' driveway and headed toward Mettler Ridge.

CHAPTER TWENTY NINE

The image of Frank and Yvonne Holder huddled together, mired in sorrow, haunted Ashley as she stared out the passenger window of the Toyota. A landscape dotted with farmhouses and fields of cattle floated past her eyes on the drive to Mettler Ridge, but all she could see were the grief-stricken faces of Beth's parents. She couldn't imagine the degree of anguish they must be going through.

She remembered how terrified she'd felt the night her ex-husband had attacked Shane. As her brother lay under the surgeon's scalpel, fighting for his life. She'd been stuck in limbo, not knowing whether Shane would live or die. How much more intense the fear must be when it was your only child who was at risk.

Ashley glanced at Daniel, his gaze focused on the road ahead. He'd been quiet since they'd left the Holders' home. She guessed he was pondering thoughts of his own. Maybe recalling events from his family's life, the way she'd been thinking about Shane.

For the first time, she realized she didn't really know very much about Daniel's personal life. He tended to be all business—all the time. He didn't wear a wedding ring and had never mentioned a wife or girlfriend, so Ashley had always assumed he was single. Were his parents still alive? Did he have siblings?

As it stood, the agent knew most everything about her—had borne witness to the worst of her troubles. And yet, to Ashley, his life was a blank slate.

She broke the silence.

"Did you grow up in Briarwood?" she asked.

The agent seemed caught off guard by the question.

"Yeah," he replied, still watching the road.

She hesitated for a moment, waiting to see if he would elaborate. He didn't. The one-word answer piqued her curiosity even further. She hoped Daniel didn't feel as though she was prying. But it had been a harmless inquiry. She decided to keep going—would keep the questions light.

"Do your parents still live in the area?"

He nodded. "My mom does. She's a teacher at East Elementary. My dad passed away when I was fifteen."

"I'm sorry," she said.

A tinge of sadness hit her. She wondered if that was the reason his first answer had been so short. Maybe she should have kept her mouth shut.

After all these years, it was still difficult for Ashley to talk about the battle her mother had lost to cancer. She realized it could be the same for Daniel.

"Dad was a cop," the agent volunteered, surprising her. "Killed in the line of duty. He'd responded to a domestic call. Things seemed okay when he and his partner first got there. But then this guy …" His voice trailed off for a second, as though he was struggling to keep emotion out of his tone.

"This lowlife piece of scum pulled out a gun and fired at his wife. Dad pushed the woman out of the way. He saved her, but he was hit. He died on the way to the hospital."

The quick flash of pain that had crossed Daniel's face felt like a dagger to Ashley's heart. The sudden urge to reach out to him—to grab his hand and try to soothe his troubled memory—swept through her like a wildfire.

But she sat frozen in place. Afraid to touch him. Fearing that the intense feelings Daniel had awakened in her at the creek—that she'd buried deep within her soul—would resurface.

She didn't know what to say. Another *I'm sorry* just wasn't enough.

"Your father was a hero," she finally uttered, her voice soft.

"Yeah. He was."

The lights from the minimart cut through the darkness, illuminating the interior of the sedan. Ashley let her gaze drift back to Daniel as she unbuckled her seatbelt. His expression remained solemn as he pushed open the driver's side door. She wished she'd chosen a better time to quiz him about his family. But he was a dedicated professional. She knew he'd shove his memories aside and focus on the case.

Ashley stepped through the door of the convenience store. She was met by a giant cardboard spider, its legs curved around a bin of Halloween candy. She wound past the display and headed toward the check-out counter. She noticed that Daniel had stopped in front of the bin. She shot him an amused look. It seemed he was always hungry.

She figured he must spend a lot of time at the gym. There was no other logical way for him to stay so fit.

She waited while he rifled through the candy, pulling out of couple of chocolate bars. But instead of joining her, he meandered toward the back of the store and began browsing the drink cooler.

"You thirsty?" he mouthed.

Ashley shook her head.

Daniel selected a bottle of soda and then made his way toward her. He approached the cashier first, placing his items on the counter. Ashley recognized the woman at the register.

Reyna Lynch. The older sister of Shane's ex-girlfriend, Robin.

"How have you been, Reyna?" Ashley asked.

The woman picked up one of the candy bars and scanned the barcode.

"Pretty good, I guess," she replied, a sheepish expression covering her face.

Ashley guessed Reyna was embarrassed by the way her younger sister had treated Shane. Dumping him just when he'd needed her support the most.

"Were you working yesterday between two and three in the afternoon?" she asked the woman.

"Yeah, I was here. Why?"

Ashley was surprised they'd gotten so lucky. She'd guessed since Reyna was working a late shift tonight that the woman's schedule would have been the same the prior day.

"Did you notice a man in a green jacket with a skull on the back hanging around outside?"

She nodded. "I seen him. He came in and used the bathroom. Gave me the heebie-jeebies. He never did buy nothing."

"Do you have any idea what his name is or where he's from?"

"No. But I can tell you that he ain't from around here."

There was no way Reyna could know every single person in the area. *Around here* could encompass Cedar View.

"What makes you so sure that this man doesn't live nearby—like maybe in Marcum County?"

"He might now, but he ain't from there. He's got a Yankee accent. A real heavy one."

In Laurel County, the term *Yankee* meant someone born north of the Mason-Dixon Line. The man must have spoken with Reyna, otherwise she wouldn't know about his accent. Ashley realized that what sounded like a heavy northern inflection to the local woman's ear would most likely seem mild to those living in Briarwood or other parts of the state.

"What all did this man say to you?"

"He asked for the bathroom key, and I told him the men's room ain't locked. He thought that was funny. He called me angel."

So far Ashley hadn't really heard anything that would make the man seem menacing. Except for the fact that he was a stranger. For some of the residents of Laurel County, that could prove to be enough.

"What was it about this man that made you feel uncomfortable?"

"His eyes. I seen evil in them. Like he would slit your throat if you turned your back."

Ashley guessed that could do it.

Daniel plucked a pack of peanuts from the display next to the register and added it to his haul.

"Have you seen him today?" the agent asked the woman.

"Nah. Not today."

"Do you know where he went?"

Reyna shook her head.

"Ashley." A familiar voice interrupted from behind her, addressing her by name.

She turned around and locked eyes with Randy Boatman, her friend from high school who was now a bartender at the Bobcat Saloon in Cedar View.

"Hey, Randy," she said, surprised to see him.

"I didn't mean to eavesdrop," he told her, "but I couldn't help overhearing. You're looking for that guy with the green skull jacket?"

"That's right."

It seemed Randy had encountered the man as well.

"I ran into him just a few minutes ago in the diner parking lot. He asked me for money to buy a hamburger. I gave him a few bucks."

The trouble with the typical panhandlers in Laurel County was that when they claimed they wanted money for food, quite often, what they really sought was alcohol or drugs. But this man wasn't from Laurel County.

"Do you think he could still be hanging around the parking lot?"

"I saw him go inside."

Ashley looked at Daniel. She guessed he was sharing her thought—if they hurried they might be able to catch the stranger before he left.

The agent tossed a twenty on the counter and didn't wait for the change.

"Thanks, Randy," Ashley called as she rushed toward the door.

"No problem."

The diner was located just a couple of blocks away. Ashley barely had time to fasten her seatbelt before Daniel slammed the Toyota into reverse. He whipped the sedan out of the parking lot and sped down the street.

CHAPTER THIRTY

Ashley scanned the parking lot as Daniel wheeled the Toyota into a space near the diner's front entrance. Around a half-dozen cars sat scattered across the lot—typical for this hour on a Monday night—but she didn't see any pedestrians wandering about. She hoped that meant the stranger in the green skull jacket was still inside.

As she pushed open the sedan's passenger door, Daniel's cell rang.

"It's my boss," he told her, glancing at his phone's screen.

Ashley nodded, sliding out of the Toyota to give the agent some privacy. She hoped everything was okay. That Daniel's boss hadn't changed his mind and decided to fire her from the case.

A cold gust of wind hit her as she made her way toward the entrance to the diner. The temperature had dipped into the high forties. She wished she'd brought along a heavier jacket than the denim trucker she wore.

Shivering, she pulled the glass diner door open and went inside.

Her eyes swept the dining counter and then the booths. To her left, in the booth farthest from the door, she spotted a dark-haired man with a beard. Although she couldn't see the man's back, he wore a green canvas jacket. Quick to avert her gaze, not wanting to alert the man, she slid onto a red vinyl-covered stool at the counter.

Lou Ann, Ashley's former neighbor, was working tonight—appearing to be the only server on duty at the moment. She picked up her order pad.

"What'll it be, Ashley?" she asked, her long red ponytail swaying behind her.

"I'll have a large coffee in a to-go cup—black."

"That's all?"

She didn't want any food, but she would like some information.

"Lou Ann, I'm going to ask you a question and I need you to keep your eyes on me. Don't look at anyone else in the diner, okay?"

The server sighed. "I don't know nothing more about Sarah."

Ashley could understand Lou Ann's further reluctance to talk about the murdered woman—she'd already given up Squeaky's real name—but the server shouldn't have any qualms discussing an outsider.

"I just want to know about the stranger in the green canvas jacket."

"Oh, him," she replied in a hushed tone.

The expression that crossed Lou Ann's face spoke volumes. It appeared that, like Robin's sister Reyna, the server felt uneasy around the man.

"Are you the one who greeted him?"

"Yeah. We're short-handed tonight, so I waited on him. He ordered a burger and fries."

At least the man had been honest about the reason he'd wanted money from Randy.

"What kind of impression did you get from him?"

Lou Ann met her gaze. "He reminds me of a guy from a movie. The one that chases his wife and little boy with an axe."

Ashley assumed the server was talking about *The Shining*. From the glimpse she had gotten as she walked in, the stranger didn't really resemble Jack Nicholson—his beard and hair were too long—but she guessed it was the man's demeanor that had sparked the similarity in Lou Ann's mind.

"Is tonight the first time you've seen this man?"

The server shook her head. "He's been coming in for a couple of days. But this is the first time I've took his order." After a second she added, "I didn't want to."

"What all did he say to you that made you feel so uncomfortable?"

Lou Ann thought for a moment.

"It ain't really what he said," she finally replied. "It's the way he looks at you. It's creepy."

Ashley heard the diner door open behind her as a draft chilled her skin. It was Daniel. He motioned for her to step away from the counter.

Apprehension wriggled inside her chest.

She hoped the TBI hadn't found Beth's body. It was hard to tell from the agent's current poker face.

She slipped off of the stool and moved toward the door.

"The search warrant came through for Stanton's place," he told her in a low voice. "We've got agents tearing his cabins apart. So far, they haven't found anything. They don't think Beth was ever there."

Disappointment crept into Ashley's heart. She had hoped that Mr. Stanton's alternate personality would prove to be the killer and that they would find Beth alive and well somewhere on his property.

Daniel tilted his head toward the booth where the man in the green jacket sat, while keeping his gaze fixed on Ashley.

"Looks like we found the stranger," the agent said.

She nodded. "Lou Ann told me that he's been hanging around the diner the past couple of days. Right now, he's waiting on his burger and fries."

Lou Ann placed Ashley's to-go coffee on the countertop.

"He want anything?" the server called, motioning toward Daniel.

The agent trailed behind Ashley as she made her way back to the counter.

A male voice boomed from the other side of the pass-through window that led to the kitchen. "Order up."

Ashley noticed that a cheeseburger and a pile of French fries topped the white ceramic plate the cook had positioned onto the warming shelf.

Daniel looked at Lou Ann.

"Is that the stranger's order?" he asked her.

She glanced at the plate sitting in the window behind her. "Yeah."

"Can I take it to him?"

The server nodded. "That'd be great. He makes my skin crawl."

Lou Ann retrieved the order and handed it to Daniel.

Ashley slid the money for her coffee—including a generous tip—toward the server and picked up the to-go cup. She followed Daniel across the diner to the stranger's booth.

The agent placed the plate of food on the table in front of the dark-haired man.

"Cheeseburger and fries," Daniel stated. "Hot off the grill."

The man looked up. A smile formed on his lips, but his dark eyes were as cold and empty as death. A large backpack rested on the bench beside him. Although he was seated, Ashley could tell the stranger was tall. He possessed a solid build with broad shoulders. The type of man who could easily overpower a one-hundred-twenty-pound woman like Beth.

Ashley studied the placket of his coat. The buttons were silver in color—like the one found at Violet's house—but the man sat too far away for her to determine whether they were a match, or if any were missing.

There was one thing she noticed that differed from the description Beth's mother had given them. Beth had reported that the stranger's hair had looked greasy—unwashed. This man's hair and beard appeared clean, as though he'd taken a recent shower. Where had he gone to clean up? Had he stumbled onto an empty hunting cabin in the forest? Was Beth there now?

"Thank you," the stranger said with a nod.

"Do you mind if we sit down?" Daniel asked.

"I don't own the property rights to the booth."

Ashley noticed that the man dropped the sound of the second *r* in the word *property* the way a New Englander would.

The agent motioned for Ashley to sit first. Once she was seated, he slid onto the bench, directly opposite the stranger.

"How long have you been in Mettler Ridge?" he asked.

The man picked up a bottle of ketchup, shook it, and then twisted off the cap.

"What does time matter when you have plenty of it?" he countered, dumping a puddle of ketchup next to his fries.

Daniel didn't seem amused.

"Where are you staying?" he asked the man.

The stranger lifted the top bun from his cheeseburger and added a layer of ketchup to the meat before answering.

"The world, in all her glory, is my shelter."

Ashley could tell that the agent was losing his patience.

"My name is Daniel Lansing. I'm a special agent with the Tennessee Bureau of Investigations. This is Ashley Hope. It would be in your best interest to answer our questions."

The stranger smiled again, and a hint of evil flashed in his eyes. At that instant, he reminded Ashley of her serial killer ex-husband, Ethan.

"I was wondering how long it would take you to find me," the man statcd, his voicc calm.

"What made you think we were looking for you?"

Ashley guessed there was likely a warrant out for the man's arrest. She wouldn't be surprised to learn that he had a rap sheet a mile long.

The stranger shoved a French fry into his mouth, avoiding the question.

Daniel stared at him. "I need to see your identification."

The stranger chewed his food. Swallowed.

Ashley wondered what the heavy-looking backpack contained. The man appeared too composed for her liking. As though he had a plan. Could explosives—a pipe bomb—rest inside the stranger's bag?

"The polite thing would be to let me finish my meal first," the man said.

"I don't have time to be polite."

Since the man wasn't behind the wheel of a car, and the agent didn't actually have probable cause—only suspicion—there was no law in Tennessee that required the stranger to identify himself. Ashley guessed that Daniel was hoping the man wasn't aware of that fact.

"I didn't realize that you were in a rush, Mr. Lansing. My ID is in my wallet, in the rear pocket of my jeans. Would you like me to stand up, so you can frisk me?"

"If you wouldn't mind."

As the stranger gave a slight nod, Ashley's hand snapped to the grip of the pistol holstered in her waistband. She didn't trust the man's movements. Feared that he could press the button of a detonator at any moment. That he would blow up the diner and everyone inside the place.

The stranger removed the napkin from his lap, folded it, and placed it onto the table next to his plate. Sliding out of the booth, he stood and raised his arms.

Ashley held her breath. She still wasn't convinced the man wouldn't make a sudden move. Terrified that he would try to overpower Daniel and kill everyone in sight.

As the agent began patting the man down, she heard footsteps coming toward them. She looked up to see one of the sheriff's deputies, Chris Carter, walking toward Daniel.

"Is everything okay, sir?" the young freckle-faced deputy asked the agent.

"Could you run this for me?" Daniel asked Chris, handing the deputy the driver's license belonging to the stranger.

"Sure thing."

The deputy disappeared out the diner door, most likely heading to his patrol car.

Seeming satisfied that the stranger possessed no weapons—at least not on his person—Daniel motioned toward the booth.

"You can sit down," he said.

Ashley realized that the agent couldn't lawfully search the stranger's backpack. Not yet.

The man slipped back into the booth and returned his napkin to his lap.

"Do I have your permission to finish my meal now?"

"Be my guest," Daniel said, reclaiming his seat on the bench. "You can answer my questions while you eat."

"And when will your lovely partner be allowed to speak?" the stranger asked, shifting his gaze to Ashley.

The man's dark eyes bored into her, revealing a soul as black as soot. Feeling a chill race down her spine, she looked away.

"Anytime she wants," Daniel said, glancing at her.

Although Ashley didn't really want to talk to the man, she also didn't want him to know that he frightened her. That he'd frayed every nerve in her body.

"Why don't you tell me your name so I'll know who I'm speaking to," she said, working hard to keep her voice firm and steady.

The man nodded, fixing his cold eyes on her.

"Well, angel, my name is Joseph Thornton. But you're welcome to call me Joe."

The tone of the man's voice sounded almost pleasant. As though he planned for them to become friends.

Ashley forced herself to meet his gaze, but his eerie stare stripped her thoughts from her mind. She couldn't remember what she wanted to ask him.

Deputy Chris Carter reappeared at the booth.

"That's not his name," the deputy stated, holding out the stranger's driver's license. "This is a fake ID."

Ashley knew that providing a fake driver's license was a misdemeanor. Daniel now had an excuse to arrest the man.

The agent rose from his seat.

"Looks like you need to come to the station," he told the stranger.

"I'm disappointed, Mr. Lansing. I see that you're not a man of your word."

Ashley caught the flash of anger that crossed Daniel's face.

"What?"

"You gave me permission to finish my food but now, you're forcing me to leave."

"We'll get you a carry-out box."

Daniel looked at Chris.

"Cuff him," he told the deputy.

The imagined scene flashed before Ashley's eyes: the stranger reaching for a detonator. The backpack exploding. The diner, the customers, and the employees blasted into a burning pile of rubble.

Not until after she heard the click of the cuffs locking into place did Ashley release the breath she'd been holding.

The agent dropped enough cash onto the table to cover the stranger's bill and then motioned toward the dining counter, getting Lou Ann's attention.

"Get the server to box his food," Daniel said to Ashley.

She nodded, grabbed her coffee, and scooted out of the booth. While she waited for Lou Ann, Ashley peered through the window and watched as Daniel and Chris led the stranger toward the deputy's patrol car. She wondered why the man had given the agent a fake ID. What did he have to hide?

Was the stranger a serial killer like Ethan?

Ashley hoped they would find the answer when they reached the sheriff's office.

Before Beth's time ran out.

CHAPTER THIRTY ONE

Daniel drummed his fingers on the deputy's desk as he waited for the outdated inkjet printer to spit out the final page of the stranger's criminal history. As he had suspected, the report was a long one. He tucked the paper into the manila file folder with the rest of the documents and headed down the hallway toward the closet that served as his temporary work space. He couldn't fault the sheriff for the accommodations. The department's seventy-year-old building was bursting at the seams, and the agent knew the county lacked the funds to expand.

As he pushed the door to the room open, Ashley glanced up at him. The police cadet's laptop computer and textbooks topped the small wooden table that rested against the far wall of the room. Daniel realized she had probably fallen behind in her academy homework. She'd been devoting all of her time to the murder investigation. And he was proud of the job she'd done.

Ashley closed her laptop.

"Were you able to get a fingerprint match on the stranger?" she asked.

"Yeah. His real name is Joseph Woodson. He's got open arrest warrants in New Hampshire. The guy's running from assault and rape charges. There's more than one victim involved."

Daniel wanted to spare her the gory details. She didn't need to know that Woodson had tortured two of his ex-girlfriends, holding them hostage for several days.

"Do you think he could be the person responsible for the murders of Sarah and Violet? That he's the one who kidnapped Beth?"

"It's possible," Daniel replied. "The sheriff's ready to give him the needle."

But then Sheriff Vance had also been convinced that every other suspect they'd identified had been guilty. It seemed as though he just wanted to close the investigation and get the TBI out of his hair.

Although part of Joseph Woodson's MO fit their case, there was a major difference. The man had left his victims alive. He'd turned the women loose. Their injuries had been horrific, but not life-threatening. Could it be that Woodson had stepped up his game?

If he had taken Beth, where was she now? Was she still alive?

Daniel glanced at the clock hanging above the table. 11:48 p.m. If Woodson proved not to be the killer, then based on the previous two murders, Beth only had around six hours left to live.

He had to find her.

He turned his attention back to Ashley.

"It's pushing midnight," he told her. "Why don't you call it a day?"

A slight look of disappointment crossed her face.

"Is it because Joseph Woodson is an outsider that you don't need me to help with the interrogation?" she asked.

"I always need you," he replied without thinking, surprised to realize that the statement rang true in his mind. "But you need to be fresh and alert. Go grab some sleep before your class in the morning."

The fact that Ashley had an early class at the police academy was only part of the reason he wanted her to go home. The real truth was that he didn't want her anywhere near Joseph Woodson. The man's record proved him to be a sadist. He also had a penchant for holding a grudge. Daniel just hoped Woodson would forget Ashley's name. That he wouldn't come looking for her years down the road.

"I'm not the least bit tired and I'd really like to stay—as long as it takes," she said, determination clear in her eyes.

"You've been going nonstop. And if you fail your classes, you won't graduate. I want you to go home now and get some rest. That's not a request, it's an order."

Daniel admired her dedication. She had everything it took to make one hell of a cop. He slid her laptop into its protective sleeve and then stuffed it into her backpack. He held the flap open as she added her textbooks.

"You want me to carry this to your car?" he asked, grabbing one of the backpack's straps.

He'd noticed her flinching a few times during the day, as if her arm muscles were sore. He knew from experience that the physical training at the academy could be brutal.

"Thanks, but I've got it."

He slid the backpack onto her shoulder.

"Don't forget I've got a meeting in Briarwood tomorrow afternoon."

The TBI all-hands-on-deck meeting scheduled for the following day had been declared mandatory. He didn't want to take precious time away from the case, but it couldn't be avoided. Not if he wanted to keep his job.

She nodded. "Just text me in the morning and let me know how Woodson's interrogation went."

"Will do."

Daniel watched Ashley as she headed off down the hallway toward the rear exit of the sheriff's department. He wondered how she was doing emotionally. Whether the investigation had pushed the memories of the trauma she'd endured during the hunt for her ex-husband to the forefront. She had also suffered the breakup of her engagement. Daniel knew she'd been devastated to learn that her ex-fiancé was cheating on her. The man was an idiot.

Brett Holbrook had never deserved the love of a woman like Ashley.

The memory of holding her at the creek—after she'd slipped on the rock—floated into Daniel's mind. It had taken every ounce of his self-control to stop himself from kissing her.

Ashley wasn't like the other women he'd dated. He felt drawn to her in a way that he couldn't quite understand. As though they'd known each other for years. In the past, he'd always found it difficult to talk to anyone about his father's death. Even Melody. And he hadn't told his ex-wife how his father had been killed until after they'd become engaged. But when he'd been in the car with Ashley, the words had just tumbled out of their own accord.

The feelings he'd developed for her ran deep.

But he knew he couldn't act on them. Ashley fell under his direct supervision. She was his partner in this investigation. It wouldn't be appropriate for him to step over the line. And he had seen what could happen when partnered cops became entangled romantically. A good buddy of his on the force in Briarwood had almost lost his life when he'd let his emotions distract him from the job at hand.

And there was Ashley's history to think about. She was no doubt vulnerable from her recent breakup. There was no way he'd ever want to be the rebound guy.

Whatever it was that he was feeling for her didn't matter. Ashley was off limits.

Daniel tucked Joseph Woodson's file beneath his arm and headed for the interrogation room. He arrived outside the doorway at the same time as the suspect. He watched while the guard led Woodson into the room and then took his seat at the dingy white table.

"You'll be extradited back to New Hampshire tomorrow afternoon," Daniel informed the man.

The agent wasn't happy with the timeframe, but the authorities in the suspect's home state had insisted.

"Will your lovely partner be joining us, Agent Lansing?" Woodson asked, his gaze veering toward the closed door of the interrogation room.

Daniel resisted the urge to punch the suspect in the face.

"Don't worry about her."

Woodson smiled, but the expression failed to reach his dead eyes.

"I'm not concerned about Ms. Hope," the man stated. "But I do enjoy her company."

Upon hearing the suspect utter Ashley's name, a bolt of anger raced through Daniel's bones. He wanted to wipe Woodson's memory with his fists. Make the man forget he'd ever met the police cadet.

Fighting to hide his fury, the agent pulled a photo of Beth Holder from the file and placed it on the table in front of Woodson.

"An eyewitness saw you with this woman," he said, failing to mention the day and location of the sighting on purpose.

Omitting the fact that the missing woman had been the witness—that she'd reported the incident herself—was justified. He hoped the suspect's response would reveal whether or not the man had been following Beth. If he had stalked her, waiting for the opportune moment to abduct the woman.

Woodson picked up the photograph.

"Yes, I remember her. We spoke briefly at the convenience store on Spring Street."

The admission matched the information Beth had given to her mother.

"Where is she now?"

The man shook his head. "Unfortunately for you, I don't have an answer to that question."

"You're not willing to answer? Or you don't know?"

The man was a pro at doublespeak. A trait that infuriated Daniel.

"I have no idea of the woman's current location."

The agent couldn't get a proper read on Woodson. It was hard to guess whether or not the man was telling the truth.

Daniel removed the photos of Sarah Lester and Violet Perry from the folder and slid them across the table.

"Tell me about these two women," he said, leaving the question open-ended.

Woodson arranged the three pictures in a line, seeming to study them.

"I would have to say that they're very attractive," he stated.

There was no hint of recognition on the man's face or in his body language. But this suspect was unlike any Daniel had ever questioned. It was as though he had no soul. No feelings at all whatsoever.

"Do you know what happened to these women?"

"They were murdered."

The blunt response surprised the agent. But the words didn't feel like a confession. They seemed more of an observation. However, the photographs had been taken when Sarah and Violet were still alive.

"Did you kill them?"

"Me? No, I'm not the person you're looking to find."

Woodson sat back in his chair as though the interview bored him.

"Then how do you know they're dead?"

"Do you really have to ask me that question? The answer is too obvious. If the women were alive and well then you'd have no reason to show me their pictures. Am I right, Agent Lansing?"

Daniel pressed his lips together, holding back the expletives that he wanted to shout. He was tired of the man's game.

"Did you harm any of these women?" he asked, his voice betraying his ire.

The man snickered as he shook his head.

"Looking at their pictures makes me wish that I had. But as I said before, I'm not the man you were hoping to find."

Hearing Woodson admit that he enjoyed torturing women made Daniel want to rip the man's throat out.

"Where have you been staying?"

Whoever had abducted Sarah, Violet, and Beth had to have a cabin or some other type shelter where the women had been held captive. A place the murderer had kept the victims for roughly twenty-four hours before their deaths. A search of the man's backpack revealed that he didn't own a tent. At least, he didn't have one currently in his possession. And Woodson also wasn't carrying any weapon. If he had fired the rifle that had killed Sarah and Violet, where was the gun now?

"Your town has a lovely church over on Main Street. The pastor was kind enough to offer me a small room with a cot in the rear of the fellowship hall."

It should be easy to confirm or disprove the information. But if the man's story checked out, where had he kept the abducted women? There was no way Woodson would have been able to hide the three victims in the fellowship hall of the church.

"How did you get to Mettler Ridge?"

Another problem Daniel saw in relation to Woodson's guilt was that the man had to have a way to transport Sarah and Violet to the remote locations of their deaths. Did the stranger have access to a car?

"I arrived by way of the thumb express," the man answered, a smirk on his face.

"You hitchhiked from New Hampshire?"

"That's correct."

"You never borrowed a car along the way?"

"I'm assuming by the word *borrowed* you're asking whether I stole a vehicle. The answer is no. I lack the skills that would require."

The man's rap sheet ran long, but no instances of car theft appeared in the report. Although Daniel was convinced Woodson possessed the potential to be a cold-blooded killer, the agent lacked evidence to connect the man to Sarah and Violet. Woodson had no viable place to hide the women and he had only been seen on foot—never in a vehicle. Instinct told Daniel that the stranger was telling the truth. He was not the man they were looking for.

Daniel shoved the photographs back into the file folder and rose from his seat. He marched out into the hallway and closed the door to the interrogation room behind him. The idea of forcing Woodson to spend the night cuffed to the interview table flashed through the agent's mind. The soulless man didn't deserve the pleasure of sleeping on one of the uncomfortable metal bunks in the holding cell. But even though Woodson had proved to be a worthless piece of scum, he was still a human being.

The agent nodded at the guard on duty.

"Keep the prisoner in the interrogation room for about an hour," he told the guard. "Then take him back to the holding cell."

Glancing at the time on his phone, Daniel headed out the rear entrance of the sheriff's department and into the parking lot. The knowledge that he had come no closer to finding Beth gnawed at him. He couldn't shake the image of the distraught faces of Frank and Yvonne Holder from his mind.

The killer's timeframe was almost up and there was nothing the agent could do about it.

He hopped into his Toyota and started the engine. He'd catch a couple of hours of sleep at the motel and then return to the sheriff's department at first light. Maybe by then he'd be able to dig up a new lead.

He only hoped it wouldn't accompany Beth Holder's body.

CHAPTER THIRTY TWO

The door to the old RV creaked open, filling Beth Holder's heart with dread. She knew better than to hope that the footsteps echoing toward the bed where she lay belonged to someone who'd come to rescue her and set her free. Her abductor—the man hiding behind the rubber clown mask—had removed the gag from her mouth. He'd made it clear that they were located miles from civilization. That there was no one around who could hear her screams.

Her arm muscles ached from being chained to the cabinet above her head and the side of her neck burned from the needle prick. The temperature in the motorhome had skyrocketed during the middle of the day causing her to sweat beneath her blue fleece jacket. When the sun had finally set, the cold air that pressed against her damp skin had sent chills through her body. Now, her throat felt dry as sand, her stomach growled from hunger, and she needed to use the bathroom.

She wondered what the man had injected her with. If she had to guess, it had most likely been a surgical anesthetic. The kind they used at the animal hospital. This led her to suspect that the clown might be a former co-worker, or a fellow student at the veterinary college.

The hours spent alone had given her time to think—to search her memory for a match to the clown's voice. The man sounded familiar, but she'd come up blank. She had no idea why she was here or what the clown planned to do to her.

But he had hinted that he would let her go home.

The overhead light switched on. Beth's breath caught in her throat as she saw the clown's face towering over her.

"I didn't plan to be gone all day," he said. "But I had a lot of things to do."

He sat down on the bed next to her.

Beth flinched as his hand brushed against her leg.

"I need to use the bathroom," she said, her voice sounding weak in her own ears.

"Okay."

The clown stood and moved toward her feet. He tugged off her left sock and then her right.

Beth pressed her eyes closed as a tear rolled down her cheek. It seemed her abductor wanted what she feared the most. That he planned to rape her.

But instead of stripping off her jeans, the man moved toward the head of the bed. He unlocked the chain from the metal ring bolted to the cabinet.

"Get up," he ordered, pulling on the chain.

She scooted off the mattress. With only inches between them in the tight space, she could smell the fake plastic hair protruding from his mask. The scent sickened her. He opened the door to the tiny bathroom and pushed her inside. The faded vinyl floor was cold beneath her bare feet. Why had he taken off her socks? It made no sense.

"Could I have some privacy?" she asked, hoping he would let go of the chain and shut the door.

The man chuckled and then turned his back toward her.

Zip ties fastened Beth's wrists to the chain, but she was able to unbutton her jeans and slide them down. She waited until she had her pants secured back around her waist before she flushed the toilet. She didn't want the clown to turn around too soon.

The man yanked on the chain, pulling her close.

"Do you want to live?" he asked, his voice just above a whisper.

A knot of fear formed in her chest.

"Yes," she replied.

"Then you'll follow my rules. You'll do everything I tell you, and you won't ask questions."

She nodded.

"I didn't hear that."

"I'll do whatever you tell me to do."

"Good girl."

He tugged the chain, leading her a few steps down the aisle that ran between the cabinets lining the walls of the RV. She wondered whether the anesthetic he'd used on her was stashed inside one of the storage compartments. Would she get the opportunity to search for it?

The clown shoved her onto one of the bench seats that flanked a small table.

"I brought you something," he said, his tone smug.

He locked the chain onto another metal ring—this one bolted to the table. He turned toward the cabinet behind him and lifted a small white box and a package of plastic cutlery out of a paper grocery sack. He placed both items on the table in front of her and then flipped the lid of the box open.

"It's your favorite," he remarked.

A red velvet cupcake with cream cheese frosting rested inside the box. The clown was right; it was her favorite. How had he known?

"I almost forgot the best part," he said, reaching back into the grocery sack. He pulled out a package of small red and white striped candles and ripped it open. He stuck one of the candles into the center of the cupcake.

"It's a little early, but there's no reason we can't celebrate your birthday now."

A shiver ran down Beth's spine. It was only two weeks until her birthday. The man knew her, which meant that she knew him. Why couldn't she place his voice?

If she could figure out who he was, she might be able to find out why he'd kidnapped her.

"Have we celebrated my birthday together before?" she asked.

The clown hesitated. "Once," he finally said. "A long time ago."

"Where were we?"

"Shut up," the man barked. "I told you not to ask questions."

He pulled a disposable lighter from his pocket and flicked the striker wheel. He inched the flame toward her. Held it beneath her chin. Beth pressed her back against the bench seat.

The heat from the flame licked her neck.

She held her breath, afraid to move.

Seeming to realize that she would obey his commands—that she understood he could mutilate or kill her at any moment—the clown chuckled again. He withdrew the flame and lit the wick of the birthday candle.

"What will you wish for?" the man taunted.

She knew he expected her to ask to be set free. But Beth decided to change the script. Instead of allowing him to see her fear, she'd act as though she wanted to befriend the man. She'd had a lot of experience dealing with feral cats at the animal hospital. The first thing she'd learned was that you had to earn the felines' trust. Otherwise, their claws could rip you to shreds.

The clown wasn't a feral animal, but he was definitely dangerous. If she could get him to trust her—to see her as a friend instead of an object—she would have a better chance of being let go unharmed.

"My wish is to get to know you," she told him, trying to push a note of sincerity into her voice.

Although the mask concealed the man's facial expression, she could tell by his body language that the answer had surprised him. It seemed to leave him speechless.

He turned back to the counter and retrieved two cans of Riddle's Root Beer from the grocery bag. Placing the cans onto the table, he popped them open. He slid into the bench opposite her.

"Go ahead," he said. "Blow out the candle."

Beth inhaled, closed her eyes as though she was making a wish, and then blew a stream of air toward the candle. The flame went out, but an orange ember glowed at the end of the wick. A millisecond later, the flame reignited. She wasn't surprised. She'd recognized the trick candles by their familiar striping. When she was a child, her father had bought the same brand several years in a row, just to make her laugh.

"Don't worry," the clown said. "You'll still get your wish. We'll get to know each other really well."

The words hit her like a spike made of ice, chilling her to the bone. But she refused to allow her fright at his veiled comment to show on her face. Instead, she forced herself to smile.

"That sounds good," she told him.

The clown pulled the still-burning candle from the cupcake and tossed it into the small steel sink across from the table. He ripped the package of plastic cutlery open and offered her a fork.

"I hope you like it."

Beth glanced at the cupcake. She wondered whether the man had laced the treat with poison. But if he wanted to knock her out, he could just use the same anesthetic that he'd jabbed into her neck. And she didn't really think he wanted to kill her just yet. It felt as though he had something more planned.

She accepted the fork from his hand. She wanted to plunge the utensil into his heart, but she knew the weak plastic tines would break. They weren't even rigid enough to leave a mark on his skin.

Painting the smile back onto her face, she stuck the fork into the cupcake, broke off a bite, and scooped it into her mouth. The rich frosting oozed around her tongue, reminding her of how hungry she'd grown.

"It tastes good; like homemade."

Although the cupcake had a nice flavor, she could tell in an instant that it was store-bought. But she wanted to appear appreciative. To make the clown believe that she approved of his efforts.

She broke off another bite and held the fork out to the clown.

"Don't you want some of the cake?" she asked.

The man froze, appearing stunned by her action.

"I've decided to keep you for a while," he stated after a moment's hesitation. "A day or two longer. Then I'm gonna let you go."

They weren't the words Beth had wanted to hear. She'd hoped the clown would set her free tonight. Right now. She'd have to work harder to gain his trust—to force him to see her as a real person.

She heard a jingle emitting from the man's pocket—a phone ringing.

There was cell service in the area. That meant they were most likely parked on a ridge, not in a valley. But that fact didn't narrow down their location. Laurel County encompassed five hundred square miles. Like the clown had told her, they could still be out in the middle of nowhere.

The man scooted out of the booth, pulled his cell from his pocket, and turned his back toward Beth.

"Yeah," he said into the phone, aggravation clear in his voice.

There was a brief pause as though he was listening to the person on the other end of the call. She wondered how difficult it was for him to hear through the rubber mask. She guessed the material was thin around the ears as it didn't seem to hinder him.

"Okay. I'll be there."

He ended the call and shoved his phone back into his pocket.

The clown stepped toward Beth and ran his fingers along the edge of her jaw. His cold touch sent a wave of fear radiating through her body, urging her to recoil. But she willed herself to remain still.

"Bad news," he said. "I'm gonna have to go for now. But don't worry, Beth. I'll be back. Real soon."

CHAPTER THIRTY THREE

Ashley spotted the cardboard box—stacked on top of a mountain of plastic bins containing her mother's belongings—in the far corner of the attic of her father's farmhouse. The label bore her name and a description of the contents written in large block letters. Ashley had packed the box and stored it away nine years earlier, right after making the worst decision of her life—marrying, and moving in with, Ethan Barrett.

Standing on her tiptoes, she pulled the box down from its perch. A layer of dust rained on her face, stinging her eyes and itching her nose. Ashley sneezed, lost her balance, and stumbled backwards a few steps. She was lucky she hadn't fallen on her behind. Resting the heavy carton on the floor, she bent over and shook the dust out of her hair.

She remembered the night a barn rat had jumped onto her head and she shuddered.

At least she hadn't seen any rodents in the attic. For that, she was grateful.

She grabbed the box and headed down the narrow stairs that ended in the hallway adjacent to the living room. Shane sat in his wheelchair next to the sofa.

"You done found it?" he asked her. "That was quick."

"Yeah, it was right where I remembered it would be."

Of course, it wasn't her recollection alone that had helped her locate the box. The large hand-printed label had been instrumental as well. Inside Ashley had stowed memorabilia from her high school days, including the four yearbooks the school had issued to the students at the conclusion of each of their four years of attendance. She dropped the carton onto the floor in front of Shane's chair and lifted off the lid.

The yearbooks were stored with their spines facing upward. She pulled out the one from her senior year and flipped the book open. Handwritten messages filled the inside cover, spilling over onto the first page. Sentiments from her classmates. The message from Randy Boatman caught her eye.

To the smartest girl I know.
Thanks for helping me make it through chemistry.
Let's celebrate in Cedar View this weekend.
Friends till the end!
Randy

But she'd hadn't celebrated with her friends that weekend. Instead, she'd run off with Ethan and gotten married.

"Look up Sarah's pictures first," Shane told her.

Ashley turned to the back of the book, to the index listing the names of all of the students and the page numbers where their photos could be found. She had worked on the yearbook committee. The group had made sure to include at least one candid shot of each of the students. These were the pictures she sought. Images that might give her some insight into the lives of the abducted women.

Something that would tie them all together and help her to find Beth.

Ashley had barely been able to concentrate at the academy that morning. She'd been terrified that she would receive a text informing her that Beth's body had been found. It pained her to think about what the woman must be going through. Not knowing where to look for her former classmate ate away at Ashley's nerves.

Every second that ticked by reduced their chances of finding Beth alive.

Although the TBI had scoured Mr. Stanton's property and had been unable to find any evidence that Sarah, Violet, or Beth had ever set foot on the former teacher's land, Ashley was convinced that something, or someone, from Laurel County High School would prove to be the missing link to the killer.

For now, Mr. Stanton seemed to have been cleared of the crimes, but the other faculty members, students, and anyone else associated with the school had not.

Sheriff Vance, on the other hand, had made it known that he believed Joseph Woodson was guilty of the murders. The stranger had fled from warrants in New Hampshire for assault and rape. But according to the phone conversation she'd had with Daniel after her classes at the academy that afternoon, Woodson had traveled to Laurel County by hitchhiking. He didn't own a car. If he had killed Sarah and Violet, how did he transport them out into the middle of nowhere?

The women certainly didn't walk to the places where they were killed.

Ashley hoped the TBI's forensic team would be able to locate a match to the tire treads found on the shoulder of the road where Violet had been murdered. If they knew the make of the vehicle that had brought the woman to the field, they might be able to identify the driver—aka the killer.

"I think we should check out the photo of Beth first since she's still missing," Ashley told Shane as she plopped down onto the sofa next to his wheelchair.

Running her finger down the index, Ashley located the entry for Beth's candid shot. She flipped through the book until she found the right page.

A young Beth Holder stared up at her. The woman looked exactly as Ashley had remembered her. Kind eyes and a big smile. Beth sat in the middle of a group of students behind a long table in the corner of Laurel County High School's gymnasium. She had chaired a committee selling tickets for a raffle that benefitted a local homeless shelter.

Ashley studied the photo, quick to notice that neither Sarah nor Violet had been a member of the group. She spun the yearbook around so that Shane could get a better look at the picture.

"I don't remember her," he said.

Shane would have been a freshman at the time, so it was likely he'd never come into contact with Beth.

Turning back to the index, Ashley zipped down the list to Sarah's entry. The photograph had been taken just inside the main entrance of the high school. Standing on a stepladder, the then teenager held a poster advertising the school's homecoming dance. Ashley scanned the faces of the students surrounding Sarah. Violet and Beth weren't among them.

"Only one more picture left to go," Ashley said, as a feeling of hopelessness began to creep into her heart.

She paged over to Violet's candid shot. The woman had been one of only a few female members of the high school's angler club. In her photo, Violet showed off her catch: a seventeen-inch largemouth bass, weighing just under three pounds. She had failed to place in the statewide fishing tournament held at Mettler Lake, but the smile on her face let the viewer know that she wasn't concerned with winning. She was having the time of her life.

Again, the other two women, Sarah and Beth, were not included in the group of fishing enthusiasts.

Ashley's hopes sank. Maybe she'd been wrong about Laurel County High School being the killer's connection with the women. They were all the same age and grew up in the same town. Naturally, they would all attend the same school. But the three women each had a distinct personality and differing interests.

What did a charity raffle, the homecoming dance, and a fishing tournament have in common?

Nothing, as far as Ashley knew. But still, she couldn't shake the feeling that her hunch was on target.

With a sigh, she closed the yearbook.

"We should get started on your physical therapy now, Shane," she told her brother.

Her failure at uncovering a clue that could help find Beth had sent Ashley's nervous energy skyrocketing through the roof. She couldn't sit still. Daniel was still tied up in his TBI meeting in Briarwood, and she had no leads to follow up on. At least she was able to help Shane.

"You're gonna be surprised," her brother stated. "I been pushing myself hard. Staying up late at night."

She was delighted to hear that Shane had kept his promise to exercise.

Rising from the sofa, she followed her brother as he wheeled himself toward the door of the small pantry in their father's kitchen. Instead of a standard knob, the door featured an antique D-ring handle with a thumb latch.

"Don't help me," Shane said. "Let me do it by myself."

Her brother secured both ends of a red elastic resistance band to the door handle making a large loop. He placed the band around his right ankle and rolled back a few feet, extending his leg straight out in front of him. After locking the brakes on his wheelchair, he looked up at Ashley and smiled.

"Watch this," he said.

Shane pulled his ankle down toward himself, not stopping until his foot was completely beneath his chair.

Ashley's heart soared. Her brother's strength and range of motion had improved by a tremendous amount. He obviously hadn't been exaggerating when he'd told her that he'd been pushing himself. She watched as he repeated the motion ten times.

“I’m so proud of you,” she said. “Have you shown Daddy and Kyle that you can do this?”

He shook his head. “I wanted you to see first.”

Her father had gone into Mettler Ridge to visit her older brother at the auto repair shop. Although Spencer’s doctor had forbidden him to resume work, he enjoyed hanging around the shop and talking with the customers.

“I want you to give them a demonstration as soon as they get home,” she said.

Shane nodded and switched the band to his other ankle.

“I been thinking about Sarah,” he said. “Killers on the news, they ain’t the people you expect. Like the Cumberland River guy. He was real good at blending in. Didn’t nobody suspect him.”

Shane was right. Elmore Wilcox, the serial killer who’d left a trail of bodies along Tennessee’s Cumberland River, had been a nondescript man with a normal background. The authorities had suspected and questioned several people close to Wilcox, but they had overlooked the man himself. He’d seemed too ordinary—harmless. His co-workers had described him as a *nice guy*. Someone they trusted. If the man’s neighbor hadn’t stumbled onto a bag of the victims’ possessions in Wilcox’s garage, the killer might still be walking free.

A realization hit Ashley like a bolt of lightning.

“Shane, you’re a genius.”

She raced back to the living room and grabbed her yearbook off the sofa. She’d been viewing the photographs of Beth, Sarah, and Violet in the wrong way. Searching for something that wasn’t there, while overlooking the one thing that was obvious.

She flipped back through the candid shots, confirming her suspicions.

Hearing Shane’s wheelchair roll into the room, Ashley looked up at her brother and smiled.

“I found the missing link between Sarah, Violet, and Beth,” she declared.

A wide grin spread across her brother’s face.

CHAPTER THIRTY FOUR

Ashley flipped the pages of the yearbook to the candid shot of Sarah and placed it on the coffee table in front of Shane's wheelchair. She couldn't believe she'd missed the one detail that was now so clear. But she'd been trying to find a shared interest between Sarah, Violet, and Beth—one that didn't exist.

"Take a really good look at this photograph," she instructed her brother.

Shane leaned closer to the coffee table.

"She's fixing to hang up a poster for the dance," he noted.

Ashley paged back to Violet's picture, hoping her brother would catch it—that he would see the connection.

"Think about the photo of Sarah while you look at this one."

Shane nodded. "Violet done caught her a nice bass."

Ashley wondered whether her younger brother was overlooking the obvious, the same way that she had done originally.

She turned to the final shot—the photograph of Beth.

"Now look at this picture and think about the other two you just saw."

Shane paused, as though he was inspecting every detail visible in the shot.

"She's selling raffle tickets."

"Yes, but what Beth is doing is not what's important. What do all three of these photos have in common?"

Her brother shook his head, hesitated for a moment.

"I don't see it," he finally told her, confusion apparent in his voice.

Like Ashley had done when she'd first studied the candid yearbook shots, Shane seemed to be focusing on the activities the women were involved in rather than what was actually important.

"That's because it's not an *it*—it's a *who*."

Ashley slid her finger across the page of the yearbook, stopping beneath the face of a teenage male.

"Yeah," Shane said, his tone revealing that he couldn't believe he'd overlooked the teen. "Rippy's in all three pictures."

Rippy.

Or as she knew him now—Deputy Troy Luckadoo.

Hearing the man's high school nickname brought forth a slew of memories—things Ashley had forgotten. She recalled that several students had ridiculed the teen—had taped a pair of men's underwear to the outside of his locker—but Rippy had seemed to take their pranks in stride.

Although Sarah, Violet, and Beth had been surrounded by students in their candid shots, the teen was the only person who appeared in all three of the photographs.

Another detail caught Ashley's eye. Rippy sat at the end of the long table in the gymnasium, two students over from Beth. A soda can rested in front of him.

Riddle's Root Beer.

Ashley remembered visiting the location where Sarah's body had been discovered with Daniel. The agent had told her that the forensic team had found an empty Riddle's Root Beer can at the scene. Although that detail—along with the fact that Rippy had been featured in the photos of Sarah, Violet, and Beth—didn't prove the man was the killer, it certainly placed him on the suspect list.

"I have to get this information to Daniel," she said, grabbing her purse and pulling out her cell.

She knew she couldn't interrupt the agent with a phone call during his TBI meeting, but she could send him a text.

"Where does Rippy live now?" she asked Shane as she typed out the message to Daniel.

"I ain't got no idea."

It was possible that Beth was being held at the man's house at that very moment, fighting to stay alive.

"Daniel will be able to find out through the DMV records. I'll ask him to send a TBI agent over to Rippy's place to check it out."

She wished she could access the TBI's database and get the information herself, but the agency software was only installed on Daniel's laptop—which he had taken with him to Briarwood.

Ashley finished typing the text and hit *send.*

"Do people still call him Rippy—even now?" she asked Shane.

"Yeah," he nodded. "Everybody does. But ain't nobody ever told me how he got that name."

Since her brother was three years younger, he hadn't been a student at the high school when Rippy had earned his nickname.

"They call him that because of something that happened our junior year," she explained. "All the students in the school—freshman through senior—were gathered in the auditorium for a presentation. I'm not sure what the topic was. Anyway, the speaker had a bunch of displays on the stage and he wanted one of them moved. Rippy went up onto the stage to help."

Ashley paused for a second, surprised at how clear the memory had become.

"He was wearing a pair of blue chino-type pants that were really tight," she continued. "I'm pretty sure they were hand-me-downs from the donation box at the church. He had his back to the audience, and when he squatted down to pick up the display, the seat of his pants ripped. I remember his white cotton underwear peeking out. And as you can probably guess, the whole auditorium exploded in laughter. I can't remember who first decided to call him Rippy, but it stuck, and pretty soon everyone was calling him that."

She recalled feeling really terrible for her classmate at the time, knowing that he had suffered a humiliating experience.

Shane smiled. "Wish I'd been there."

Ashley wondered if being called by the nickname was a sore spot for her former classmate, or if he'd gotten so used to hearing the moniker that it had become meaningless. Something he could laugh about now.

Even though she'd found evidence to suggest that Rippy was connected to the three woman, the idea that he might be a cold-blooded killer sounded insane in Ashley's own mind. He'd always seemed like such a nice guy—one she'd trusted. But then again, Ted Bundy's friends had all been shocked to learn that the law student was a rapist and murderer. Like Shane had pointed out, serial killers were usually revealed to be the people you least expected. People who—on the surface—appeared normal.

She needed to find out where Rippy lived. Beth's life was poised in the balance—the clock ticking. Ashley couldn't just sit around and wait for Daniel and the TBI. Unzipping her backpack, she pulled out her laptop and booted it up on the coffee table. She clicked on her browser and conducted a search on Rippy's real name—Troy Luckadoo.

Although she got a few hits for her former classmate's social media, she couldn't find any information that led to his home address.

"Do you know who Rippy's friends are now?"

Shane shook his head. "I seen him at Mack's a bunch of times. I never paid no attention to who was with him."

Mack's was a dive bar located on the highway that led to Cedar View. Ashley never would have pegged Rippy to be a regular there, but she reminded herself that her memories of the man were from several years ago. She didn't really know him anymore. And she realized she'd probably never been privy to his true nature—even back in high school.

She glanced at the clock on her phone. 5:49 p.m. It was a little early for barhopping, but she might find someone she knew at Mack's. Someone she could finesse into telling her where Rippy lived without raising their suspicion.

Ashley grabbed her purse and stuffed her phone back inside. Then she stowed her laptop in her backpack and hoisted it onto her shoulder.

"I'll be back in a little while," she told Shane.

"Don't you do nothing stupid," he said, his face a mask of concern.

She touched her brother's arm.

"There's no reason for you to worry about me," she assured him. "I'm not about to confront Rippy or do anything else that will get me in trouble."

Ashley planted a light kiss on the top of Shane's head and then hurried out the front door of her father's farmhouse and ran toward her sedan.

CHAPTER THIRTY FIVE

The thick blanket of cigarette smoke stung Ashley's nostrils as she strode through the front entrance of Mack's and scanned the faces of the patrons scattered around the room. An ancient country tune—Hank Williams's "Your Cheatin' Heart"—reverberated off the walls of the dive bar, drowning out her thoughts. The music and the outdated décor gave her the distinct feeling that she'd somehow traveled through a swirling time portal and had been deposited decades in the past.

Although she'd driven to Mack's to conduct a clandestine investigation—to question Rippy's friends and find out his address—a part of her had hoped to find her former classmate in the bar. If Rippy had been here, that would mean that he wasn't with Beth. But she didn't see the man anywhere. She realized it was likely he was at work—at least she hoped that was his location.

Unable to spot anyone that she knew, Ashley hopped onto a stool at the bar counter.

"What'll it be, darlin'?" the bartender—a man with wavy gray hair who seemed almost as old as the song that was playing—asked.

"Can I get a club soda with lime?"

He looked at her as though he thought she was joking and hesitated—like he was waiting for her real order. Ashley knew that most of the customers came here to drink beer or whiskey, although they might serve fruity alcoholic drinks to the females. A virgin order was most likely as rare as a snowstorm in June. When the bartender realized she was being serious, he smiled.

"Comin' right up."

She pulled some cash from her purse and slid it across the counter. While waiting for her drink, she spun around on the stool and surveyed the room again, checking all the tables, trying to decide who looked like they would be someone Rippy would befriend. Or at least, who knew him. But then she reminded herself that she had no idea of the kind of person her former classmate would associate with now. He wasn't the same man she'd known back in high school. The fact that he liked to hang out at Mack's proved that point.

Not that the honky-tonk was necessarily a rough place—it was fairly tame. But back in the day, she remembered Rippy had been known as a straight arrow. Dive bars hadn't really been on the list of his preferred places to frequent.

"Here you go, darlin'."

Hearing the bartender's voice behind her, she turned back around. The man seemed just as likely a candidate for her questions as anyone else in the joint. Bartenders were known for their listening skills. He might have more information on her old classmate than any of the customers.

"I was hoping to meet an old friend of mine from high school here," she told the man. "Maybe you know him. He goes by the name of Rippy."

Recognition flooded the bartender's eyes.

"Yeah, I know Rippy. But he don't come in here on Tuesdays. He's a weekender."

Ashley wondered whether that meant that her old classmate's friends were only here on the weekends as well. She was about to ask the bartender another question—was already making up an excuse as to why she needed to get in touch with Rippy—but the man turned and headed toward a customer at the other end of the bar before she could speak.

She took a sip of her club soda. Inside, her nerves began to fray. Beth was being held hostage somewhere, could be mere moments away from death, and Ashley lacked the power to help her.

A cool burst of air cut through the stuffy bar, causing her to glance over her shoulder. She caught sight of a man walking through the entrance, a curvy blonde on his arm. She recognized the couple. It was her cousin Nathan and his wife, Gloria.

Ashley watched as they made their way to a table near the wooden dance floor. Nathan slipped off his Sherpa-lined denim jacket and draped it over the back of one of the chairs. The couple hadn't noticed her yet. She picked up her drink and headed for their table.

"What in tarnation are you doing here, Ash?" Nathan asked, giving her a brief hug.

The man was a younger copy of her uncle: tall and lean with auburn hair.

"It's really good to see you both—it's been a while," she said.

The last time Ashley had seen the couple was at her engagement party to Brett. She hoped they wouldn't ask about her former fiancé. She didn't want to take the time to discuss the reason she and Brett were no longer together. She needed to find out whether her cousin knew where Rippy lived as fast as possible.

Gloria motioned toward one of the chairs. "Sit down," she told Ashley. "Talk with us for a spell."

The woman's turquoise earrings bobbed as she spoke. The color of the stones just a shade lighter than her eyes.

Ashley sank into the chair.

"Ladies, I need to make a pit stop," Nathan said.

Instead of sitting down, he headed toward the men's restroom.

"So tell me how you've been doing," Gloria said, leaning toward her. Likely so that her voice could be heard over the music. "Shane said that you broke up with your beau."

Leave it to her younger brother to spread the word to the family. He'd probably spilled all the gory details as well. Knowing Shane's big mouth, at least she probably wouldn't have anything more to explain.

"I'm actually doing really well—moving on with my life."

"That's good to hear."

It was time to switch the subject—to get to the reason for Ashley's visit to the bar.

"Do you and Nathan ever come here on the weekends?"

Gloria nodded. "All the time."

"Shane told me that an old friend of mine from high school likes to hang out here. Do you know a man named Rippy?"

Both Nathan and Gloria were several years older than Ashley. They'd both graduated from Laurel County High before her freshman year had even begun. So it was possible they'd never met her old classmate.

"Sure, I know Rippy," she said, a smile spreading across her face. "Are you sweet on him?"

Ashley decided to play on Gloria's assumption, to pretend she was romantically interested in the man. That would definitely be a good excuse to ask questions.

"He doesn't know about my feelings yet, so don't tell anyone, okay?"

"You ain't gotta worry. I won't say nothing, especially not to Nathan. He's got a big mouth."

A pretty blonde server appeared at their table.

"What can I get you two to drink?"

Gloria didn't hesitate to answer. "Me and Nathan both want beer. And a plate of them hot wings."

The server scribbled down the order and then looked at Ashley. The glass of club soda was still almost full.

"I don't need anything right now," she told the server.

Once they were alone again, Ashley picked up her conversation with Gloria.

"I'm sure Rippy has probably changed a lot since high school," she said. "What all can you tell me about him?"

"You mean, is he dating somebody?"

Ashley nodded. She realized that could be useful information. Especially if the woman Rippy was going out with had light brown hair and blue eyes.

"He ain't right now. Not that I know of anyway. The last woman he was seeing, Holly, used to work here. But they broke up over a year ago."

"Do you remember what she looked like?"

"She was pretty, but not as pretty as you. She had brown hair."

"Light brown or dark?"

"Light. Golden like. She couldn't hold a candle to you though, so don't worry about her."

The description of Rippy's former girlfriend seemed to fit the profile. Of course, Gloria hadn't mentioned the woman's eye color, but Ashley realized it would sound weird to ask about that detail.

"Do you know where this woman works now?"

"Honey, I'm telling you, she ain't no competition. So don't be thinking that you need to sneak a look at her. She ain't even around here no more anyway."

Ashley wondered where the woman had gone and what had been the reason for her to leave.

"Did she move to another town?"

Gloria stared at Ashley.

"I didn't want to say nothing, cause I know you've been through a rough patch. And you take things to heart. You don't need to be dwelling on sad stuff."

The woman paused for a moment as though she was debating whether or not to divulge the information.

"Holly just up and disappeared," Gloria finally said. "Rippy was real tore up about it. Her family's still hunting for her. They called the Nashville TV stations and everything. Some rich man her daddy knows even put up a reward."

The news hit Ashley like a cyclone. She hadn't wanted to let herself believe it—had hoped that she would find evidence that would clear her old classmate—but now she knew the truth in her heart.

Rippy had murdered Sarah and Violet.

He had kidnapped Beth.

The question now was: where was he holding his latest victim? And how much time did she have left to live?

Ashley had to find her.

The information Gloria had relayed brought up additional troubling questions. Did the man have other girlfriends who had disappeared? When did his killing spree really begin? Ashley realized it could have started years ago.

And she was determined to stop it.

"Rippy used to live with his parents back when we were in high school, but that house has been torn down since then. It used to be located on Spring Street—right where they built the minimart. Do you happen to know where he lives now?"

Gloria smiled again. "You planning on going to see him?"

She planned on doing much more than that.

"I'm hoping to drop by his house tonight, but remember, I don't want you to tell anyone else. So do you know where he moved to?"

"You really got it bad for Rippy. Can't blame you though, he's a nice guy."

Ashley wanted to shake the woman. If Gloria had the information, she needed to spit it out.

"Just tell me—do you know?"

"He don't live with his folks no more. He's got a trailer up on Bullinger Road."

She was familiar with the area. There were miles of trailers on that road.

"Where exactly?"

"You know the Medfords' farm? It's the trailer on the right just past their barn."

As an image of the location popped into her mind, Ashley jumped up from her chair.

"Tell Nathan that I'm sorry I ran out before he got back, but I really need to go."

Gloria shook her head, a look of surprise on her face.

"I ain't never seen you this worked up over a man."

She didn't have time to reply to the comment. Ashley flew through the door of the bar and raced into the parking lot.

She had to get to Beth before it was too late.

CHAPTER THIRTY SIX

Ashley slowed the sedan just as the Medford family's barn popped into view. She'd driven to Bullinger Road in record time, breaking all the speed limits along the way. As she rolled past Rippy's mailbox, she scanned his driveway, searching for his car, wondering if he was at home. She didn't see any vehicles and no lights shone in the trailer's windows. If Beth was there, it was quite possible that she was alone.

There had been no word yet from Daniel. Ashley assumed that meant he was still dealing with TBI business in Briarwood. She wondered if he'd had a chance to read her text message and whether an agent was already on the way to Rippy's house. But there was no time left to wait for backup from the TBI. And given Rippy's job as a deputy, she couldn't risk phoning the sheriff's office. While she had no evidence to link Deputy Kevin McConnell—Rippy's ride-along partner—to the crimes, she couldn't rule out the idea that the two might be partners in more than just law enforcement. Although it felt like a stretch, there remained a slight chance that Kevin could be involved in the deaths of Sarah and Violet.

Her only choice was to go it alone. If Beth was tied up in Rippy's trailer, Ashley had to save her.

A wave of sorrow washed through Ashley's heart as she realized that Beth was likely already dead. If Rippy had stuck to his previous schedule, he would have murdered the woman early that morning. It was quite possible they just hadn't found Beth's body yet. She could be lying in a remote area of the county, vulnerable to the wildlife. It might be weeks before they found what was left of her.

Ashley remembered that a small cemetery shouldered the road just ahead on the right. She wheeled the sedan onto the gravel parking area and killed the engine. The thought that her car might appear suspicious parked at the graveyard at night flickered in her brain, but then she reminded herself that this was Laurel County. Teenagers here utilized cemeteries as make-out spots and places to drink and smoke weed. The locals probably wouldn't give her sedan a second look.

Reaching into the back seat, she grabbed a black jacket—heavier than her denim trucker—and slipped it on. According to her sedan's instrument panel, autumn had chilled the mountain air to thirty-nine degrees. She stuffed her cell phone and a flashlight into the pockets.

Dread filled her soul as she thought about what she might find inside the trailer. She recalled the conversation she'd had with Violet's younger sister. Eva had asked whether Violet had been tortured. Ashley hoped she wasn't about to enter a house of horrors. She took a deep breath and hopped out of the car.

Guided by the bright moonlight, she trotted along the side of the road toward Rippy's place. The lot where the trailer rested had once been part of a cornfield. There were no trees to hide behind, nothing to camouflage her arrival. She'd have to dart up the side of the property and then make a beeline for the mobile home. She just prayed the man wasn't home, staring out one of the windows.

The ditch flanking the road fell deep, but the girth was narrow. Ashley jumped across and ran, skirting the wire fencing that bordered the cattle pasture to the left of Rippy's property. As she drew even with the trailer, she stopped and knelt next to a fence post.

The cold air morphed her breath into fog as Ashley surveyed the land, searching for movement. The single-wide mobile home sat still and quiet. She glanced back toward the road. There were no headlights approaching and no audible hum from a vehicle engine. She rose and sped toward the shelter of the wooden front porch.

The bottom step creaked under the weight of Ashley's foot. She froze in place and listened. After a few seconds—hearing nothing—she crept to the double window and peered inside the trailer. Moonlight revealed the shape of a sectional sofa in the living room. She couldn't make out anything else.

Leaving the porch, Ashley skulked along the front side of the building toward the window at the end. A pair of closed blinds met her, blocking her view into the room. She rounded the mobile home's corner and climbed onto the rear deck. The window here afforded her a view into a hallway. The angle of the moon highlighted a utility closet with open bi-folding doors. The closet housed a washer and dryer, nestled side-by-side.

Ashley paused at the back door. Should she knock, or should she return to the front door? What if Rippy answered? What excuse would she give him for showing up at his house unannounced? She needed to keep the fact that she knew the man was a murderer hidden. She couldn't let him get the upper hand.

If Beth was inside, she would hear Ashley knocking. If the woman was alone, maybe she would call out and let her presence be known. If that happened, Ashley would have a solid reason to break the door down.

Balling her hand into a fist, she pounded on the rear door.

She waited and listened for movement—for a scream—inside.

Nothing. She wrapped her fingers around the knob and twisted. To Ashley's surprise, the door popped open.

An eerie sensation engulfed her. Was she standing at the gate to hell?

Rooted at the threshold, Ashley drew her Smith & Wesson. Should she go inside? Did she have the legal right?

The suspicion that someone needed help inside of a dwelling was legal grounds for entering. Odds remained high that Beth lay bound and gagged in one of the trailer's rooms. The woman could be unconscious. Drugged. And if Beth was here, it was definitely against her will.

Ashley had no choice but to go inside. Beth's life was more important than protocol.

Stepping into the hallway, Ashley paused and listened, checking the air for the scent she would never forget. The smell of human decay.

"Beth?" she called out. "Are you here? It's Ashley Hope."

Silence filled the mobile home.

Keeping her back to the wall, Ashley edged to her right into the living room. Aside from the furnishings, the space and the adjoining kitchen appeared to be empty. She moved back through the hallway and entered a bedroom. Only one window graced the room, the blinds closed, blocking out the moon's glow. Ashley switched on her Maglite and swept the beam across the small space.

A desk rested against the far wall, a wooden bookcase to her right. She didn't see a computer. Rippy most likely owned a laptop. He probably had it with him. She checked the closet. Winter apparel—a heavy coat, a couple of jackets, and some flannel shirts—hung from the rod.

At the end of the hallway, past the laundry closet and an empty bathroom, Ashley found a second bedroom. The beam from her flashlight revealed a queen-sized bed and a wooden chest of drawers. The closet held nothing more than clothing.

Beth wasn't there.

Ashley felt a mixture of relief and fear. Relief that she hadn't found her old classmate's body, and fear that Beth had been murdered in one of Laurel County's many forests. She hoped for a third option: that the woman was still alive and being held at another location.

As she returned to the hallway, Ashley glanced into the utility closet. A plastic basket—piled high with laundry—topped the dryer. A garment that trailed over the side of the basket caught her eye. The long-sleeved shirt sparked a memory. The distinctive plaid cotton fabric appeared identical to one she'd studied online.

A shirt manufactured by Z.L. Holt.

Directing her flashlight toward the garment, she inspected every inch. The silver-colored buttons—stamped with the company's name—that dotted the shirt's placket matched the one found at Violet's house. Ashley slipped each button on the front of the garment into its corresponding hole. They were all there.

She realized that shirts were often sold with extra buttons. Did Rippy repair the garment? Or would Ashley's suspicions prove to be unfounded? All the evidence she had linking her old classmate to the abductions of the women remained circumstantial. Was her gut instinct wrong? Had she accused an innocent man?

Wondering whether she'd jumped to all the wrong conclusions, she slid her hand down the right sleeve of the shirt. A jolt of reality hit her as she looked at the cuff.

A blue thread dangled from the fabric. A thread that had once secured a button.

Her instincts had proved true. The shirt's missing button sealed the case in Ashley's mind, removed all of her doubts. Rippy had murdered Sarah and Violet. Ashley needed to get out of the trailer before he returned. But more important, she needed to figure out where he had taken Beth.

When she got back to the cemetery, she'd text Daniel and let him know what she'd found. She was pretty sure the agent would be able to secure a warrant for Rippy's arrest. Once she received confirmation that her text had been delivered, she'd head back to Mack's bar. Hopefully Nathan and Gloria would still be there. She'd fill them in on the truth about Rippy. They seemed to know a lot about her old classmate. Maybe they had information that could help her locate Beth.

Ashley prayed the woman was still alive.

She pulled Rippy's back door closed, flew off of the deck, and raced back toward the cemetery.

CHAPTER THIRTY SEVEN

Rippy flipped up the bolt handle of the rifle and pulled it back. He pressed five cartridges into the magazine, pushed the bolt forward, and chambered the final round. He had everything set to go at first light in the morning. For a moment—a weak moment—he'd almost changed his mind. Had almost talked himself into keeping Beth for a week or two. However, he'd since realized that would be a mistake. She'd tried to charm him with her offer of cake—and the implied offer of other things—but he knew how she worked. She was leading him on, just as she had in high school.

She wanted to make a fool out of him again.

He glanced out the county SUV's passenger window, scanning the parking lot of the minimart. Sheriff Vance had driven by a few minutes earlier, setting his nerves on edge. Everybody was searching for the missing veterinary student. There was even a poster featuring her photo plastered on the door of the convenience store. He'd smiled when he'd seen it.

Knowing that she would soon share his bed.

He stowed the rifle in the rack between the front seats and checked his minimart haul. Three different kinds of chips, a pack of peanuts, a few candy bars, two bottles of water, and of course—root beer. Beth hadn't been fed all day, and she'd obviously be hungry. He knew she'd appreciate real food from the diner, but he'd eaten dinner there. He couldn't afford to draw suspicions by ordering another meal. There should be something here that she would eat.

Prisoners deserved a final meal before their execution.

Too bad Holly had missed hers. But his former girlfriend hadn't deserved the granting of any final wishes. A female infinitely more vile than Sarah, Violet, or Beth, she had publicly humiliated him. At the club. In front of his friends.

It surprised him how easy it had been to kill Holly. Without her shoes, she couldn't run fast enough to get away. He'd taken his time. Fired several rounds, missing on purpose, just to instill fear into her heart. She'd begged him to spare her life. Promised that she would change her ways and admit in front of his friends that she'd been wrong—that everything had been her fault. His response had been to laugh in her face. He was the one in control. He'd never let her make a dunce of him again.

Rippy remembered the satisfaction and pleasure that had flooded his soul when he'd fired the final bullet into the woman's brain.

To further exert his power over her, he'd denied her a proper burial—denied her meddling family the closure of knowing what had happened to Holly. As luck would have it, the woman had died mere yards from an old abandoned well near the ruins of what had once been a homestead in Tucker Holler. He'd dumped her body into the well, never to be found.

After Holly's disappearance became known, he'd played the role of a heartbroken ex-lover-turned-friend like an academy-award-winning actor. Garnering sympathy from everybody around him. Rippy was such a nice guy—a friend to all who knew him. Willing to give you his last dollar if you needed it. Nobody suspected him of the crime. Not even Holly's parents.

It was his success in pulling off Holly's murder that had encouraged him to right the other wrongs he'd suffered. To settle the score with the other women in his life who'd used him for their amusement. Who'd made him into a fool.

From now on, Rippy would make sure he always got the last laugh.

He started the SUV's engine and shifted the transmission into reverse. He had one more thing left to do before he returned to the RV. Before he could enjoy the night of fun he had planned. He hoped it wouldn't take long.

Beth was waiting for him.

CHAPTER THIRTY EIGHT

Jumping at the sudden sound of her cell phone ringing, Ashley almost veered off the road. She'd been driving on autopilot since leaving Rippy's trailer. Her mind had raced, focused on one thing alone—sorting through her high school memories, trying to figure out where the man had taken Beth.

Reaching into the passenger seat, she tried to grab her phone while keeping her eyes on the traffic in front of her. But her fingertips bumped the case and her cell flew into the floorboard, too far away to grasp. The phone jangled a second time. It could be Daniel. She had to answer the call before it switched to voicemail.

The diner sat to her right. She swerved into the parking lot, unfastened her seatbelt, and stretched toward the passenger floorboard. She snatched up her cell just as the third ring hit her ears. A quick glance at the screen confirmed her hunch. It was Daniel.

"Hello?"

"Are you okay?" he asked, his voice filled with concern.

She guessed that although she'd been successful in her search for evidence at Rippy's house, the agent had probably worried that she'd put herself in danger. Most likely felt that she should have waited for the TBI instead of busting into the trailer alone. But what if Beth had been there? She couldn't sit back and wait if there was even the slightest chance that she could save the woman's life.

"Yeah, don't worry about me—I'm fine. We just need to get Rippy into custody and find out where he's holding Beth."

She heard a siren blaring in the background. She assumed it was coming from Daniel's vehicle. He must be racing back to Laurel County.

"You sure he's our guy?"

There was no doubt in her mind.

"I'm just as sure that Rippy killed Sarah and Violet as I am of my own name. He's the only person who we can prove is connected to all three women. And his button was found at the exact spot where Violet was abducted. On top of that, he knew that Sarah's boyfriend was in the county jail and that she would be home alone on the day she was abducted. His ex-girlfriend—who has light brown hair and blue eyes—has been missing for months. My gut tells me that I'm right, Daniel. You have to believe me."

"It's not that I don't believe you. We just have to be careful. This guy's a cop. We don't want to accuse him unless we're positive."

She realized it was a sticky situation and she would never do anything that would jeopardize the career of a dedicated police officer. But Rippy wasn't an honest cop. He was a killer. And she knew it with every fiber of her being.

"The evidence—even though it's all circumstantial—is more than we've had against any other suspect. It should be enough to justify arresting Rippy for suspicion of murder."

"Well right now, I can only get a search warrant," he told her. "And it's in the works. The arrest warrant will come after we collect the evidence. After we're sure we've got a case."

Ashley felt disappointed, but she understood how the justice system worked.

"Do you have any idea how long that will take?"

"I put a rush on it. Maybe an hour. Where are you?"

At this juncture, an hour felt like a lifetime to Ashley.

"I'm sitting in my car in the parking lot of the diner—why?"

She wondered whether there was somewhere else Daniel needed her to be.

"Because this is the third time I've called," he said, his voice sounding strained. "I was worried."

For a split second, Ashley thought she heard something in his tone. Something more than just normal concern. But she pushed the thought aside, telling herself that she was only hearing what she wanted to hear. Not what was really there.

"I had to drive through a valley to get back to town from Rippy's place," she explained. "I guess I lost the cell signal."

"You shouldn't have rushed into the trailer alone. If he'd been there …" The agent's voice trailed off for a moment. "Just don't take that kind of risk in the future."

She appreciated Daniel's concern, but she'd had no other option.

"There was a good chance that Beth was tied up inside—that she needed my help. I couldn't just walk away."

"I get that. It's just—"

The agent didn't have time to finish his sentence. He was interrupted.

Voices from Daniel's police radio echoed through her phone. She could only make out a few of the words, but she heard enough to know it was regarding the search warrant.

"An agent's en route to Rippy's right now," Daniel informed her. "We should have the warrant by the time he gets there."

"Okay. I'll head back over to Mack's and talk to my cousin and his wife and find out if they have any ideas about where Beth could be."

She just hoped Nathan and Gloria would still be at the bar. There was no time left to try and track them down.

"I hate that it took so long to get back to you," the agent said. "But I just got your texts about twenty minutes ago. I got called into another meeting—high-level security. They made me leave my phone outside the door. I tried calling you as soon as I read the messages."

"I knew there was a good reason for the delay—that it was the TBI's fault and not yours."

A firsthand witness to Daniel's dedication to his job, she'd realized that responding had been out of his control—that he would reply as soon as he was able.

"We got some new information. You know those tire treads we lifted at Violet's crime scene? They're from the front wheel of a small tractor. A John Deere. So they're probably not connected to the murder."

Ashley couldn't imagine Rippy carrying Violet to the field on a tractor. The tire tracks had likely been made by a farmer who lived in the area. John Deeres were about as common as barns in Laurel County. There was one in every pasture.

"Well at least we have the button that Eva found that connects Rippy to Violet."

"Probably hair and fibers too."

She realized that the TBI's forensic team had collected hordes of microscopic evidence that would no doubt trace back to the man.

"I'm on my way," Daniel assured her. "Go talk to your cousin. But be careful. And watch your back."

Ashley tapped off the call. She'd been disappointed to hear that the tire tracks weren't from Rippy's vehicle. An image of the field where Violet's body had been found popped into Ashley's mind. Except for the bend where the John Deere's tracks had been found, there was no other viable location for a vehicle to stop, pull off the road, and park for any length of time. The shoulder that flanked both sides of the highway was too narrow.

A memory surfaced and a realization struck her.

It had been years since she and her brothers had ridden four-wheelers through the area where Violet had been murdered, but she was pretty sure she now knew how Rippy had transported the woman to the field.

She shifted her sedan into gear and pulled into a parking space next to the main entrance of the diner. The location should be close enough to access the eatery's public Wi-Fi network. The manager had posted the password—*#1finestdiner*—on a large sign behind the serving counter. Not the most original password, but one that was hard to forget.

Hoping that she would be able to spot what she was looking for, she hoisted her backpack from the rear of her sedan and brought it to rest on the passenger seat. She pulled out her laptop and booted it up.

It took a few seconds to log onto the diner's network. Once she was in, Ashley clicked on her browser and pulled up the satellite map for Laurel County. She zoomed in the view around the highway where Violet had been murdered.

It was just as Ashley remembered.

In the forest behind the field where Violet had met her death, Ashley could see a distinct thin line running north to south. A break in the tree cover. It was an old logging road. Not labeled on any map.

Sarah's murder had also taken place near a logging road.

Because of the tire treads, they—Ashley, Daniel, and the TBI's forensic team—had thought that Violet had been running from the direction of the bend in the highway. But they'd been wrong. The woman had been fleeing the forest.

Rippy had probably held both Sarah and Violet captive in a tent he'd set up next to the logging roads. The roads cut through remote areas that were seldom traversed. A lot of the land surrounding them, especially the areas where the timber and been cut and trees replanted, was now state owned. About ten years prior, the land had been closed to hunters. The only people she knew for sure who still utilized the roads were the employees of the Tennessee Department of Agriculture's forestry division. And they only checked the areas a couple of times per year. Unless you were a long-time local, you wouldn't even know the roads existed.

Was Beth being held hostage in a tent in the forest?

It seemed unlikely that Rippy would choose to hide Beth on one of the two roads near where he'd killed Sarah and Violet. But Ashley remembered there was a third logging road, on the other end of Laurel County.

She zoomed out the map and then homed in on the area where she thought the road was located. And there it was—clear as day. A thin, straight break in the tree cover. This time the line ran east to west. The third logging road.

Was Beth there now? Was she still alive?

Ashley had to find out. She had to make sure Rippy didn't murder another innocent woman. She'd made a promise to Beth's parents to do everything in her power to bring their daughter home safely.

And that was a promise she intended to keep.

Grabbing her cell phone, she typed out a text message to Daniel filling him in and letting him know where she was going. If she gave him the information in a phone call, she knew he'd be worried about her heading to the logging road alone. He'd want her to wait on him. But they didn't have the luxury of time.

She had to get to Beth—now.

Ashley decided not to hit *send* until she reached the logging road. That way, it would be too late for Daniel to stop her. After returning her laptop to the rear seat of her sedan, she backed out of the parking space.

"Hold on, Beth," she said aloud.

She circled out of the diner's parking lot and sped toward the logging road.

Ashley just hoped she'd reach Beth before it was too late.

CHAPTER THIRTY NINE

Apprehension grew in Ashley's chest as she steered her sedan off the highway and onto the old dirt logging road. Somewhere up ahead she hoped to find a camping tent with Beth inside—alive and well—but she feared she might be too late. Rippy could be here at this very moment. He may have already killed Beth.

Shifting her car into park, Ashley grabbed her phone. She read through the text she'd composed to Daniel while in the parking lot at the diner. The message included detailed directions to the logging road. Satisfied that he would be able to find her, she hit the *send* arrow and then switched her phone to silent mode.

Glancing through the windshield at the path cut by her headlights, she realized Rippy would be alerted to her presence well before she reached his campsite. But she couldn't make the trek on foot—there wasn't time. The logging road stretched several miles long and he'd most likely placed his camp at the far end. She gazed up at the night sky, gauging the amount of moonlight that filtered through the branches of the trees hugging the road. There was only one choice. Ashley killed her headlights. If she hoped to rescue Beth, she would have to proceed guided only by the moon.

The tall weeds striping the center of the old road scraped the undercarriage of her car as she rolled forward, her field of vision shaded in spots by the canopy of trees that had yet to yield their leaves to the autumn air. A flash of movement caught her eye and she slammed on the brakes. The shape of a buck—antlers held high—crossed her path. A thought flickered in her mind. If it had been Rippy in front of her car, would she have run him over? Although she hated the man for what he'd done, the answer was no. She wanted him to stand trial in front of a jury. For him to be convicted and face either life in prison or the death penalty, whichever the judge deemed appropriate.

The road ran straight, but potholes littered the surface. As she continued on, Ashley mashed the accelerator, increasing her speed. The sedan bounced hard enough to jar her teeth, but she had no choice.

Rippy had killed both Sarah and Violet on the mornings following their abductions. If Beth was still alive, she was living on borrowed time.

Up ahead to her right, just off the road, Ashley caught sight of a large white object reflecting the moonlight. An old battered RV. The cab of the motorhome sat facing her.

A knot of fear formed in her chest when she realized she'd been right about the logging road. She knew that Beth—or the woman's body—was inside the RV. Was Rippy here as well?

She pulled her sedan off of the left side of the road, as far as she dared, resting beneath the branches of a large pine tree. She wanted to try and camouflage her car—to hide it from Rippy—but at the same time, she worried about getting her tires stuck. She realized she might have to make a quick getaway.

Ashley cut the sedan's engine. Making sure the car's interior light was switched off, she slid out of the driver's seat, careful to press the door closed without making too much noise. She stood still and listened. A soft breeze rustled through the boughs of the pine, but she didn't hear any footsteps.

Drawing her Smith & Wesson, she crept toward the old, dusty RV. No lights shone from the inside. What appeared to be brown cardboard covered the interior side of the windows of the living compartment. All was quiet. The only sound was her own heartbeat pounding in her ears. She inched toward the motorhome's cab. She peered through the passenger window, but she couldn't see anything beyond the two front seats. Circling around to the other side of the cab, she looked through the driver's window. The view from this angle remained the same.

Ashley tried the door handle. Locked. Looping back around the front of the vehicle, she checked the passenger door. It was locked as well. She assumed the door to the living compartment was secured also. Testing the latch, she found out she was right. The only option was to break in.

Scouring the ground along the logging road, she found a large rock with a pointed end. She holstered her weapon, shielded her eyes with her left arm, and slammed the rock against the passenger window. The glass cracked, forming a white line, but it didn't break. Using all her strength, she whacked the window again. This time, the aging glass collapsed. She knocked out the remaining shards and then hooked her arm through the window and pulled up the door handle.

Her breath caught in her throat as the passenger door popped open.

She switched on her Maglite and drew her Smith & Wesson.

Easing into the passenger seat, she turned toward the living compartment. The beam of her flashlight cut through the gloom, revealing cabinets with a miniature stove and sink to her left and a built-in table flanked by bench seats to her right.

"Beth, are you in here? It's Ashley Hope—from high school," she called out.

"Ashley!" a frightened voice screamed. "I'm back here. Help me!"

Relief flooded Ashley's soul and tears sprang to her eyes. She'd made it on time. Beth was alive.

Realizing she could be walking into a trap—that Rippy could be hiding in the shadows—she readied her pistol and inched along the narrow aisle between the cabinets. A built-in bed rested in the rear left corner of the living compartment. Beth lay on the thin mattress, her arms raised above her head. Ashley was grateful to see that the woman was fully clothed.

She directed the flashlight onto her former classmate's hands. Thick plastic zip ties secured Beth's wrists to a heavy metal chain that had been bolted to the cabinet above. Ashley holstered her weapon. The only way to free Beth was to cut the zip ties.

"I need to find a knife or scissors or something else that's sharp to cut you loose," Ashley told the woman. "Have you seen anything like that in the RV?"

"He's got a hunting knife, but he takes it with him."

Ashley's hopes sank as she realized Rippy probably hadn't left anything sharp enough to cut the plastic behind in the motorhome. He'd likely been afraid that Beth would somehow get the upper hand and stab him.

"Are you okay—did he hurt you?"

"He drugged me with something. I think it may have been a surgical anesthetic. He hasn't hit me or raped me. Not yet. But I could tell he was planning to."

Ashley was glad to hear that Beth was physically okay, but she knew the woman would most likely be left with deep emotional scars.

To the right of the bed, a door yawned open. Ashley panned her light across the space. It was a bathroom, the size of a tiny closet. Noting the storage cupboard hanging on the wall, she stepped across the threshold. She searched the shelves of the cupboard, hoping to find a razor or a small pair of scissors, but the only things inside were first aid supplies.

"There's nothing in the bathroom that I can use to cut the ties," she told Beth. "Maybe I'll find something in one of the cabinets."

"Hurry," the woman replied. "I'm afraid he'll be back any minute."

Ashley feared the same. She rifled through the drawer next to the stove where cutlery would normally be stored, but all she found were plastic forks and spoons. She was about to push the drawer closed when the flashlight beam hit something in the back right corner. Behind a package of birthday candles, she spotted a disposable lighter.

She could melt the plastic zip ties.

As her fingers closed around the lighter, she heard a noise to her left. Jerking her hand from the drawer, she reached for her pistol, but it was too late.

A heavy object slammed into the side of Ashley's head, shooting pain through her skull.

Darkness pushed in around her as she fell to the floor.

CHAPTER FORTY

Ashley struggled to stay conscious as she felt herself being dragged across the floor of the RV. Her brain screamed at her to fight, but the message failed to reach her arms and legs. It was as though a switch had been flipped, turning off her ability to control her own body.

She felt Rippy lifting her up off her feet as dizziness overcame her, racking her stomach with nausea.

A light switched on overhead. The sudden brightness stung her eyes. She looked down, away from the light, and saw her hands on the table in front of her. She realized her wrists had been zip tied to a metal ring.

She pressed her eyes closed as bile rose in her throat. Her head throbbed. She wondered what he had hit her with. It was possible she might have a concussion.

"Nice of you to join us, Ashley," Rippy said, his tone heavy with sarcasm.

Ashley opened her mouth to speak, but she couldn't seem to put her thoughts together, couldn't get her words straight.

"TBI," she finally pushed out, the letters feeling strange on her tongue. "They know … they know who you are."

Rippy laughed.

She looked up at him, forcing her eyes to focus. At first she thought she might be dreaming. That she had fallen unconscious after all, but then her vision began to clear. A clown stared back at her. Spiky red hair and a bulbous red nose. Rippy had on a rubber Halloween mask.

"And who do they think I am?" the clown taunted, as though he was convinced he was safe.

"You're Rippy. But the TBI knows your real name—Deputy Troy Luckadoo."

Ashley heard Beth gasp. It was obvious the woman had just learned the identity of the man who had held her captive.

Troy ripped off the mask and threw it onto the table.

An expression of fury replaced the hideous clown face.

"I'm gonna enjoy killing you, Ashley."

"No!" Beth screamed from the bed.

Troy turned on his heel and marched toward the woman.

"Guess we don't have time to get to know each other after all," he said to Beth. "But we can still have a little fun."

Fear raced down Ashley's spine as she saw Troy pull a hunting knife from a sheath on his side.

"Don't hurt her!" Ashley heard herself yell, her brain still out of sync with her voice.

There was nothing she could do to stop him. She was bound to the table with no way to escape.

"I'm not gonna hurt her," Troy stated. "I'm gonna let her go."

"Let Ashley go too," Beth said. "And we won't tell anyone what you've done. You can get away."

"Do you want to live?" Troy asked the woman, seeming to ignore her plea.

"Of course I want to live, and so does Ashley. Let us both go."

The deputy chuckled. "Maybe I will. But you're going first. And if you try anything stupid, I won't hesitate to ram this knife in your gut. You understand?"

Beth didn't answer.

"I said, do you understand?"

"Yes," the woman replied. "I won't do anything stupid."

Ashley watched as he cut the plastic ties binding Beth's wrists with the hunting knife.

"Troy, you have me now to use as a hostage," Ashley said. "Set Beth free and I'll help you negotiate with the TBI."

Ashley decided to use his given name, hoping he would listen to her. She recalled that when the deputy had reintroduced himself at Sarah's crime scene, he'd used his real name, Troy, not Rippy—the name he'd received in high school and the one that would have brought back the most memories. She guessed he hated the moniker. That it was still a source of humiliation. But as he had done in high school, he likely pretended to embrace the name, refusing to let anyone know that it galled him. If she showed him the respect of addressing him as Troy, maybe she could reason with him.

"Shut up," the deputy barked.

"Think about what you're doing, Troy," Ashley urged. "You can stop all of this now and I'll get you the help you need."

The deputy glared at her. He pushed Beth down the aisle toward the door of the RV. Ashley glanced at the woman's feet and noticed she wasn't wearing shoes.

"Beth," she called out. "Run as fast as you can because he's planning to shoot you."

"I told you to shut up," Troy warned.

She realized he had a rifle hanging over his shoulder. It had probably been the butt of the weapon that he had slammed into the side of her head.

Troy shoved Beth down the steps and then out of the RV, closing the door behind them.

Ashley tugged at her restraints. She sawed at the zip tie on her right wrist against the metal ring. She knew it would take hours for the friction to generate enough heat to soften the plastic. But what other choice did she have now?

Better options had been open to her before Troy had arrived. But she'd acted like a rookie again—had made the all the wrong choices. Why had she holstered her weapon? She should have just sat next to Beth on the bed, guarding the woman, her Smith & Wesson aimed at the RV's cab. Then Troy wouldn't have been able to sneak up on her. And she should have texted Daniel sooner. If she had, maybe he—or another TBI agent—would be here by now.

As it stood, her mistakes would likely get Beth killed.

A wave of dizziness hit Ashley as she slid down, bracing her feet on the opposite bench. She pressed her eyes closed and willed the world to stand still. Pushing against the bench, she pulled hard on the zip tie, trying to stretch the plastic as she scraped it back and forth against the metal ring.

The tie bit into her flesh, but she gritted her teeth and ignored the pain.

Somehow, she had to get free. And fast.

CHAPTER FORTY ONE

As he hopped down from the door of the battered RV, Troy yanked Beth's arm and pulled her around to face him. In the glow of the moonlight, he could see the fear in her eyes. Like that of a condemned criminal being led to the electric chair. Her panicked expression made him smile. She deserved to be afraid. Deserved what was coming to her.

Although she'd been a pro at pretending, Beth had never cared for him. She'd played him for a fool. He'd suffered her treachery years before, but the memory still stung as if it were yesterday. She had teased him and led him on, brushing her hand against his arm—acting as though it had been an accident. But he'd known it was on purpose.

Charming him with her coy smile, she'd lured him in with those big blue eyes, calling him Troy instead of the stupid nickname the morons in the school had foisted upon him. She'd even sat next to him in the cafeteria at lunch. Had shared half of the turkey sandwich her mother had packed in the small, pink, soft-sided cooler. She had tricked him into believing that he mattered to her. That she wanted to be with him. But when he'd leaned in to kiss her, she'd pushed him away.

"*Stop it!*" she'd yelled, disgust on her face.

It had all been a joke. A trap. A game to humiliate him.

Her voice had echoed through the cafeteria. Everyone had turned to stare. She had made a mockery of him in front of all of his friends.

But now, who would be the fool?

It was time to play a game of his own. A game of revenge. He'd be the one leading her on this time. He'd make her believe that he was setting her free. That she was going home. And then he'd hunt her down and kill her like he'd killed Sarah and Violet.

And when he was finished with Beth, he'd come back for Ashley. The sweet girl he remembered from high school had obviously grown up to be a nosy, high-minded bitch. He'd make the TBI consultant sorry that she'd interrupted his plans.

Troy slid the blade of the hunting knife along the curve of Beth's cheek, the cold metal glinting in the moonlight.

“Do you want to live?” he asked, taunting her.

“Yes,” she said, her blue eyes wide.

“Then you’ll do what I say. I’m gonna let you go. But you can’t tell anyone what I did, or I’ll kill your parents first, and then kill you. Understand?”

She nodded, eyeing the rifle that dangled from his shoulder.

He laughed, his breath a puff of fog billowing in the cold night air. The jig was up. Beth knew she didn’t stand a chance. That he was toying with her. But it didn’t matter. The hunt was the fun part. The fact that she had already realized that she wouldn’t survive the night didn’t take away the thrill.

It would be harder for him this time—he didn’t have a night scope—but he’d still be able to find Beth beneath the silvery glow of the moon. The darkness actually made the hunt more interesting—more of a challenge. Which would ultimately lead to a more satisfying ending.

Once he let Beth go, he knew she wouldn’t get far. And he wasn’t worried about the TBI. That agent—Lansing—wasn’t even in town. He’d gone to Briarwood and likely wouldn’t return until the morning.

Ashley had no doubt been bluffing when she’d said the agent knew Troy was responsible for the murders. If that were true—if Troy were even a suspect—he would have sensed it from the sheriff and the other deputies. Especially from his partner, Deputy Kevin McConnell. The man had never been able to keep a secret. And if the TBI had an inkling that Troy was the killer, they would never have allowed Ashley to come here alone.

He didn’t know how, but the TBI consultant had stumbled onto the RV and had deciphered his identity by herself. Without backup. And she would pay for it.

Troy tightened the fingers of his left hand around Beth’s arm.

“I didn’t hear your answer.”

“I understand,” she said, her voice shaky. “I won’t tell anyone what you’ve done.”

He smiled. They both knew Beth would never get the chance to talk.

“Good girl.”

Pushing her forward, he led the woman across the old logging road. She slipped in the tall weeds that had sprouted along the center of the lane, her bare feet likely numb from the cold. He jerked her up and shoved her toward the edge of the forest.

"When I say *go*, you run," he told her. "Like your life depends on it."

He chuckled. "Because it does."

Excitement raced through Troy's veins as he steered Beth in the direction he wanted her to flee—into the area he'd already mapped out—and propelled her toward the tree line.

"Go!" he shouted.

As Beth raced off into the woods, he stuffed the hunting knife back into its sheath and pulled the rifle from his shoulder.

The game had begun.

Smiling, he strode into the forest.

CHAPTER FORTY TWO

Ashley tested the zip tie fastened around her right wrist. She'd managed to stretch the plastic a bit as she'd sawed it against the metal ring bolted to the table in the RV, but still not enough to slip her hand out. Panic filled her heart. She knew she was running out of time.

She jumped as she heard the door of the motorhome burst open.

"TBI!" a familiar voice shouted.

Ashley's hopes soared. It was Daniel. He'd received her text. The agent entered the RV with his weapon drawn.

"You have to go and find Beth before Troy kills her," she told him. "He's chasing her through the forest right now."

"Did he hurt you?" Daniel wanted to know, an expression of angst plastered on his face.

The agent pulled a small folding knife from his pocket and sliced through the zip ties that bound her to the table.

"No, I'm fine," she said, her temple still throbbing.

She didn't want to tell him that Troy had hit her in the head, that she thought she might have a concussion. She wanted him focused on saving Beth.

With her arms free, she scooted along the bench and out from beneath the table. As she stood, Ashley noticed for the first time that Troy had taken her gun. She kept her mouth shut. If Daniel found out she was unarmed, he'd likely make her stay behind, locked in his vehicle.

Following at the agent's heels, she rushed down the steps and hopped from the door of the RV onto the ground.

The crack of a rifle echoed through the trees. Troy was firing at Beth.

"I'd like to kill that worthless sack of scum," Daniel said.

But Ashley knew that like her, he wouldn't. Not unless the agent had no choice.

They ran toward the sound of the gunfire, Daniel outpacing her, but not by much. The cold night air filled her lungs, clearing her head. The nausea had left her. She pushed herself harder, catching up to the agent.

Ashley heard a muffled cry behind her—coming from the opposite direction as the gunshot blast. In the darkness, Beth must have circled around and headed back toward the logging road. It had been daylight when Troy had murdered Sarah and Violet. She doubted he had a night scope on his rifle. Beth might be able to hide from him in the shadows.

Daniel stopped short and met her gaze. He must have heard the scream as well.

"I'll go after Troy," he told her. "You find Beth."

Ashley nodded and took off toward the sound of the cry. The underbrush snagged the legs of her jeans as she raced through the forest. She was thankful that Troy hadn't taken her hiking boots. As she wound her way around a large cedar, a wave of dizziness hit her. She stumbled, catching herself just before she fell. She inched forward and leaned against the trunk of an oak, trying to regain her balance, trying to compel the world to stop spinning.

As she pressed her eyes closed, another gunshot split the air.

Her brain cloudy, she couldn't determine the direction from which the blast had come, or how far away Troy had been when he'd fired. But she feared he was closer—that he was gaining on Beth.

Another thought struck her—one she didn't want to consider. What if Troy had fired that shot at Daniel? The agent could be wounded. He could be bleeding out in the forest. Or he might already be dead. If he'd been shot, it would be her fault. She was the one who'd charged into the RV without backup. And if she lost Daniel …

Ashley forced the horrible image from her mind. She had to push forward.

As the world around her settled back into its proper place—the ground below her and the sky above—Ashley plowed ahead. She couldn't let her thoughts drift back to what could be happening with Daniel, or she'd drive herself crazy. She had to focus all of her energy on finding Beth.

With pain still pulsing through her head, she sped between the trees. When a third shot rang out, she slowed her pace, trying to gauge the distance of the blast. This one definitely sounded closer. Troy seemed to be advancing at an alarming rate. How long before he caught up with Beth?

Cursing the deputy under her breath, Ashley crossed over a felled tree next to an outcropping of limestone.

"Ashley," a voice whispered from behind her.

She turned around and saw Beth, her back pressed against the large slab of rock.

"Are you okay?" she asked the woman. "I heard you scream."

"I stepped in a groundhog hole and twisted my ankle. I can't run anymore."

There were several broken branches lying near the felled tree, snapped off when the trunk had crashed down. Ashley picked up a long branch and tested its strength. It was sturdy enough to use as a crutch. She helped Beth stand.

"Here." She held out the branch. "See if you can walk with this, if not, you can put your arm around me and I'll support your weight."

Beth took a few steps with the makeshift crutch.

"It works," she said, a note of triumph in her voice.

Ashley grabbed another branch—shorter and heavier—to use as a weapon, since she didn't have her pistol.

"Come on, let's head back this way, toward the RV," she told Beth, motioning to her right.

She wanted to get the woman into the safety of her sedan.

"How the hell did you get loose?" Troy's voice boomed behind her.

Panic surged in Ashley's chest. She turned around.

The deputy stood just a few feet away, his rifle aimed at her heart.

Ashley dropped the branch and raised her hands. She wanted to step to her right, to put her body between the gun and Beth. But if she moved—even an inch—she feared Troy would pull the trigger.

"There's no reason for you to kill anyone else," she told the deputy. "You have another option—another way out of this mess."

If the man would put down his rifle, she'd help him work out a deal. She could try to get the death penalty taken off the table.

"You think I'm gonna surrender? Think again."

Ashley could feel the hatred radiating from the man's cold eyes.

"Just let Beth go and you and I can talk this out. I can help you if you'll allow me to."

He shook his head. "You know what they do to cops in prison."

She did know. In the general population block, he might not last a week.

"We could work out a deal and try to get you into a segregated block."

"I don't think so. This is the deal: First, I'm gonna kill you. And then I'm gonna finish what I started with Beth."

Ashley heard a noise behind Troy. It was the buck she'd seen earlier on the logging road.

The deputy started to spin around, obviously thinking there was a person sneaking up on him.

Keeping her center of gravity low, Ashley charged. She plowed into Troy, knocking him off his feet. The deputy hit the ground hard. His rifle slipped from his grasp and flew behind him.

Rising to her knees, she scrambled after the gun. Troy grabbed her jacket and pulled her back. He flipped over on top of her, pinning her to the ground.

The deputy's fingers clamped around Ashley's throat.

Her lungs burned as she struggled for air. The man was going to kill her and then he'd kill Beth. He might even kill Daniel—if the agent wasn't already dead.

Out of the corner of her eye she glimpsed movement. Beth slammed the tree branch into Troy's head, knocking him to the side. He climbed off of Ashley and lunged toward Beth. He grabbed the woman's good leg and she tumbled backwards.

Ashley coughed, inhaled deep, and pushed herself up off the ground. She had to stop the deputy before he hurt Beth. Before he killed the woman.

She grabbed the rifle.

When she turned around she saw Troy straddling Beth. The deputy yanked his hunting knife from the sheath on his belt.

"Stop, Troy!" Ashley yelled, aiming the rifle at his heart. "Or I swear, I'll shoot."

She wouldn't let him kill another innocent person.

The deputy glanced at her and smiled. It seemed as though he wanted to be shot. That he would rather die than go to prison. He raised the knife, ready to plunge the blade into Beth's chest.

Beth screamed.

Ashley squeezed the rifle's trigger.

The bullet pierced Troy's heart. His body flopped to the side as the knife slipped from his fingers.

It was over. She hadn't wanted to kill the man, but she'd had no choice. And now, Troy would never be able to hurt anyone ever again.

Beth wriggled out from beneath the deputy's body.

With her ears ringing from the blast of the gunshot, Ashley never heard footsteps approaching, but she felt Daniel's presence at her side.

Thankful that he was still alive, the sudden urge to hug the agent washed over her, but she pushed the feeling aside.

"I saw what happened," Daniel told her. "You did the right thing. I was taking aim at Troy myself right when you pulled the trigger."

He patted her on the arm and then went to help Beth.

As Ashley watched Daniel lift Beth to her feet, an image of Frank and Yvonne Holder popped into her mind. A smile played across her face as she thought about the family being reunited. She'd kept her promise. Beth was safe and she'd be home soon.

Ashley's smile faded as her thoughts switched to the families of Sarah and Violet. There was nothing she could do to erase the pain of their losses, but at least now, the families would receive the truth about what had happened to their loved ones. And they had the solace of knowing that Troy had been stopped.

In just a few weeks, Ashley would graduate from the police academy. She wasn't sure where life would take her, but she knew that she wanted to help other victims like Beth, Sarah, and Violet. She wanted to track down criminals like Troy and get them off of the streets.

The search for Laurel County's serial killer hadn't ended the way she had hoped—with the deputy facing trial. But with Troy's death, justice had been served.

CHAPTER FORTY THREE

Three Weeks Later

A crisp breeze rustled Ashley's hair as she stepped out into the bright sunshine in front of the auditorium on the campus of Highland Rim State University. Her hard work and the long hours of physically demanding training had paid off. She'd graduated from the police academy at the top of her class. The ceremony—which had concluded just a few minutes earlier—had honored thirty-seven graduates whittled down from a starting class of fifty. The number of successful cadets proved the rigors of the course.

As she flitted down the concrete steps of the building, feeling lighter than air, Ashley was met by her former defensive tactics instructor, Sergeant Paul Newell.

The man shook her hand.

"Congratulations," he said in a hearty voice.

"Thank you, sir."

Although she was no longer under the command of the sergeant, the air of respect remained.

"You've got a lot of promise, Hope. And you're tough," he told her, his eyes reflecting his sincerity. "That's the reason I was so hard on you. I knew you could take it. I knew it would make you a better officer."

The compliment surprised her. And she realized for the first time that she was grateful for his method of training. If he hadn't saddled her with the kettlebell—if he hadn't driven home the point of keeping her center of gravity low—she probably wouldn't have been able to tackle Troy and knock him to the ground. The deputy had been twice her size and had completed the same training.

"I appreciate your kind words, sir."

"They're not kind, Hope. They're honest."

Ashley smiled, realizing the man held respect for her as well—even if it was just a small amount.

She glanced across the courtyard and saw her family waiting for her. Shane met her gaze and waved as she strode toward them, his wheelchair angled next to the park bench nestled underneath the branches of a massive oak where her father and Kyle sat.

Ashley's heart warmed as her eyes shifted to the man standing next to her younger brother.

She hadn't asked Daniel to attend her graduation—assuming he'd be too busy to make the hour-and-a-half trip to Cedar View from Briarwood. But the agent had surprised her. And she was glad to see him. She'd been fighting hard to shake the feelings Daniel had kindled within her at the creek, but they were still there. Hidden just below the surface.

Her father rose from the bench.

"I'm proud of you, baby girl," he told her, his eyes sparkling.

"Thank you, Daddy."

Spencer pulled her into a hug. Although she knew he still hadn't fully recovered from his heart attack, his grip felt stronger and a healthy sheen glossed his skin.

Kyle hugged her next.

"Guess this means I'm gonna have to quit speeding," her older brother said, a playful expression on his face. "Don't wanna get a ticket."

"I'll have to find a department that will hire me so I can start writing citations," she teased back.

She glanced over at Daniel and he returned her smile.

Ashley hadn't yet decided where she wanted to work. Sheriff Vance had praised her for saving Beth and had hinted that he wanted her to apply at the Laurel County Sheriff's Department. But she wasn't convinced that replacing Troy would be the best idea. Especially since several of the former deputy's relatives lived in the area. They no doubt hated her for taking the man's life, even though Troy had murdered two women and was suspected of killing a third—his former girlfriend, Holly.

"She ain't gonna let you slide, Kyle," Shane added.

"I believe I saw someone else speeding today—you in your wheelchair."

Her brother had learned to maneuver the chair like a pro and she could tell he was getting stronger every day.

“I got a surprise for you, Ash,” Shane said, a wide grin spreading across his face. “But you gotta close your eyes and don’t open them until I tell you.”

“Okay.”

Ashley pressed her eyes closed and waited. She wondered what her brother had brought her.

“You can open them now,” Shane said, his tone serious.

Joy flooded Ashley’s soul at the sight before her. A two-wheeled walker had been placed in front of Shane’s wheelchair. With a look of determination on his face, her brother grasped the handles of the walker and pushed himself up onto his feet. Although his legs appeared a bit shaky, he took one step forward, and then another. Tears streamed down Ashley’s cheeks as Shane completed a third step.

At that moment, she knew her brother would make it. That he would reclaim his life and live it to the fullest.

“This is the best present anyone has ever given me, Shane,” she said, her voice thick with emotion.

And she meant it.

As Shane pivoted the walker and returned to his wheelchair, Ashley felt Daniel’s hand press against the small of her back. The agent guided her a short distance away from her family as though he wanted to have a private conversation.

“Thank you for coming to my graduation,” she said, touched that he had taken the time out of his schedule.

Daniel’s blue eyes locked with hers and she felt her heart stir.

“I wouldn’t miss it. I got you a little something.”

He held out a gift-wrapped box adorned with a blue ribbon.

“You didn’t have to go to the trouble of getting me a gift.”

She hadn’t even expected him to show up, let alone buy her a present. His thoughtfulness brought a smile to her lips.

“Open it.”

Ashley ripped back the paper and lifted the lid of the box. Inside rested a silver pen, engraved with her name in a classic script font.

“It’s beautiful—I love it.”

It was. And she did.

“When working out in the field, special agents with the TBI take lots of notes,” Daniel told her as a smile danced across his face.

What was he hinting at? She was almost afraid to ask.

“Special agents?”

He nodded. “There’s an opening in our criminal investigations division. I got you an interview. That is, if you’re interested.”

“Are you kidding me right now? Of course I’m interested.”

Excitement flowed through Ashley’s veins. She couldn’t believe it. She’d wanted to apply for a job with the TBI but knew the competition was fierce. She’d feared they wouldn’t even consider her since she had no prior police experience.

“Thank you, Daniel,” she said, grateful for his recommendation.

Ashley let her gaze drift back to her family, laughing beneath the orange leaves of the oak. She felt so thankful that her father’s health had improved, happy for Kyle’s success in running the auto repair shop, and proud of Shane for the progress he’d made after his injury. Her heart waxed full.

Ashley’s future had never felt brighter.

She heard Kyle’s phone ring. A second after he answered the call, a look of panic washed over her older brother’s face.

She felt her heart stand still.

Something was terribly wrong.

“Okay, I’m on my way,” Kyle said into the phone, anguish clear in his voice.

“What’s going on—what’s happened?” she asked, rushing toward him.

Her older brother met her gaze.

“The auto shop’s on fire,” he said, as though he couldn’t believe the news.

“Follow my car,” Daniel told them. “I’ll turn on my lights and siren.”

Ashley grabbed the handles of Shane’s wheelchair and steered him toward the parking lot as fast as she could go, Kyle and her father at her heels. The auto repair shop was the sole source of income for not only her family, but her Uncle Russ’s family as well.

In her heart she knew the fire wasn’t an accident. It was a direct result of Troy’s death.

This was payback.

But she was a fighter. And there was no way Ashley would allow the former deputy’s relatives to win.

NOW AVAILABLE!

LET ME LIVE
(An Ashley Hope Suspense Thriller—Book 3)

Ashley Hope is an average Southern woman, happily engaged—until dark secrets from her past tear her life apart. Now a member of Tennessee's state police's violent crimes division, Ashley is summoned when victims are found murdered in a similar way within the same geographical area. In a mad race against time before the killer strikes again, Ashley must enter the killer's mind and understand: what do these murders have in common? Where will he strike next?

A dark crime thriller full of mystery and suspense, the ASHLEY HOPE mystery series is rife with twists and jaw-dropping secrets as it unfolds into a riveting psychological thriller. Join this brilliant new female protagonist as she hunts down a serial killer, keeping you spellbound and turning pages late into the night. Fans of Rachel Caine, Teresa Driscoll and Robert Dugoni are sure to fall in love.

Future books in the series will soon be available.

Kate Bold

Debut author Kate Bold is author of the ALEXA CHASE SUSPENSE THRILLER series, comprising six books (and counting); and the ASHLEY HOPE SUSPENSE THRILLER, comprising three books (and counting).

An avid reader and lifelong fan of the mystery and thriller genres, Kate loves to hear from you, so please feel free to visit www.kateboldauthor.com to learn more and stay in touch.

BOOKS BY KATE BOLD

ALEXA CHASE SUSPENSE THRILLER
THE KILLING GAME (Book #1)
THE KILLING TIDE (Book #2)
THE KILLING HOUR (Book #3)
THE KILLING POINT (Book #4)
THE KILLING FOG (Book #5)
THE KILLING PLACE (Book #6)

ASHLEY HOPE SUSPENSE THRILLER
LET ME GO (Book #1)
LET ME OUT (Book #2)
LET ME LIVE (Book #3)

www.ingramcontent.com/pod-product-compliance
Lightning Source LLC
Chambersburg PA
CBHW030619310726
48979CB00003B/784
9781094393803